KA·E·RO·U

KA•E•RO•U

Time to Go Home

B. Jeanne Shibahara

Independently published
KA-E-RO-U Time to Go Home © 2018 B. Jeanne Shibahara
All rights reserved.

Though the characters seem real, they are not. With the exception of public figures, any resemblance to persons living or departed is coincidental. The opinions expressed are those of the characters. Certain long-standing institutions, establishments, governments, and places are mentioned for the benefit of the story. Historic events are used fictitiously. The moral right of the author has been asserted.

Original paintings for KA-E-RO-U:
Another Springtime with You and *The Stream of Fireflies*, courtesy of Shinko Yamaguchi (山口真功).

Photoshop design by RobertLyall.ca

Poetry is from *Shinkokinshuu: A New Collection of Poems Ancient and Modern* translated by Laurel Rasplica Rodd.

All other translations are the author's.

"Memorial Day" by Jeanne Williamson.

ISBN: 9781719859264

Author's note: Japanese words in KA-E-RO-U aren't italicized.

"KA-E-RO-U is a testimony to the human spirit that bridges differences and overcomes divisions, so different from the spirit that prevailed in the 1930s and 1940s and sent our grandparents and parents to war."

—Elaine Gerbert, University of Kansas, translator of Edogawa Ranpo's *Strange Tale of Panorama Island*

To my private chauffeur,
my Obochama,
Akira

Contents

Desert Flower M.

Kimi	3
Greg	9
The Professor's Office	14
The God of Letter Writers	23
Louis Cunningham	24
More News	33
A Visit from the Professor	36
Coffee and Cookies	42

The Backstreets of Namba

The Birthplace of Instant Ramen	47
Something in Common	52
On the Way to Byron's School	58
The Robatayaki	60
It Doesn't Make Sense	69
Mr. Ono	75
Mixed Juice	80
Making Plans	84

Day 2 in Japan

Nara Park	93
Shopping with Fiona	103
Mrs. Quist's Maiden Name	105
A Crane Waits	107
Mr. Baba	111
The English Lesson	117

Ms. Kawanishi

On the Way Home	129

To Meryl, to Akita

The French Teacher from Algiers	165
A Goldfish in the Ikebana	169
About Akita	174
A Welcome Home Party	178
Long-legged Colts	180
Okamisan, Fireflies, a Ruddy Kingfisher	185
To Ani Town	194
The Telephone Call	199
Ayako Sato	201
Blue as the Inland Sea	206
Children of the Matagi	210
Okinawa Song	219

Returns

Wet Feathers	223
A Rice Dumpling	225
Middle Names	231
Believe Anything	233
The River Flows	236
Three Lifetimes	240

Finale

Kimono Time and Ms. Kawanishi	245
Good-bye to Ms. Kawanishi	256
Song of Tsukutsuku-boushi	261
Vanquished	265
Japanese Lessons	268
So Yummy	271

Acknowledgements

For providing information in KA-E-RO-U, I thank—

In Akita: Katsuyoshi Kanazawa, Shoko Goto, Miho Yamamoto, Michiko Takahashi, Kunio Sato, the Matagi Museum in Ani.
Iwate: Motomu and Toshiko Sasaki, Hekishou Temple Museum
Fukushima: Hiroji and Shinobu Yogiashi
Nara: Hajime Kitamura, Mineko Shibahara
Osaka: Fusako Nishikawa, Yasuko Yoshitake

I am indebted to my editors, my dear friends representing Japan, Armenia, Australia, Canada, England, Poland, and the US. They bless me with their goodwill, acumen, humor, devotion, and trust. I am honored to be in their lives. This novel is theirs.
Jo, at the right time told me to write a novel.
Darryl King, together from the start, my novel soul mate.
Elaine Gerbert, fun and funny because of you.
David Paulson, holding the carrot to my nose.
Noreen, the laughs are yours.
Jacquelyn and Robert Elliott, keeping this ride on track.
Lee Nourse, fierce, brave, bold.
Lianna Kirakosyan, naming Ani, Ani.
Yoshie Shiroma, head cheerleader.
My cousin Evvie Smith, sticking to the fundamentals.
Applause to Claudia, who I met via insightful and lucid notes on two revised manuscripts.

Thank you to friends from my youth for believing that someday I would write a novel, Aron Quist, Patti, Peter, Don and Jeanne.
And to my fathers who dreamed of becoming novelists—
Monte J. Anderson and Hiroshi Shibahara.

Desert Flower M.

*Tempe, Arizona
A hot and promising day in July 1995*

...but I never met a man I didn't like.
—Will Rogers
Kimi's motto

Kimi

EVERYBODY who knew the secretary knew she couldn't resist any chance at serving up beefy gossip—seasoned, well done, sizzling and sputtering the latest, the most titillating, the just-gotta-tell.

Her next visitor turned out to be the choicest cut of the day. Good enough for a bottle of Bordeaux.

"Um. Is this the Department of Asian Studies?"

The secretary glanced up, met a pair of legs made for a catwalk, spotted an envelope, and her eyes squeezed half shut as her lips twisted into a lemon-sucking *O*.

"Um. Would it...is it all right? This is for a professor. The first letter is *G*."

Most people didn't know how to say the last name Gieschen—g-i-e as in geezer and -s-c-h-e-n like *-tion* in flirtation.

"Sorry, I wrote the name down somewhere, but..."

Excitement pitter-pattered in the secretary's heart—

"You must mean Dr. Gieschen."

And she asked herself, Who else would a thirty-maybe-forty something, show-stopper of a leggy blond be looking for?

"Your name?"

"Meryl. This is for him."

The secretary's head swayed from side to side...The envelope for Dr. G was open. In no time—a sneaky peeky.

But from the copy machine on the other side of the office, Dr. Gieschen's graduate assistant made a preemptive move.

Loose, reddish-brown ringlets bounced at Kimi's shoulders, a hair color that someone from Japan could only get from chemicals. Twenty-seven and with the body of a typical eleven-year-old American girl...sparkling eyes, bright make-up, an anime character come to life.

Kimi envied Meryl's gazelle legs, wondered—How fast can she run?

And Kimi knew she had to butt in when Meryl said she had something for Gieschen Sensei. If the secretary got anything out of Meryl, who knew what wildfire of gossip would spread?

"I'll take you to him!"

Kimi accessorized most of what she said with perky exclamation points.

"I'm Kimi, Dr. Gieschen's assistant!"

Neither Kimi nor Meryl imagined that the secretary's arm could stretch so far.

"Meryl, give that to me. Kimi, your copies are calling you."

Kimi's ringlets bounced toward Meryl. "Shall we go?"

Kimi used *shall* in life's potentially dramatic moments.

Meryl easily approved of Kimi's spunk, smiled at the sour secretary, and left with Kimi.

Meryl, however, had no idea what to say to a professor. She made up her mind—ask Kimi to give Dr. Gieschen the envelope.

As they walked side by side, Kimi wondered if her sensei had recently met Meryl for the first time and told her where he worked. She came to surprise him. Or maybe they *had* a lunch date!

What made the stroll in the corridor that much more provocative was...Kimi had never heard anything juicy about her sensei. The only thing everyone knew—he had children and grandchildren and was a widower.

Something magical was going to happen.

Meryl had on barely any makeup but was still pretty. She had a small, oval face and her neck was as graceful as a swan's. Meryl wasn't at all like most of the American women Kimi knew. No bulging here and there, no bra lines, no ripples making her back look like a roly-poly manatee's. If she wasn't so tall, she would look great in a kimono. And her hair...like glistening honey!

Kimi often wished she were blond. If only she could dazzle in fluffy pastels and that luscious shade of bubblegum pink lipstick.

And for Kimi, compatible couples had to look cute together, complement each other...like wasabi complements soy sauce.

Wasabi, Meryl. Sensei, soy sauce.

Sure, her sensei had wrinkles, but each was in the perfect place. His nose curved like one on an Italian sculpture. Plus his nostrils sometimes flared, signaling a simmering passion. And his nose was *long*.

Everyone knew what that meant. At least the women she knew in Japan knew what that meant. American women looked perplexed whenever she mentioned the length of a man's nose. Maybe they didn't talk about it because most American men had big noses. Not even the secretary blabbed about it. Kimi wanted to ask her American friends about noses, but the question would be a little embarrassing, "In America, if a man has a long nose, does that mean he also has a long...ahem?" if the answer was NO!

Anyway, Gieschen Sensei's nose was long and Meryl was tall so that should make a great fit.

His salt-and-pepper hair was thinning in the sexiest way, tempting Kimi's mind to wander in the direction of other smooth, round places and end up at a fantasy of what she thrived on the most.

And so, she was curious about the source of her sensei's nookie. The *n*-word she learned from another older man with a long nose, a chemistry professor from Stone, England. She liked the name of his town because "Stone rhymes with bone." Easy to remember, like "A cookie after nookie!"

That intimate thought—about her sensei's nookie—spawned a plain question.

"Are you a professor too?"

Kimi had a rowdy mouth with more teeth than it should have to hold, crooked and bucked, the left-front tooth slightly overtaking the right.

Meryl's head tilted sideways on her graceful neck as she sighed—her son's boyhood and his bucktoothed buddies...He had been such an adorable child. If only he could always stay seven or eight or even nine or ten. She wished he would call.

"It's my first time in a building at a university," Meryl said.

Kimi squeezed her dainty lips over her teeth, halting a naughty smile.

"My son used to be Dr. Gieschen's student. His name was in one of my son's old files."

"I think I know who your son is."

Meryl's plan to ask Kimi to give the envelope to the professor slipped her mind.

"Maybe same legs." Kimi opened the stairwell door for Meryl.

Up they climbed.

"Not the same nose." Kimi had admired Byron's nose.

"It's so easy. Your son must be Byron. Byron Quist."

"You *do* know my son."

"Yes, yes. He's soooo handsome! I was his tutor for grammar drills. His Japanese is good."

They entered the second-floor corridor.

"You taught Byron?"

"Yes, yes. I'm always like this to him." Kimi shadowed her eyes with her hand as she did in the glaring sun, dropped her head of merry ringlets back as far as it would go, and looked straight up to the yellowed ceiling...not at all like the color of Byron's perfect teeth. "Because he's soooo tall! Smile soooo bright!"

Her beguiling face returned to a more comfortable angle, and they walked on.

"Is he fine? Still teaching in Osaka? What does he think of Japan? I told him everyone would love his smile."

The giggles from her playful mouth sounded as cheerful as a bag of circus-colored jellybeans pouring into a glass bowl.

"Have you met Dr. Gieschen before?"

Dr. Gieschen! Meryl's shoulders tensed. What was she going to say to a professor? She shook her head no and tried to give Kimi the envelope. "I'm sure the Professor will know what to do. Please give—"

"He's nice with a very long nose." In a split second, Kimi's hand clamped her mouth shut.

Meryl felt as if she were poolside and had gotten splashed by a belly flop. "All the better to smell you with?"

"No! Not me! The Professor would never smell me!"

"Of course, not you. It's the big bad wolf in *Little Red Riding Hood.*"

Kimi's face was blank.

"What I said would be funny if you knew the story. Really."

"Yes, yes. Byron's soooo funny too!"

"He is?" Meryl thought her son was always soooo serious.

"Yes, yes."

They moved on, Meryl hooked and pulled by Kimi's lure.

"How tall are you?"

"Baby giraffe size."

"That's what I thought!" Kimi glanced down at Meryl's sandals.

"Godzilla-size eleven."

"You're the tallest woman I've ever met. With the biggest feet! I know. I'm the shortest for you. With the smallest feet! Byron said to me—I am for him too!"

Kimi...someone's little girl, all grown up, and on her own far from home...like Meryl's son. Meryl wished they could go for a cup of coffee and Kimi would prattle on and on about Byron.

Instead they arrived at the Professor's office.

Butterflies fluttered in Meryl's stomach. If there had been a chance to leave the envelope with Kimi, she had passed it by.

Behind the office door a samba was playing. Kimi bobbed her head to its rhythm. Her spectacular smile flashed, overbite and all. "Please tell Byron Kimi says hi!" She knocked, the music stopped, and the Professor's voice called out.

Meryl took a deep breath and followed Kimi in.

"Byron Quist's mother is here!"

One look at Meryl and the Professor leapt from his seat—"This is a pleasure. Greg Gieschen."

And was shaking her hand with overwhelming enthusiasm.

Meryl hadn't stuck it out. She almost muttered, Oops!—and wished Kimi would say something.

But Kimi stepped away. Gieschen Sensei never introduced himself as Greg—always Gregory.

And he did something Kimi had never *seen* him do. He didn't look at who he was talking to. "Kimi, thank you." His gaze was on Meryl.

In a moment, her sensei and Meryl would be alone *and* together! How Kimi wanted to see into her sensei's mind.

She backed out of the room, shutting the door in front of her as if someone had played a movie in reverse.

Meryl looked over her shoulder. But before she could say good-bye, Kimi was gone.

Greg

IN A BLINK of an eye, the Professor found himself in an airy cathedral...beams of light streaming down on Mrs. Quist through narrow panels of jewel-colored glass...his voice reaching plump, pink cherubs in the heavens on ceiling frescos.

Greg Gieschen saw the glow. No—the aura. No—the divine effervescence. Words couldn't describe it. That same light had surrounded another woman over thirty years earlier. Greg knew in his heart Mrs. Quist was sent from heaven.

Glory to God in the highest, Hallelujah, and Amen!

AND GREG didn't believe in God.

Though he had grown up under the Lutheran sky of Nebraska and had spent Sundays with churchgoing parents, a deep, lasting faith always seemed out of reach.

It was true Greg marveled at the world's beauty, nature's miracles. But he believed everything came about from a series of coincidences, which happened to have worked out well...especially for human beings. His students sometimes asked if there was a God. "The vagaries of nature," he told them, "and the proclivities of people are matters too miniscule to hold God's attention. The Almighty is on the other side of infinity—nodding off." He never said that he didn't believe in God or the afterlife. He knew his students wanted to live forever.

Greg had eloped in graduate school.

Janice spent her time running the house and taking care of their children, giving them what she hadn't had. She welcomed them home from school...encouraged their interests, which—by what she called *the charm of coincidence*—happened to be hers...art, music, dance, and literature.

Greg sometimes overheard their teenage children tell her, "You have to go out and be your own person." And her reply, "I am my own person. I love my family and my husband...your father."

A woman like that by his side...he knew he could get away with anything.

Instead of sprinkling out his love every day in the simple things, he planned to thank her for graciously supporting his career after he retired. They would travel. First stop, England for her favorite plays—*King Lear*; *A Midsummer's Night Dream*; and *The Tempest*, the one they had seen together when they were students. At times, he confessed that he kept her like the enslaved sprite Ariel...he, the demanding magician Prospero.

Had the Professor studiously observed his wife as he had his career, he would have noticed the weight she lost and her movements slowing, her shiny hair dulling, her glowing blush carefully applied. He would've asked why she said good night to him earlier and earlier each evening, would've insisted on her going to a doctor. No, he would have taken her himself.

He got into their bed one night and felt that he was in an unfamiliar place, aglow in silver-blue moonlight. His darling hadn't drawn the curtains. But he didn't get up...It was a still, comforting light.

Janice was on her side facing the window, her voice soft. "If you were gone tomorrow, I wouldn't know what to do. I love you so."

"I'm not going anywhere. You're stuck with me for the rest of your life."

He snuggled up to her, his hands moved across her shoulders, down her back. At once, he trembled. She was so small. When had her skin become this thin cover for her bones?

"If you weren't here, would you want me to fall in love with someone else?"

What was she saying? Hadn't he told her he wasn't going anywhere? Panic spread through him. His throat tightened, as if he were choking by the grip of his own hands.

"I would, you know. Love again." Her voice was kind...as heartbreaking as a whisper of leaves in a frosty wind.

Love again? He couldn't live without her. Surely she must know that he wanted his life with her more than anything else in the world. Why did she think he was leaving? What outrageous blunder had he made? Was she so worried she could not eat?

Janice said, "I would do everything that I didn't do with you."

Greg grappled with his voice.

"Beginning tomorrow we'll do anything your heart desires." He managed to sound strong and decisive. "Anything you've wanted to do but haven't been able to...because of me."

"Everything precious I have is because of you."

He ignored the quiver in her voice. And for the first time in a long, long time, romance filled his heart.

"Let's get a flight to London. Loan out the children to Mom and Pop. We're headed for the stage and your first love, Shakespeare."

Janice turned over on her back. Her eyes were closed. "My first love is you."

In the dim light, Greg studied the outline of her face. "The first time I saw you, heaven opened and God sent an angel to me."

"You don't believe in God."

"I believe in angels. You were even wearing a white dress...let's say a rapturous shade of ivory. I couldn't speak. Only ridiculous lines of British poetry came to mind."

She opened her eyes. "You were rambling on and on about seaweed in sweetened vinegar, about Japanese pickles."

"And you still married me?"

He barely made out the smile playing on her lips.

His wife told him she wanted to be a man in her next life.
"A man as wonderful as you."

"Well then, I'll be a woman as marvelous as you. I'll fall in love with you all over again and do everything for you without a peep of complaint. You can have all the freedom I've taken for granted."

"You won't be bored?"

"What nincompoopery! Bored? With you, a man like me?"

"Never!"

Janice giggled in the magical light of the moon. A spell had been cast, and they were both once again students who had fallen in love for the first time.

They spoke a few minutes longer until Janice fell asleep.

Greg was at peace, more than he had ever been in his life. He told himself Janice would gain weight and whispered, "Everything will be fine."

But how small she had become.

He decided to take time off for their trip to London.

Then late that night, when moonlight fell on the ever so delicate face of Greg's wife and he murmured her name in a dream he would never be able to recall...her heart stopped beating. Janice had wanted to be sure she wouldn't groan in pain. The amount of painkiller she had taken was too much for her weak heart.

Greg learned the details of her illness the morning of her death. The tumor had grown slowly, had been difficult to find. And there was nothing that could have been done.

She had hired a neighbor to help around the house. Christmas and graduation presents were in the hall closet...plus an envelope. On it, she had written *A Date With Shakespeare*. Inside was a bank check for a trip to England.

Janice left poems about their children and a letter to Greg.

She couldn't bear telling anyone that her body was getting ready for the eternal rest, that her life was on the last page of its storybook. No tears. Her family didn't need to stop what they were doing because her soul was moving on. And she had pretended Greg would join her to meet death; what a

comfort to imagine they would be together on that stairway to heaven.
My greatest sorrow is knowing you'll be lonely for a while. She ended with her last wish.
Greg covered his lips with his hand and began to weep.
I'll be your guardian angel. And your magical Prospero—leading you through the storm of grief to happily ever after. You will fall in love again.
Thoughts of eternity had overcome any thoughts of rivalry. Janice only wanted someone to love and care for her Greg.
He thought Janice was mistaken.
He would never love again.
But she proved Greg wrong, the day Kimi stepped into his office with the woman who came unannounced and had brought something unexpected.

It suck'd me first, and now sucks thee,
And in this flea our two bloods mingled be.
—Donne, "The Flea"

The Professor's Office

GREG waited for Meryl to speak...remembered the line, "There's nothing more mysterious than the silence of a beautiful woman." And reveled in his heart—Yes, that's it! You know something grand is about to happen when you recite absurdities of British poets in your ol' noggin.

Meryl didn't say a word.

"I usually don't meet my students' parents. But...well, this is a surprise...a pleasant one."

The Professor felt self-conscious at the intimate sound of his voice, then somewhat giddy at feeling self-conscious...then somewhat at a loss to hide his giddiness.

"Please have a seat."

From the chair, he took his pilot's flight case, a gift his wife had once wowed him with, and set it in a low bookcase—keeping his eyes on Meryl.

He could barely stay upright; his knees now had something in common with a spoonful of jell-o. He sat down across from Meryl. "I have an envelope with something I think you'll be interested in."

Her glance skipped off the side of his face and landed at the top button of his polo shirt.

He looked down. Lo and behold, on his chest, left side, right side, poking against his polo shirt...

As everyone in the Language and Literature Building agreed—Greg's clothes fit him nicely.

He felt a flush rising from his chest, invading his neck, ready to conquer his earlobes. He'd recently started shaving a few hairs growing there, but that morning he didn't check to see if any were sprouting.

Mild regret pranced around him.

And an instant later, his ridiculous emotional roller coaster took him to the top of the world.

What a swell of emotions in a matter of moments!

Meryl put her envelope on his desk.

In Greg's now-addled noggin, he truly was only thinking about a letter from her son that he wanted to show her when he asked, "Would you like to see *mine* first?"

Big Freudian slip.

"My envelope...well, I didn't write it...It's a letter from Byron. I opened it yesterday. You see...I was at a conference in Hawaii. Got back two days ago." That was odd. He never told anyone what he did. "Yesterday, on campus—late afternoon—I was sure Byron was walking ahead of me. He's quite *outstanding* in a group of people, isn't he?"

Surely his wordplay on Byron's height would tickle her funny bone.

But nothing, not a sign of camaraderie. Humor was the finest path to intimacy, and he had tripped.

"I tried catching up with him, but he was gone...as if he'd been in a mirage."

Greg leaned forward in his chair as Meryl sat up straighter in hers.

She didn't know what a professor was supposed to be like...but *this* professor was a little silly and stumbled over his words.

Then again, she hadn't even said hello. She hadn't expected to talk to the Professor, but now that she was about to, how could she chitchat about Byron...with what she had brought?

"Has Byron changed his plans and suddenly come home, Mrs. Quist?"

She moved her head from side to side.

Most everyone called her Meryl or Meryl Jeanne. But she was Mrs. Quist, Mrs. Peter Quist.

"Mrs. Quist?"

"Please...would you...look at...?"

She opened her envelope and pulled out a folded piece of thin cloth, discolored with age, stained in faded blood...a Japanese flag from WWII. There was writing on it in black ink.

A smaller envelope—with a note from her cousin—fell out unnoticed and landed on the floor under the desk.

"I've heard about flags like these, seen them in old newsreels, but never..." Greg spread it across his desk, then took out his glasses.

Meryl touched the edge of the flag, wishing she hadn't seen it—

Wishing her cousin hadn't gotten it from a neighbor—

Wishing it hadn't been in a desk drawer of the neighbor's father—Where had he gotten it? Why had he kept it?

Hadn't there been enough *red-white-and-blue* flags? Neatly pressed, folded into tight triangles—given to families, to mothers, to wives.

And then a different war and tens of thousands of more caskets...and Peter's flag for her.

Wishing none of it had happened.

Her cousin's peppy letter—

Take this flag to Japan and see Byron. Change your boring life...go on an adventure!

Meryl had called her father, asked him what to do with it, but he sounded as if he was in cahoots with her cousin—

"Get out and see something new of this old world. I had a lot of fun in Japan."

Peter's flag had been hers for a lifetime, their son's lifetime. And now she was supposed to go on an adventure? What happened to only wanting Peter to come home?

Meryl wished the Professor would say something.

He lifted his glasses to the top of his salt and pepper hair, and set them in the slight dip on his skull, which was used to them.

"When a Japanese man was drafted, his family bought a flag. Relatives, friends wrote messages like these. And before combat, the soldier would wrap it around his waist...under his...fatigues..."

Greg squeezed his lips together. Mrs. Quist *and* those details—*wrapped...waist...around...under.*

STOP.

"Or the soldier put it in his helmet. A kind of good luck charm, so to speak. Something from home."

Greg brought his glasses back down to the bridge of his long nose.

"These large kanji characters"—he pointed at the top of the flag—"are 'bu-un-chou-kyuu.' 'Bu' (武) means 'strength during battle.' This one, 'un' (運), is 'fortunate fate.' And 'chou' (長) means 'a long time.' So does 'kyuu' (久).

"It's something like, 'fight strong until victory.' Come home in one piece.

"This is 'Tennouheika banzai' (天皇陛下万歳). Simply put, 'Hooray Emperor.' But during the years of Japanese imperialism it meant, 'I give my life to the Emperor,' or 'Sons of the Emperor.' "

Greg glanced at Meryl—

Tiny, dewy drops dotted the line of her upper lip.

And he wondered. Still hot from being outside? A little nervous? Because of...? Greg wasn't sure. But wouldn't those drops taste salty?

"He got this flag in the seventeenth year of the Showa (昭和) era. 1942. He was born on September twenty-fifth. A coincidence. Depending on the calendar year, it's celebrated as the night of the *loveliest* moon."

INAPPROPRIATE.

"He was nineteen. If he had been a little younger, he wouldn't have gone to war."

And we *wouldn't* be here *together now.* What tortuous schemes of tragedy fuel the whims of Cupid!

Greg waved his hand over the flag. "Beautiful lettering, isn't it? What we'd expect from artists. Fluid lines, widening and tapering, balanced." He traced over some of the curves, as if his finger were a calligraphy brush.

A possibility of tracing over hers?

Right before his eyes the flag had become a stepping-stone to romance. Even the bloodstains disappeared.

Futile war. What have you become in the light of love?

Greg knew he must respect the dead...but at that moment he rejoiced because he was alive!

"Perhaps someone," he said, "still prays for him, thinks a-bout him."

Greg hadn't noticed Meryl's hands in her lap.

She was twisting her wedding band around her finger, thinking how the flag reminded her of the one Byron kept in his room...Peter's. And they were nothing at all alike.

"Kouichiro was his first name. One meaning of 'kou' (功) is 'success in any endeavor.' 'Ichiro' (一郎) means 'first son.' His family name is an unusual combination of characters. This is 'kuzu' (葛), the name of a vine indigenous to Japan. Our government planted it in the mid-thirties to help reclaim the wasteland that had given us the Dust Bowl. You see, it puts nitrogen back into the soil, controls erosion."

Greg picked up his pen and asked himself, Sounding like a hopeless idiot?

"Now kuzu is right at home in the Deep South, where they call it cud-zoo."

Mrs. Quist didn't say she knew it—she wasn't from anywhere kuzu grew.

This little discovery sent a thrill down to Greg's toes.

"In Japan, kuzu fiber is made into paper and cloth."

His wife, bless her, would've asked him to Please return the lid to the soup pot a few sentences back. But Mrs. Quist listened so earnestly that his tongue kept flapping out words.

"Its root is used in confections for the tea ceremony...has medicinal value..."

Under his breath—

Dull smarty-pants.

He tapped his temple with his pen, wondering where the connection had gone, then pointed to the second character in Kouichiro's family name.

"This means 'west.' The city he's from should also be here, but only..."

A flurry of lines.

He paused, as he did during his lectures, praying to his god of the opportune question for one to rise up in front of him.

"Do you think anyone would...want it now...after so long?"

Prayer answered.

"I imagine his family would be happy to get it back."

Meryl's hand moved near the flag.

Ah, the poor woman has seen the bloodstains. Who wouldn't have?

But we're here together...two *bloods mingled be*. Yes—another British poet!

Greg cleared his throat.

"*Happy* isn't the right word. Forgive me for explaining so much, Mrs. Quist. May I?" And with her nod he said, "The government didn't bring home the remains of fallen soldiers. No belongings. There were fire bombings in over sixty cities. Families were left with nothing."

"Wasn't only Tokyo?...Well, and the atom bombs." Her voice was low. "So many cities?"

Greg could hardly hear her.

"Many cities." Speak love, not war. "It would be something—finding his family."

"Maybe...could you...find them?"

"Wouldn't Byron be interested in this? Searching for someone he doesn't know, in a country he loves. There's the chivalry of a medieval knight in it, as if returning a holy relic—immense kindness, something your son has.

"Byron could start with the city's public records. The family might have moved and is now in Osaka."

Meryl took a deep breath.

She didn't want Byron to see those bloodstains.

"Have you thought of visiting Japan while Byron is there? Think of the people you'd meet and what you could learn."

Greg asked if she had a passport.

Byron insisted that she get hers when he had gotten his. But she hadn't planned on using it.

Meryl begged herself to please think...Excuse, excuse. About to sound like a five-year-old, but—
"My father...will worry."
"Byron would be your interpreter and guide. Your father won't worry, will he?"
Meryl's eyes opened wide. Next excuse?
"I can't leave my dog."
Greg's nostrils flared.
The tidbit he'd been waiting for...No husband...No boyfriend. Hallelujah! Only her dog!
"The rascal who buried Byron's homework?"
Was he being too familiar? He surrendered completely.
"I'll take care of...*him*?"
"Her." And Meryl was out of excuses.
TRIUMPH.
"She's not trained to attack Japanese teachers, is she?"
Another humor misstep, but Greg maneuvered magnificently by implementing practicality. "My place has a large yard." And then wielded lonesome self-pity. "I haven't had a canine around for a long time and would enjoy the company."
Meryl thanked him but said no.
"My backyard is always open." Like a gallant knight, he said he would try to find where the flag should go.
She fumbled folding it.
Greg put the letter that he wanted to show her on his desk. "From your gregarious son. Says he's going to need housing for married students when he gets back. Congratulations." Greg decided to ask her to lunch. "Something to celebrate."
The flag slipped from Meryl's hands and fell to the floor—a burst of air blew her cousin's letter farther under the desk.
Greg swooped down and got the flag.
"I hope I didn't let the cat out of the bag." But the look on her face told him he had.
Asking her to lunch went out the window.
Meryl put her hand on the edge of the desk and stood up.
"Mrs. Quist, if there's anything else, please—"

"I have to get back to my car, but...I don't...I wa. far."

"You must've parked in one of the visitor parking lots, next to the bookstore or Grady Gammage, the auditorium. It's a pink-bronze color...has pillars, fancy loops and golden balls...like a palace spreading across an Arabian night." How could he keep her longer?

"I think near that palace place."

Greg opened the door, something he hadn't done for someone in years—for his beloved wife, the only woman he'd known who thought the gesture was still suave.

"I'm headed that way—to the library. I enjoy reading the newspaper there." Ask for her phone number?

Greg turned back to get his flight case, stuffed with newspapers that had been delivered while he'd been in Hawaii.

On the wall, his framed poster for a Stratford production of *King Lear* caught his eye...The stark simplicity looked like the setting of a kabuki play and foreshadowed doom. He had seen it with his children the year after his wife died.

In the corridor, Meryl was facing away from Greg. He locked the door, dropped his keys into his jeans pocket, freeing up his hand, then instinctively reached for Meryl's. When their hands were about to touch, she stepped away, breaking his rhythm. He caught his breath and kept his bulky case between them.

Near the library, he watched Meryl move across campus, her slip of a shadow tagging behind like a small child.

He murmured sayonara, the lovely expression filled with longing. I say good-bye only because I must.

She was gone.

Solid heat of midday, glaring summer sky—Greg skipped the library and headed back to pick up his mail from the secretary.

And as his mind searched for his next move, he started composing phrases that rhymed.

Whenever Greg was about to face a certain type of person (e.g., the secretary), he made up rhymes. Only his late wife knew he did this. Each time he had recited his poetry, the twinkles in her eyes twinkled more.

He walked by his favorite red brick building, one that captured the spirit of the Old West and its headstrong will to catch up with the rest of the country. Completed in 1898, its design united two styles named after British queens and portrayed the dignity and moral stature of higher education the founders had hoped students would aspire to.

And then Greg finished.

There once was a woman with a proclivity.
She gossiped and spoke quite uncivilly.
Her mouth was as wide
as Godzilla's backside;
Her caboose spanned to infinity!

He spotted Kimi, curls bouncing and giggles ready to say hello.

"You didn't take Mrs. Quist to lunch?"

The Professor was dumbstruck by Kimi's question, surprised that she knew what he wished he had done—

"You two make a lovely couple, I think."

A bit abashed at her intimacy.

"Byron told me his mother never dates. His grandfather chased the men away!"

In the next second, Kimi looked as serious as her cheery makeup allowed. "Did he tell you his father was a pilot in the air force? He died in Vietnam."

Vietnam. Greg had been a university student, exempted from the draft.

He guessed Kimi didn't know Mrs. Quist had been given the flag that was draped over her husband's casket.

Greg also guessed that Kimi didn't know what Mrs. Quist had brought him.

"His mother was only nineteen then," Kimi said.

She tilted her head to one side. Her sensei's quick goodbye puzzled her—so did his fast pace back to the Language and Literature Building.

The God of Letter Writers

IN his office, Greg stood at the poster for *King Lear*. He had hung it there years ago after his wife's death. But it still seemed that Janice kissed him awake every morning.
    Yet he couldn't stop thinking about Mrs. Quist.
    If he had known about her husband's death, had seen the abiding grief in her eyes...he winced. And he had been the one who told her that her son was getting married.
    If he knew her phone number or address...but what reason did he have to contact her?
    The gloomy despair in the poster grabbed at his heart. He murmured his wife's name.
    And a moment later, a thrill raced through him and caught him off guard, a thrill that reminded him of the first years of their marriage...Janice at his side, tapping his shoulder to get his attention. Her voice came to him as clear as the summer sky.
    Put away that bleak poster and live!
    He wiped the frame with a few tissues, wadded them up into a ball, aimed for the wastebasket, took the shot, dove for the rebound, and found...the small envelope. Meryl's name and address were on it.
    Hallelujah!
    Greg looked upward, praising his god of letter writers.
    Sing, plump cherubs, sing!

Louis Cunningham

ABOVE the sofa in Meryl's living room was an abstract of Venice, a masquerade of the buildings along those romantic canals—rooftops cloaked in terra cotta; facades dressed up with plumes of canary, parrot, and peacock. A bridge of indigo zigzags and loops fastened the buildings together. All fading reluctantly into a faraway place.

Meryl had painted it when Byron was a university student, when she was caring for her mother and bolstering her father's weary spirit.

The painting became a mask for her heart.

By the time the painting was framed, her son had graduated, her mother had died.

Meryl had started dabbling in art when her son was old enough to scribble. She spent the lonely nights with paints and pastels while her single friends were out looking for love. Meryl didn't, however, have an artist's ambition. Most of her art only saw the light of day in her own house or on homemade holiday cards.

Morning light would shine on a house palm on top of a ceramic elephant from Thailand, skillfully painted and gaudy, the last gift her husband had sent. Its trunk pointed toward the front door.

The sun was high now. Rays sifted through pointed, narrow leaves of an olive tree and dappled in the shape of tiny elf shoes on the path in Meryl's yard. She hadn't yet come back from the university. Near the painted elephant was her ever vigilant English springer spaniel, freckled chin between freckled paws.

Meryl's father was sitting on the sofa. He had enjoyed lunch at his house but still felt a little hungry.

LOUIS CUNNINGHAM'S belly showed no sign of his childhood in the Dust Bowl of Oklahoma when the land had given up on itself and had blown away in billowing clouds, leaving behind soil unfit to till. Pantries and cupboards, once filled with the preserved goodness from the once bountiful earth, became empty and stayed as barren as the land.

Louis' father owned a barbershop and from 1923, was the justice of the peace in Shidler, Oklahoma.

Twelve years later, Roric Cunningham was asked to step down from office. Funds had been found missing. The country was smack dab in the middle of the Great Depression. And the Dust Bowl was blowing most of the Plains into poverty and hunger, forcing millions to give up their homes and look for jobs elsewhere.

His children never talked about why he'd pocketed the money. But Roric loved his whiskey and his cards—a onetime card shark on the showy steamboats of the Mississippi. Whiskey had ruined his skill...and then it seemed the hand of providence kept the Cunningham family from doing all right when others no longer had spare change for a shave and a haircut—or for most anything.

Roric's barbershop folded.

Louis' older brothers walked out the front door and forgot the family they left behind.

His mother packed up her novels and books of poetry. She used to read to her children in happier times, her voice peppering the romance and adventure with savory dramatic flair. When she died, Louis' teenaged sisters hitchhiked across the country to California. His oldest sister stayed, watching over him when she could. Decades after his mother's death, his sisters said it had been cancer. But Louis knew otherwise. After her books were sold, if any food was in the house, it was on the plates of her children and their tag-a-long, bug-eyed friends. Hunger had taken her.

Louis wasn't about to let hunger nail his coffin shut.

He perfected his aim with his slingshot—ammo, old ball bearings—and ate a lot of birds. He honed his skill catching soft-shelled turtles and scavenged alleys for anything to sell or barter...swept out old buildings for any coins under the trash...worked any job, but there were few to go around. He made a lot of friends and showed up at their homes during supper.

Things that didn't belong to him ended up his sometimes.

And once in a while, people gave him secondhand clothes and shoes, but he wore mostly rags that didn't fit; his shoes had holes, or he went barefoot. He was a child but looked like a bum.

Louis didn't know where his father was during a few of those bad years.

Much later in life Louis and his sisters talked about their father. "He did his best."

Their house burned down in 1935. Louis remembered the year, but not because of his father's fire. It was the same year the nation's most loved satirist and Oklahoma's favorite son died in a plane crash, Will Rogers.

An insurance agent—who still missed the baby-smooth face he'd gotten from Roric's razor—inspected the property, his back to the yard and a pile of furniture, undamaged.

Setting a fire for insurance money was common news. Louis saw his share of businesses burned to the ground...the shoe store, the dry goods store, the movie theater, and even the machine shop, which was next door to the fire station and owned by the fire chief.

Roric lost his insurance money at poker tables, sipped it from shot glasses.

But Louis still loved his father because "He's my father."

Louis could spin a yarn about the time he earned a nickel for the stinking hours it took plucking a turkey only to have Roric tell him to go down the road for some tobacco. Louis had been happy to do it without thinking much about the bread a nickel could buy.

When the Cunningham family fell into the deep pit of poverty and hunger, Louis was too young to understand the reasons why. When he understood...he thought a lot less of his fellow man, those who had plundered the topsoil for decades causing it to blow away in fierce windstorms—and also of his father, the one who had stolen years of happiness. And Louis believed, had gambled away his mother's life.

It was for certain. Hunger had shaped the boy's heart.

The wrong and right of his world was in black and white. There hadn't been enough cozy times in his childhood for him to think over any shadowy doubts.

Food on the table was what mattered.

Their preacher once spouted off a rip-roaring sermon of fire and brimstone and "Man can't live on bread alone." Louis' scrawny arms had shot up. "Yes, we can!"

Religion was for full bellies.

Happiness was only possible without hunger.

Education! He hadn't heard a word in class. His brain battled the tiny demons spearing pitchforks into his empty stomach.

Louis thought public schools should provide breakfast and lunch. Some parents couldn't.

All his mother's love hadn't kept him from being hungry.

And Louis sorely knew...a person who had never starved would never understand how everything besides food was a luxury.

Louis didn't even care for money. "If there's no food to buy, a thin dime is something else you can't eat."

But hunger hadn't kept Louis from growing six feet three inches tall. Meryl's height came from her father.

His favorite ice cream was Tastee Freez soft vanilla, swirling up from a crunchy cone into a curlicue. Sometimes on his way driving home, he would buy a large one, lick once or twice, then finish it off in big bites, each time wishing the ice cream filled the cone all the way to the bottom. It never did.

IN 1943 the Allied Forces in the Pacific Theater advanced into New Guinea and the Solomon Islands.

Louis and his lanky buddies found themselves at a pool hall, thinking.

Would they let the draft lead them down the path to certain death, the kind that came from having your guts blown out? Or not?

The vote was unanimous for the *not* option with the stipulation of joining the Merchant Marines...If you're hauling war supplies from one port to another—the logic went—you won't be armed so no one will care enough to shoot.

Those Oklahoma boys had been half right; they weren't issued guns. The Germans shot at them in the Atlantic; the Japanese, in the Pacific. By some luck, a bullet from those thousands flying around Louis didn't have his name on it.

Then back home after the War, Louis drove a truck for his brother-in-law's company until he found out that George Anderson had been exempted from military service due to an oversight—his medical records were switched with those of another George Anderson. That really galled Louis. His oldest sister still praised the Lord, "It was a miracle." Louis' blessed brother-in-law had stayed stateside; the cursed Anderson had fought—hell if they knew where—suffering from cirrhosis.

Louis bid a speedy farewell to peacetime civilian life. He joined the army.

Next stop: Osaka City.

The Japanese had been trying to annihilate Louis' army the year before. But now women on trains bowed and offered their seats to the Americans. Louis always stayed standing, thinking of his own mother.

Once in a downpour, a woman ran from her house and pushed an umbrella into his hands. He thanked her and made up his mind to bring it back the next day. But when he tried retracing his steps, the narrow streets ran together like a maze within a maze. He fretted for that woman. Her skin hung from her bones as his mother's had the last months of her life.

Louis had been hungry when he was a boy, but he didn't remember being polite or giving anybody anything. He fell in love with Japan and wondered why in the world there had ever been a war.

When Byron said he was going to Japan, Louis didn't try to stop his grandson as some grandfathers would have, the ones who had fought through the bloodbaths on any number of Pacific islands. Louis was pleased his grandson wasn't following the same road he and his son-in-law had been on.

Byron was going to be a scholar.

Louis served his country in three wars, two on the administrative end. His haircut was the same as the first one he got after joining the Merchant Marines, cropped close. His head looked like a scrub brush.

But a comfortable military pension didn't stop him from airing his views.

"My entire life this lousy government's been fighting some other pig-headed country—one nobody ever heard of before or could find on a map if someone paid them. Still hasn't learned a gosh-dern thing about diplomacy."

Louis could swear with the best of them, but it had offended his good-hearted, God-fearing wife. For her, he softened the cuss words he'd grown up with, kept them soft even after she was gone.

Louis was proud Byron was a civilian in Japan.

The only thing he warned his grandson about was the fish.

"Sometimes they eat it raw. When they do grill it, the head *isn't* chopped off—so while you're eating, it's eyeballing you straight through supper."

LOUIS had seen a lot of good men die. And women too.

But the most painful loss Louis ever knew was that of his son-in-law. He never saw a heart as shattered in grief as his daughter's had been.

If Meryl didn't have Byron to love—it was too terrible to imagine.

Byron had filled each of their days.

Louis had been in command of his grandson's boyhood, but it was an easy duty. There wasn't a rebellious bone in Byron, and he was blessed with brains that put the brakes on doing anything dangerously dumb or foolhardy. Most boys were born rascals, Louis knew. He'd been one himself.

Byron never had to compete for his mother's attention. Meryl didn't date. And Byron had a good mother. Maybe it was hard to be a rascal with a mother as sweet as she was.

But Byron committed the worst infraction any boy could. He grew up and left his mother. On top of that, Byron didn't move down the street. He moved clear across the world to Japan, a short journey from Vietnam—the country where his father's jet had gone down.

Byron was there now. Vietnam. He hadn't told Meryl.

Louis was going to.

LOUIS called to Meryl's dog—

"Freckles, I've got something to say to you."

Took her paw.

"No more thinking about your own tail-waggin' self."

Freckles' floppy mouth opened. Her tongue lolled out and flapped back in.

"You've been letting Meryl hang on to you for too long."

RIGHT FROM the start Louis hadn't liked the idea of his little princess getting married. But Meryl's husband had been a gem, had even bought a house in a neighborhood close by. And around the time Louis was getting used to the idea of having a son-in-law, he was gone.

When Meryl's mother was ill, Louis didn't know what he would've done without his daughter's comfort. When the good Lord saw fit, what was he to do? Meryl looked after him and didn't boss him around too much. Played checkers with him.

And with what gratitude did he repay his princess?

Getting remarried.

He met a nice woman a few months back. They hit it off and got married. A perfectly natural thing to do, wasn't it?

Louis considered the possibility that he most likely had kept Meryl from at least trying to find a man she could share the rest of her life with. He hadn't introduced her to anyone who might ask her out. The word "date" never made it past his lips.

HIS FINGERS worked their way around Freckles' soft ears as he reprimanded—
"It's not right to hog Meryl's attention."
And gave orders.
"You have to push her to find someone she can bum a-round with...someone not as furry as *you* are."
He looked into the springer spaniel's eyes.
How they saw into his heart—already knew that he was going away for a short time, leaving Meryl.

Yes, the news for his daughter that day: her son was in Vietnam and her father was going on a trip with his new bride.
"We've got to get her moving on. Her cousin thinks so too. Daffy as a looney tune...sending a dead man's flag. Bet it's stained in blood. Didn't think what it would mean to Meryl. Can you believe Lee wants Meryl to take it to Japan? 'For an adventure...maybe meet a nice man.' And I'm supposed to go along with her lame-brained idea."

Louis rubbed his hand across the top of his bristly head and remembered one more thing.

On a lamp table was a painted ceramic bear in hobo dress, comically posed upright, a crooked walking stick in one paw, in the other, a misshapen lantern.

He lumbered to it, speaking as if the bear would put its lantern down and reply.

"I know some little girls who'd like to make your acquaintance."

Its suspenders stretched, and its buttons bulged. A tuxedo hat topped its jolly head. Trousers bunched in generous folds above worn-out shoes. Patches and pockets, a tulip in its lapel, the bear was in all the colors of a boy's childhood—lime green, tangerine, lemon yellow, and cherry red.

Byron had painted it in the arts and crafts program at the community center during summer one year.

"That was a nice program for children. Too hot to play outside."

Louis picked up the bear.

For its eyes Byron had glued on two clear plastic half-spheres backed in white. Each encased a black bead the size of a popcorn kernel. The beads wobbled around whenever the bear was moved, coming to rest at the center bottom, making the bear look ready for its next meal down the road.

Long ago, Louis had gone down endless roads for many next meals. He knew he was a lucky man.

He only wished his daughter would find someone to love. Her husband had been a prize with the common sense of a man from cattle country. But now Louis wished his son-in-law had been a good-for-nothing reprobate. Meryl would've forgotten him, been glad to be rid of him.

She would've wanted to find someone else.

No matter how much of a prize he'd been, Louis didn't want his daughter spending the rest of her life thinking of a dead man.

...it seems that I alone am
unaltered from what was then
—Ariwara no Narihira, *Kokinshuu*

More News

IN the university parking lot, Meryl tried not to think about Peter's flag...about how many bombs he had dropped on Vietnam.

And then the news of Byron's marriage.

She needed to hug her dog.

But first—the key in the ignition.

MERYL'S neighborhood...empty streets like a ghost town's, ranch style homes sealed up tight to keep the air conditioning in, the desert heat out. Palm trees towered above streetlights. Oleander and juniper hedges grew higher than the wooden fences marking property lines. Citrus, date, olive, and mulberry trees shaded lawns of spiky Bermuda grass. Cicadas buzzed madly in the trees. If stagnant heat made a sound, it would be at the same frenzied pitch as the incessant buzz of those cicadas.

The neighborhood was near her parents' and the university. Peter was going to complete his last tour of duty, go back to university, study architecture—Japanese aesthetics.

He had told Meryl that someday they'd go to Japan and she'd wear a kimono. "It'll probably reach your knees."

She had told Byron of his father's dreams...

MERYL spotted Louis' car.

"OK, Dad. You're *not* like the Professor. You don't know Byron's getting married...do you?"

She turned into her driveway—

"Why hasn't Byron told me? He must have a reason."

And took a tissue from her bag, wiped the sweat running down her face.

"A reason? That's so lame."

Inside, licks and slobbers of love. After a kiss from Meryl on her long, floppy ear, Freckles moved back and spun around, a ball of excitement bundled in deep brown and white fur.

"Aren't you a pretty girl? Mommy's pretty baby. Keeping Dad company?"

Meryl patted her father's belly, and he kissed her cheek.

Louis thought her voice sounded the happiest whenever she was talking to her dog...the best sound in the world...like when she was his little princess and laughed at everything that caught her fancy and most everything did.

"Been admiring Byron's bear." Its pupils wobbled as Louis put it back down.

"Want something to eat?"

"Nope. Only here a minute."

"That's long enough for a cookie."

She brought him a plateful.

Louis crunched into one, as thin as a silver dollar, then lowered his hand, sharing his good fortune. "Came by to say we're going on a trip."

"We are? Where? For how long?"

His thoughts regrouped.

"Aren't you taking that flag to Japan? Like Lee says, go on an adventure. See Japan for yourself. It's a beautiful country, people real friendly."

Louis knew he had pitched out a shovelful of malarkey...Not too much time had passed since that poison gas attack in Tokyo...carried out by Japanese terrorists...They sure as heck weren't friendly, not by a long shot...not like people he'd known after the War, shell-shocked and scared to death wondering if the Americans were going to change their minds about a peaceful occupation and line 'em up and shoot 'em. Sure any dummy would be friendly then, including himself.

And about it being a beautiful country...it was, but in January an earthquake had hit near Osaka. Thousands killed.

Louis started on his second cookie.

"I was talking about...me and Patricia. Two slowpokes, twiddling our thumbs in another place, that's all...No fun for you...We're going on one of those riverboats...down the Mississippi to New Orleans." He finished his fourth cookie.

Meryl blinked her princess eyes and wondered, Can this day get any worse?

Louis brushed a little dust off the ceramic bear's hat. "Thought I'd show this fellow to Patricia's granddaughters."

"You're taking him?"

"Byron said I could. We're leaving this Saturday. Back in two weeks."

"When did he say you could?"

"This morning."

"Byron called you?"

"Yep. He's in Vietnam."

"Dad, Byron's in Japan."

Louis pressed cookie crumbs onto the tip of his finger and licked them off. "He asked me not to tell you, but I think a mother should know the whereabouts of her son. He took medical supplies to Vietnam for one of his students, a doctor who helps a hospital there. Said he'll stop back in Japan before coming home in August."

Louis handed Meryl his spotless plate.

"Don't worry 'bout taking us to the airport. Reserved a shuttle bus."

His arm was around her shoulder. "Take that flag to Japan." He felt his heart about to break. "It's time you stop waiting for someone to come back home." Louis stooped down and picked up the bear.

"He's coming back, right?" Meryl sounded about to cry.

"He is." Louis kissed her cheek.

"Bring him home in one piece."

"Sure thing."

The door closed behind Louis, Byron's bear easy in the crook of his arm.

A cry of Hell Hounds never ceasing bark'd
with wide Cerberean mouths full loud
—Milton, *Paradise Lost*

A Visit from the Professor

MERYL lay down on the carpet next to the sofa, tried breathing in and out slowly, then reported the news to her ceiling.

"Flag arrived. Met Professor G.G. More than sixty cities in Japan were bombed. I didn't know that. Dad and his wife going down the Mississippi. Not invited. Tells me to go to Japan...takes Byron's bear. The two big headlines I saved for last. Byron is getting married. I hear that from someone I met this morning."

But Meryl couldn't say the second big headline. Her darling son was in Vietnam.

She always thought he told her everything, at least the important stuff.

"Why do you think *I've* got a phone, my favorite son? And who are you marrying? Someone I'll have to speak Japanese with? She'll take you away, and I'll never see you again—without first flying halfway round the world. And what about my beautiful grandchildren?"

Meryl pouted like a child who hadn't gotten what she wanted.

"I hate Japan."

Tears caught in her lashes. She blinked her tired eyes, twisted her wedding band around her finger, and asked the question she had asked every day since Peter's death.

"My Love, where are you?"

Waking time and reality withdrew, and before her dreams began, faint notes of music, like those coming from behind a door, played in her mind.

A door?

"I'll never see him again."

Freckles' tail wagged. She shifted from side to side on her front legs, pushed her nose into Meryl's ear, sniffed, nudged, then barked—once.

FRECKLES had barked only one other time in her life with the Quists—when their pastor had paid a visit.

The front door opened, and Freckles howled a chorus as ferocious as the alpha male's in a pack of Dobermans. Freckles leaped. So did the pastor...landing on overripe olives in the spiky Bermuda grass.

Byron caught Freckles in midair and carried her out the back door, whispering praises in a poorly affected southern accent of a television evangelist. "Laaawd Gawd Ahhh-my-dee! I doooo declare I've beheld the lungs of Sy-berry-us!"

Meryl said sorry more than once, but as the car sped off, she wondered why her gentle dog tried to attack the pastor of all people. The more Meryl wondered, the more he became suspect. Of what, she didn't have a clue. She stopped going to church. She had been a Sunday school teacher when Byron was small. Her husband had thought children should know Bible stories.

She never did care for hearing about hell.

FRECKLES lifted a paw to Meryl's shoulder and pushed down her claws.

"Ow."

A wagging tail held sway over Meryl's loneliness.

Meryl turned over on her side. "Daddy would've loved you so much."

Peter was "Daddy" whenever she talked about him to Freckles or Byron.

After Meryl had given birth, her newborn had kicked, squirmed, gurgled, burped, spat up, and dirty diapered her grief deep down in her soul. But with her son away, her mother in heaven, and her father remarried, she and Freckles were alone, and she thought of Peter.

Meryl stared at the sofa, its frayed upholstery; on one of its legs, the vacuum cleaner had left nicks. If Peter were sitting there, his shoes would be in the same place her head was.

The dirt he had brought in—she vacuumed it up twenty-five years earlier. There weren't any strands of his hair left in the carpet either...or on the old sofa...or on his pillow still next to hers. His blood wasn't on the flag that had been draped over his casket. She closed her eyes and tried to empty her mind. A wish for sleep, for an escape.

Don't think.
Don't cry.
Stop thinking.
If only.
And she couldn't stop wishing.

But one by one, each wish disappeared, and Meryl fell asleep to the soft snores of her dog.

She dozed for some time.

"Hello. Mrs. Quist?"

Freckles scratched the front door.

Greg found the knob unlocked and opened the door wide enough for a wet nose to get through. A nose, he judged, not above a set of choppers ready to chomp.

He called out again, rang the bell, waited, then pushed the door open wide.

Freckles sat before him, pawing the air.

He hesitated.

When he had been with Meryl, he hadn't thought for a moment what sorrow filled her life. Now...what memories the flag brought her, he could only guess.

But as soon as he stepped inside, he felt a peaceful comfort, one that settles in the heart at childhood and stays throughout a lifetime, every so often showing up...in a place or in a person or in the eyes of a dog. The feeling of coming home.

Greg lowered his hand. Freckles stepped closer for him to find the place of surrender and pure enjoyment behind her left ear.

He squatted down. Her dark eyes led to—even Greg could believe—her soul.

"Hello, my pretty one. Now, aren't you the best watch dog in the world? Yes, you are."

In her sleep, Meryl heard the Professor's voice and her mind conjured up a dream. His voice was Peter's. Peter had come home!

How the dream caressed her, feeling so real.

Greg stood up, expecting Meryl to walk in at any moment, startled to see him. He looked around and found her on the carpet.

"Mrs. Quist?" It was barely a whisper.

Freckles licked Meryl on the side of her face.

She woke as slowly as she could. Her lovely dream. Peter's voice. He had come home. Who had taken him?

She rolled over on her back, barely opened her eyes, saw Freckles.

"So, it's you."

Folds of fur made the dog's eyes unnaturally squinty, features mushy and dreamy.

"Yes, it's me."

Greg's face hovered over Freckles.

Meryl knew she had seen him before, such a friendly face, somewhat dreamy like Freckles'.

"Are you all right?"

She nodded, wishing she could wake up faster.

"It must seem that I've appeared out of nowhere. Forgive me."

She couldn't place him.

"We met this morning. Greg."

The Professor!

She pushed herself up on her elbows, only to feel dizzy.

Greg stretched one arm around her, then grabbed the nearest cushion, and propped it behind her against the sofa.

"Meryl Jeanne Quist." Greg sat near her. "Your initials, MJQ. My favorite kind of jazz. Modern Jazz Quartet."

She stared at the envelope he had put in her hand.

"It was under my desk."

She thought how kind professors were. She would've mailed it.

"Pretty cushion."

She pulled it out from behind her. "This embroidered part is a design I copied out of a book."

Then Meryl stroked her dog's back. "She likes you."

"Mrs. Quist, I think she'd like anyone. What's her name?"

"Freckles."

"She's gracious. Showed me right in."

Freckles got one stroke from Meryl followed by one from Greg. A thin drizzle of contentment slid over the round corner of her floppy mouth.

"She barked at our pastor."

"Not too interested in religion?"

"Byron called her Cerberus for a while."

"The hellhound? But she's such an angel to me."

"Do you think there's a hell?" At once Meryl felt uncertain and silly about asking. After all, no one knows—not even professors.

She stopped petting Freckles.

Greg's hand brushed against hers.

How he wanted to hold her hands and tell her that her husband was in heaven and she would see him again in that everlasting sweet by-and-by. It didn't matter that it was a blatant lie.

But before he answered, Meryl said, "Your students don't ask you this. I must sound like a child asking if a fairy tale is true."

"Only if I sound like a father reading a fairy tale."

She nodded yes.

Greg cleared his throat.

"My students ask the same kind of questions, contemplate on eternity. I'd rather they spend their time in the moment, see the beauty around them. There's no such place as hell—"
"Does that mean there's no such place as heaven?"
And he sorely regretted his mistake.
Meryl searched his eyes.
"There can be a heaven without a hell," he said.
"Then you believe?"
"Yes. Recently, I've started. Everyone goes to heaven."
"Even soldiers who kill?"
"Especially soldiers. Their hell is war itself."

She turned to Freckles. "You would make a wonderful god. You see, my husband died in Vietnam. But...I make-believe he's still alive...he'll come home one day. I make-believe, don't I, Baby?" Freckles licked Meryl's chin. "They brought him home. I was in the hospital...when I had Byron. I haven't been to the cemetery...his grave. Still...I want to know where he is. I wish I could've gone with him...so he didn't have to go alone. It's not that I wish I'd died with him. Byron was a newborn. But wouldn't it be wonderful to go to the gates of heaven with someone who has died...to make sure they got there and then come back home?"

Greg was thankful for her dog to pet. If he sat motionless, how would he keep back his tears? Hadn't his wife written the same in her last letter? Hadn't she wanted him to go along with her...so she wouldn't have to go alone?

He looked away.

"Whew!" Meryl hugged Freckles. "That was a lot to say to someone I just met."

Greg patted Freckles. "We don't mind, now do we?" It was time to go.

"Well, I don't know about you two"—Meryl stood up—"but I've worked up an appetite with all this talk about the ever after." And then she asked Greg a question she would've asked almost anyone.

"Would you like something to eat?"

Coffee and Cookies

THEY spoke of simple things. And halfway through lunch, strings of melted cheese dangled from Greg's chin. Meryl tapped hers. "Cheese goatee."

He glanced at his napkin, mumbling about a billy goat.

She tossed him a dishtowel in the kitchen after they finished and said Byron was in Vietnam.

"My father told me before you got here."

Greg tossed the towel back. "Children have secrets." And started washing the dishes. "They think it helps keep us sane." He swished the suds, talked about his family, then helped put away the dishes.

Meryl served coffee in the living room.

Greg looked around, commented on her good taste in paintings—

"I painted them."

And crossed the room, a plate of cookies in hand, for a closer look.

"You painted everything here?"

"Even the walls, but Byron helped with that."

Greg thought her abstract of Venice was what his stuffy, book-wormy office needed.

"Do you accept commissions?"

Meryl didn't know what he meant.

"Is it too bold to ask?" Had he come up with a brushstroke of genius? "May I hire you to paint for me, a painting like this?"

She couldn't guarantee her work.

"You see, I mix the paints to get the color I want but later forget what colors I mixed. Real artists don't forget. What I'm trying to say is...it'll be in different colors...maybe take a few years."

Meryl sipped her coffee.

"I'll wait."

A burst of confidence sped up her spine.

"Good cookies. May I give Freckles one?"

"Yes." The Professor asked permission to give Freckles a cookie! No one had ever done that. Everyone plopped cookies in front of her without asking.

Freckles took it from his hand.

"This pretty girl knows protocol."

Meryl had hand fed Freckles when she was a pup.

A feeling unlike anything Meryl had ever known took hold of her heart.

It didn't make any sense, but because a professor asked permission to share his cookies with her dog, she now believed she could do anything.

And more than anything else, she wanted to do what the Professor had suggested in his office. She would take the flag to Japan. She would show him she could do that...*and* her cousin *and* her father.

Even though Byron was in Vietnam, the teachers he worked with were his friends so she was sure they would help her find who the flag belonged to.

"Professor Gieschen, may I take you up on your offer? Would you watch over Freckles if I took the flag to Japan?"

"My house and backyard are hers."

AFTER coffee and cookies, they went to a travel agency.

"What about a hotel near Byron's language school?" Greg asked.

Out came Meryl's wallet, then Byron's business card, one side in English, the other in Japanese.

"How do you say Byron's name in Japanese?"

"Ku-i-su-to Ba-i-ro-n."

"Quist is Cristo! Like the Count of Monte Cristo?" The Japanese version of her last name—somewhat swashbuckling like Peter had been.

"A little different but close," Greg said.

Meryl would leave in a few days and stay a week...an expensive trip, but she had saved money from her widow's pension for Byron's future wedding. Now that he was eloping, she would use some of those savings for her trip.

She was about to set out on the adventure her cousin had imagined for her.

Meryl called Lee that evening, told her the plan, got some free advice, was counseled to detach from Byron and asked if any eligible hunks had taken her number at the travel agency.

"You know"—Lee had a feeling—"I think you're going to fall in love on this trip."

"You're living in La-La Land."

Then Meryl called her father.

Louis had one question. "Who's watching Freckles?"

GREG had promised to drive Meryl to the airport. She was waiting outside with Freckles when he got to her house.

He handed her the flag, then gave her what he thought was a good idea—a present, his first present to Meryl.

"A trusty guidebook. My father thought I should have one too."

Her father? Major zilch-of-romance move.

In front of the terminal, Greg surprised himself by wishing her Godspeed, what his wife had whispered to him whenever he left on a trip.

Meryl shook his hand, then kissed Freckles one last time, waved from the door of the terminal, and was gone.

Greg kissed Freckles on her long floppy ear, where Meryl had, took her home, and counted the days until Meryl's return.

The Backstreets of Namba

The Birthplace of Instant Ramen, of Conveyor Belt Sushi, the Cutter Knife...

IN her guidebook from Greg, Meryl didn't find anything about why ex-pats lived in Japan.

She didn't know that Japan's bubble economy of the '80s and early '90s welcomed foreign university graduates who couldn't get the salaries they had dreamed of in their own countries. Jobs teaching English conversation were waiting for them.

And Meryl didn't know that even though Japan had its own English teachers, roughly 98% of them couldn't *speak* English.

Those teachers knew grammar and had memorized vocabulary lists. But their side of a conversation amounted to enthusiastic nods, giggles, and a few simple questions about cities or age or favorite foods. English was pronounced as Japanese. "Thank you" became "san kyuu." "McDonald's" doubled in syllables, "Ma-ku-do-na-ru-do."

The government and private sector eventually understood if Japan was ever going to become "internationalized," Japan needed native English speakers.

Private language schools opened near subway and train stations in major cities.

Native English speakers earned three times the salary they would in their home countries during those boom years.

There had been pubs aplenty. Shopping galore. Scant violent crime. A new generation's Camelot.

When Meryl's son had asked Greg for advice on what to do first, enter graduate school or study on his own in Japan for a few years, Greg answered—Japan.

And suggested Osaka City.

Osakans didn't bother to speak English to anyone. Exceptions were found in English conversation classes.

The one drawback for Byron—Osakans didn't speak the standard Japanese in conversation textbooks.

The first word Byron learned in the Osaka dialect was the warm-hearted "thank you"—ookini. The standard Japanese is arigatou. Unlike ookini, arigatou is often said without any feeling behind it.

Meryl never would have guessed that during the Japanese economic boom jolly Osaka—the metropolis that still seemed like a provincial merchant town—was home to one of the largest stock exchanges on the planet.

And Meryl didn't know that even though this was so, Osaka had cradled plenty of thriving family-owned businesses—factories, department stores, restaurants, and specialty shops. Some stretched further back through history than governments in the western hemisphere.

Savvy businessmen had bragged, "In Tokyo, Osaka companies cream the competition. In Osaka, Tokyo companies don't stand a chance."

The bravado had been basically right. There had been relatively few chain stores, franchises, and foreign businesses in Osaka.

Each month on payday, company presidents handed out salaries in stacks of new bills in new envelopes and bowed as they thanked their employees. If the employee was a married man, he took his envelope to the overseer of the household economy, his wife, and was given back some of it as spending money for a number of possibilities. These included—a round of golf with his business friends; drinks and karaoke in bedroom-sized bars called "sunaku" where young hostesses ran up his bill; a live sex show; beer and sake with his favorite grilled food at a robatayaki. The choice was up to the man.

On behalf of their companies, Osaka businessmen brandished the latest technology, secured foreign markets, and set out to prove that perfection on any production line was not an abstract ideal. It was natural, like the sun rising. As children, they had seen egalitarian prosperity cut through poverty after the War, had seen business chances march to the beat of a better life.

If Osakans were asked what the best city in the world was, they answered Osaka.

And they had tacit understandings. Meryl's guidebook didn't mention any of them.

1. When racing up and down escalators, do it on the left side.
2. Park bicycles anywhere, even under NO BICYCLE PARKING signs.
3. Jaywalk.

A professor at the city university postulated that the success of an economy was in direct proportion to the walking speed of the people who worked in that economy. Around the world he traveled and timed pedestrians in cities of commerce.

Osaka won!

The data even pinpointed where the fastest feet were— those zipping back and forth through the underground passage from the Yotsubashi Subway Station ticket stalls to where the Kintetsu Railroad began and where two other subway lines connected in Kintetsu Namba Station.

If Meryl had been the editor of her guidebook, she would have added that bit of sociological research.

Two downtowns command Osaka, Umeda in the north; Namba, in the south.

Midosuji, an avenue lined with gingko trees, connects those two hubs. Meryl saw that avenue from her hotel room. Byron's school was minutes away on foot.

The rainy season had ended. From the wooded mountain range bordering Nara Prefecture twenty kilometers to the east, cicadas had swarmed to Midosuji's trees; their triumphant buzz, a fanfare to summer.

The first day Byron was in Namba, he telephoned his mother and told her if the sounds of musical instruments could describe a place, Namba would have four—the roller-coaster slides of a trombone...the unexpected tinkle of a triangle...a tuba's jovial oompah-pah...and that suspended thrill in the firework booms of a bass drum.

His employer owned a worldwide chain of language schools offering lessons in several foreign languages. Over 95% of the lessons in Japan were English.

Six of the schools were located in the Osaka Metropolis. Byron's was the one in Namba.

Meryl would have been proud to know that during the economic boom the school in Namba had made a profit near 30%. Most company presidents were pleased to hit 3%. Its ten classrooms had been used twelve hours a day, eight on Saturday.

Namba School's personality differed from the company's other schools, which catered to mostly businessmen.

Namba's rosters were made up of wealthy wives, university students, small business owners in Namba, and various professionals who worked away from Osaka's business districts. Why? Easy access from suburbs, south and east. And though some students took lessons because their bosses had told them to, many others came for their own reasons.

They thought highly of their foreign teachers...for the simple reason that they had left their home countries to teach English in Japan. The students showered them with gifts of appreciation, desserts and snacks, sometimes on a whim, usually during gift-giving seasons. The teachers enjoyed gourmet chocolates, mandarin oranges, and rice crackers with roasted black beans in winter. And in summer, they smacked their lips and bit into purple kyoho grapes or slurped up sweet azuki beans in jelled kuzu from plastic cups.

Few people knew (Meryl never would) that Namba School had become a place where students forgot their worries, away from family and job connections, away from their own language and culture.

The school was a place where some students filled a hole in their hearts.

They spoke their thoughts in English to a person no one they knew would ever meet.

If the students could manage a simple conversation, they had someone who would pay them full attention and ask questions—courtesies at times skipped in fast-paced Osaka— for the simple price of a lesson.

Something in Common
Their Fathers Had Come Back Home from the War

ON MERYL'S first evening in Japan, she spent time with a student from Namba School, Mr. Ono, and four teachers. Elliot, Darryl, and Jo were from the US, Fiona from the UK.

JEREMY D. ELLIOT was old enough to be his colleagues' father. They called him Elliot. For them, Elliot equaled enlightened.

He *didn't* smugly tell Darryl to cut off twelve inches of his hair, *didn't* look down his nose at Jo's business attire, *didn't* scold Fiona for slouching and fidgeting.

He certainly never gave the fatherly advice, "If you don't have something nice to say, button it."

A ruby stud winked from Elliot's earlobe. His hair was trimmed close to his head. He saw the world through frameless glasses and when he wore a shirt with a mandarin collar, looked like a guru...so his colleagues thought.

DARRYL KING, a New Yorker, came to Osaka after a short run in modeling.

No one he knew understood why the modeling agency hadn't been able to sell his perfect face, expressive eyebrows, long, dark hair, or his gymnast body, which had been good enough for the Olympics. But Darryl accepted the truth. Photos didn't capture his beauty. The opposite—the camera lens stole his soul from his eyes, his passion from his eyebrows. Darryl's curse, his cross to bear...be gorgeous and not get one thin dime for it.

The day he said good-bye to modeling forever, a friend told him there were English teaching jobs in Japan's largest cities.

Darryl left his portfolio, which had cost him a pretty penny, with his father, then packed a suitcase and tried to make another dream come true...explore the world of ikebana.

When he was a child, his mother had pointed out an ikebana arrangement. Each flower and leaf posed for him alone. The flowers spoke a serene language he desperately wanted to understand.

Darryl studied with a sensei in Kyoto City, home to Ikenobo, ikebana's classic school of flower arranging.

JO HURLEY'S vibrant health showed off her features to good advantage...full lips, mesmerizing bone structure, inspiring feminine curves.

Jo was sensual by nature. Even when her mind was focused on a serious topic, her body often surprised her with pleasant sensations. Jo didn't mind. But each of her lovers—except one—hadn't wanted her body activating itself. If a lover told her this or asked her to "Stop *it*," she abandoned his bed, took a shower, and was done with him. She was alive, for goodness sake! Who did he think he was? Pygmalion? Had she been carved from the tusk of an elephant the size of Godzilla? Could only the touch of his magic wand bring her to life?

More condoms were in her wallet than in Darryl's.

Jo spoke Japanese well and took lessons in black ink painting.

A PSYCHIC once told Fiona O'Shea that her tongue was the source of her troubles. Fiona didn't pay for the session.

Her parents had emigrated from Ireland before the War and were over forty when Fiona was born, their only child. Her mother had loved Fiona more than life itself and given her a free rein in anything that made her happy.

Little Fiona said things that none of her playmates dared say. Early on, she learned how to contort the masks adults wore with a few well-placed words and unexpected questions.

At university she studied acting. Her most devoted fan—her mother. Her father seldom spoke and when he did, the topics were on what he was fond of: reptiles and amphibians or his hobby, entomology.

After graduation, she worked for a costume designer at a local theater and auditioned for parts.

But before Fiona was ever cast, a heart attack took her doting mother from her.

Every day Fiona searched for her mother—at train stations, at the sweet shop and Woolworths, and in each room of their home. She swore she heard her mother singing an Irish melody in the kitchen. She woke up each morning thinking, Wasn't it a bad dream?...In an instant, felt she was being crushed...her throat, her chest, her entire body. Her grief wasn't a dream. It was in every muscle.

The one who had loved her the most was really gone.

Fiona wanted to get far away...told her boss. Their talk turned to Japan. "It's easier finding a teaching job in Osaka than in Tokyo." Fiona didn't ask why.

A week after the funeral she went into her father's room and said, "See you then." Never had the cases of his insect collections been wiped so clean and stacked so straight.

On her third day in Osaka, the language school hired her.

Fiona adored Japan and its genteel manners.

She loved genteel manners, especially those in one of America's great, historic romance novels.

In Japan, men didn't open doors for her or hang on her every word, as they would have done in antebellum Georgia.

Instead they bowed.

Fiona didn't care to wake up early, but sometimes she did and visited department stores at opening time—that's when the staff stood at attention inside the doorways. The moment she walked in they bowed, as if she were the Queen.

She was fond of others being well mannered.

Fiona, however, loudly blew her nose, looked at her watch when she talked to someone, yawned unabashedly whenever overtaken by boredom, and gulped her food down like a Komodo dragon.

Most people in London had never noticed that Fiona was a beautiful woman. The curves of her face didn't have enough time to seduce them before Fiona's other than ladylike words assaulted them.

But Fiona's English conversation students were unable to understand what Fiona was saying most of the time and her unpolished manner seemed natural coming from someone not of their culture.

Fiona didn't know anyone who had fallen in love with her until...

Osaka.

WHEN MR. ONO laid eyes on Fiona, it looked as if he had been smitten.

The truth—he had been in love since junior high school.

Little Boy Ono was like the other boys in his English class who tumbled headlong into a widespread illusion—if he had a girlfriend from America or England, his English would be fluent without the bother of turning a page to study.

But he had plunged deeply into that illusion. He made up a woman's face in his mind. An essence a poet or playwright hadn't put into words. A woman with shimmering golden hair and fiery emerald eyes. A woman like the woman he would meet twenty years later.

A woman like Fiona.

Every possible moment in his boyhood, Mr. Ono daydreamed of his English-speaking Vision, especially as he counted the clues in detective stories by Sir Arthur Conan Doyle. He convinced himself, at the age of twelve, that he was never marrying anyone other than his Vision—though he had invented her and in gloomy moods, knew the chance of their meeting was exactly zero.

Even after he became a newspaper reporter, that Vision comforted Mr. Ono in moments of distress, encouraged him during tedious hours. In his free time, he wrote mystery novels. His Vision was his muse and came to life as the heroine in his novels.

The week Mr. Ono met Fiona, his work had been keeping him up late.

And for each sleepless hour, more dominoes of exhaustion lined up in his mind forming a pattern of twists and turns, uphill climbs, spiraling descents.

Then as he waited for his teacher at the language school, the classroom door opened abruptly. A blast of air must have toppled the first domino into the second and so on until the last domino in his exhausted mind fell.

Standing there was his Vision, his love since boyhood.

He took off his thick glasses, the same as Clark Kent's, and rubbed his eyes to rub her out. But instead, she spoke in English with a splendid British accent. His heart palpitated. His face heated up. He knew he looked like a boiled octopus. His fingertips brushed the side of his face. As he suspected—oil glands pumping full blast. His lenses steamed. He dropped his handkerchief and wanted to bolt.

His eyes averted hers, searched for a hiding place, and ended up at the table's mahogany veneer. He could barely mumble; his lips felt as if they'd been shot full of novocaine.

Finally the bell—signaling the end of the lesson—rang.

Fiona stepped into the teachers' room.

"Mr. Ono's overdue for a facial...and he grunts."

"With you? In class?" Elliot spoke in a deliciously lascivious mode. "I didn't think he had it in him."

Darryl's perfect model eyebrows rose. "Way to go, Ono."

Jo's slinky skirt moved up her thigh as she scooted next to Darryl on a sofa. "All Ono does with me is talk about his trips up North. Nothing guttural."

"Whaaawt?"—The Irish voice of Fiona's mother boomed. "Then why do I get Mr. Monosyllabic?"

"Did he gaze," Elliot asked, "upon your radiant beauty?"

"Stop it. He glanced at me. Once. What? Do I have something in my teeth?" She looked at Elliot as if he were her bathroom mirror, her upper lip curled under, flattened against her gums.

"No." Elliot chuckled. "The answer is simple. Ono has fallen in love."

"OH NO! Not with me!" Not at all like the swaggering man of mystique she fantasized about. Mr. Ono's affection and its unwelcome manifestation in his pituitary glands humiliated her beyond words.

A flush raced to Fiona's neck.

Good Lord! she thought. As ladybird red as Mr. Ono? What if they see?

She touched her blouse.

Thank God for high collars!

But in the next breath, her heart sank.

What's the chance of being doomed to a life with men like Mr. Ono falling in love with me? Is that it? Bollocks!

Elliot peered at her over rimless glasses.

"Classic symptoms."

Jo cooed, "He's at your mercy now."

He is?

Fiona realized instantly that having someone at her mercy was advantageous somehow.

"You mean I can do anything I want with Mr. Ono?"

"He's all yours," Elliot answered like a guru.

A toss of her head, a swish of her shimmering hair—four years before Meryl comes into the picture.

On the Way to Byron's School

MERYL called Byron's school; the secretary told her to "ask at the front desk of your hotel."

But the hotel clerk didn't answer.

Giving directions wasn't easy. A street map of South Osaka looks like a child's drawing of spaghetti. Most Osakans end up stretching out their arm and saying, "Go over there. Try again."

It was quicker to take Meryl to the Noguchi Building.

She felt like a VIP escorted by her very own hotel clerk, dressed in a spiffy uniform dotted with gold buttons. Once outside she almost took hold of his arm. The sidewalk was crowded and buildings rose up around them, still lit on the inside.

At a corner, Meryl looked back. The entire block melded together like one expansive building with people scurrying in and out of so many doors.

"Byron's friends will show me which one is mine," she mumbled and tried to stop worrying.

The clerk tilted his head upward.

Meryl didn't want to make any generalizations. She had only been in the country less than six hours, certainly not long enough to be an expert like the Professor.

So far—all the men were short.

She was used to being the tallest woman in a room, but there were always men who were taller.

Then she looked at the cars—

Most were white sedans and black taxis. None were old. Not a dent or scratch on any that zoomed by. No pickups.

Then—the license plates.

The lettering and numbers were stunning, luminescent green neon!

Meryl was about to ask the clerk why, but he was already halfway across Midosuji even though the pedestrian signal hadn't changed.

She dashed after him and found herself in front of her son's office building.

A short bow and sharp about-face later, the clerk marched away like a toy soldier, his brow as shiny as enamel. The heat and humidity hadn't let up.

In the lobby of the language school, sudden panic and exhaustion from her trip made Meryl sit down on a sofa.

No one was there.

The wall clock said 8:40, but the secretary had said classes finished at 9:10.

Meryl didn't know what happened next.

It was like a dream...a woman's voice, one with a British accent.

"Good Lord. Is she even taller than her son?"

Meryl sensed she wasn't home in bed. A face hovered over hers. Not Freckles'. Not the Professor's. It was a young woman whose smile was as beautiful as her cousin's.

"Did you fly all the way to Japan to snore at your son's place of employment?"

Saying hello was the best Meryl could do.

"Here. I'll help."

Fiona slipped her hand under Meryl's neck, and on the count of three Meryl was sitting back up.

"Lucky I got out here before the students. You'd give them something to talk about. Wake up. It's time for dinner."

Meryl put on a drowsy smile. This woman was an angel. Something to eat. What could be more heavenly?

The Robatayaki

EVERY EVENING at 8:45 a security guard locked the main door of the Noguchi Building, and at 9:10 after the last lesson ended, students and teachers trailed out from a side door facing a narrow street. Most students headed to the well-lit Midosuji, but the teachers...to Namba's backstreets, what Elliot called the scenic route.

The scenic route wound through a neighborhood of pay-per-hour love hotels—each facade distinct and each cared for like a family home, only without gardens. Tantalizing aromas from ramen shops and the ruckus from pinball machines at pachinko parlors filled the air. Neon drizzled down storefronts like syrup on shaved ice at a carnival.

Across from the side door of the Noguchi Building was another office building.

On and off throughout the night, a woman stood near it. Her stilettos seemed to stem from the asphalt. Steamy nights put a glow on her skin; neon added unnatural colors to the shine of her jet-black hair. The sharp angles and shallow curves of her body seduced the shadows and made them their own.

Working that backstreet, she sometimes saw the white men leave the Noguchi Building.

They always said good evening, their lips like crescent moons. She loved that...the acknowledgment.

The New Yorker with the brows had known of this sphinx in the backstreets longer than the other teachers had.

Once when Darryl's last student canceled the lesson, he left the building early and at the moment her angles turned, smiled his model smile and introduced himself as if she were a new teacher.

She was from Jakarta...had been in Japan as long as he had been...was sending money back home.

Darryl asked the question he and the other teachers had talked about a few times.

"You're a man, right?"

She nodded.

"We thought so. You're prettier than a real woman."

Earlier that evening, Fiona—"No woman can consistently look that good."

And Jo—"I bet she's a boy, the bitch."

Then Elliot in a twang from Fiona's beloved favorite novel—"Ain' no way dat Miss a lady."

ON the evening of Meryl's first visit to the language school, the teachers asked her out to the robatayaki. Elliot went ahead of the others to see if he could get *the* table. There was only one in the cramped place. Most customers sat at the counter, near the food and the grill.

Their angular woman on the scenic route swayed softly in heels the color of turquoise green...a slender stalk of sugarcane in a breeze.

The crescent moon rose on Elliot's lips. His ruby stud winked as he walked by.

The sugarcane headed toward Midosuji.

But a familiar voice called out, then a nondescript man taking a detour on his way home was at her side. The two turned back to the love hotels. The tip of her tongue added more shine to her lips. Adoration radiated from her, and she made sure he saw her smile.

How she loved working Japanese men...clean, quick, and the size appreciated by those in her field—an S.

The teachers left the building with Meryl, waited for her to get her bearings. But she didn't.

"I have no idea where I am."

Fiona rummaged through her handbag for her cigarette case; she also had a full shopping bag from a 100-yen shop. "Suppose you're still groggy from jet lag. Makes everything seem not real." She tilted her head toward the prostitute, now strolling toward them, arm in arm with the nondescript man. "Meryl, your hotel is that way." Then Fiona's head tilted to a narrow street. "We're going this way."

Meryl turned and a shy nod greeted her.

"Japanese women," Meryl said to Fiona, "are pretty," and wondered if Byron's fiancée was as pretty and well dressed. Did she have shiny, long black hair and spiked high-heeled, turquoise patent-leather shoes? Meryl would love to slip her feet into shoes like those.

"Didn't your mother ever tell you that things aren't always as they seem?" Fiona started for the robatayaki.

Darryl broke the news. "She's from Indonesia."

"You know her?"

"She walks the street here," Jo said, "almost every night."

"Oh." Meryl didn't know what to say.

Fiona stopped, turned to them with, "And she's a boy," and went on her way.

"Oh!"

Meryl had never been in proximity to a prostitute and wasn't even sure if she'd ever seen one before. She was about to wonder everything a mother could possibly wonder in a neon-lit backstreet, but then...

"Meryl!" Fiona had come back and stood next to Darryl. "This is city life. Its nocturnal face. The innate natural drama—venomous and simmering hot."

"Sounds like the desert," Darryl said.

"It doesn't matter what it sounds like. No ignoring reality, Meryl."

The role Fiona was playing with Byron's mother was like the one she had played with her own mother—bossy, cheeky, a pushy brat hurling affection.

Meryl tried. "The person dressed as a woman seemed nice. So did the suit. I love the turquoise shoes."

"Good." Fiona threw her head up in victory. "Much better than 'Oh!' " She took a step, then..."Whaaawt? *Shoes*! You like those slut-teeeee patent-leather shoes? Now there's a bit of a wench in you."

Meryl didn't mean to but did glance down at Fiona's thick-soled loafers, then at Jo's heels, as high as the ones that had shimmied by.

"Come on. Elliot's already there, and I'm famished."

Meryl wished she could face reality with pizzazz like Fiona did. She followed a few steps behind, pondering the adventurous ring to "a bit of a wench," then noticed how narrow and colorfully lit the street was. Like a tourist entering a cathedral or a palace, in open-mouthed wonder she looked up and spotted...

"Audrey Hepburn!"

Famous lashes peeking over dark glasses, tight black dress. *Breakfast at Tiffany's*—a billboard spanned the roof of a pachinko parlor and pointed the way to a love hotel. No marketing license. A breech of copyright. It was clearly a transgression, but who would ever tell? Audrey had been Namba's urban nymph for years, and the rest of the world— even Ms. Hepburn—never knew it.

Meryl caught up with Fiona. "Didn't you think she was wonderful in *My Fair Lady*?"

At once, the phantom of déjà-vu crossed Fiona's path.

And though nothing came out of Fiona's mouth, her mind voice boomed—STOP!

But Meryl asked. "Will you speak some cockney?"

Jo and Darryl dropped back a step and smirked at each other. They had asked Fiona to do the same. Every teacher from the United States had.

Fiona felt a fuzzy fondness for Meryl and tried to stay pleasant, but her mind voice had other ideas—Why, why, and triple why do Americans ask me this within thirty minutes of meeting me? It's like clockwork. People think the Japanese all act and think the same! What does anyone know? The Americans are the bloody most ludicrously predictable people on the planet.

"No, sorry. I can't speak cockney." Fiona turned away.

"Oh." Meryl said to Darryl and Jo, "I think her voice would sound super in cockney."

The facade of the robatayaki looked like a leftover from the past. Smoky-black tiles topped its wooden over-hang. Red, waxy paper lanterns lit it up. A noren curtain hung from a thin bamboo pole above the doorframe. Its sliding doors had rows of rectangular panes of glass. The robatayaki's simplicity gave the impression of a one-story building, but eight floors of apartments rose up from it.

"Meryl, watch your head." Fiona's neck hurt. "Your son probably still has a few slivers of this doorframe in his forehead." She wasn't used to bending her neck upward so much...seldom did with Byron; it was much easier to look at the button on his shirt above his stomach.

The sliding door rattled open. A group of middle-aged businessmen, flushed from beer and sake, sprang out onto the street. Their oiled, thinning hair combed in perfect array looked like bar codes on consumer products. Jackets were flung over their shoulders, folded handkerchiefs pressed to greasy lips. They still had enough money stuffed into their wallets for the next drinking place and the next.

Inside more businessmen sat at a wooden counter, neckties loose, buttons undone, jackets draped over low-backed chairs. Cluttered on the counter were beer mugs, sake cups and squatty decanters, and various shaped dishes glazed and painted for summertime—darting dragonflies, fishing nets, the trumpet blossoms of morning glories. There were chopsticks propped on rests and moistened hand towels in narrow bamboo trays.

The counter ran along a sunken bin filled with gleaming seafood any alley cat would roll on its back for...mackerel, yellowtail, sazae turban shells, plump scallops, tangles of tentacles—octopus and squid. In another bin were shallow baskets piled high with vegetables and a variety of mushrooms. Then came colorful bowls—one held a mound of sweetly flavored hijiki seaweed dappled with thin strips of deep-fried tofu; another, boiled spinach mixed with ground sesame seeds, sake, sugar, and soy sauce. Thick slabs of deep-fried tofu waited to be grilled and topped with grated ginger root.

Behind the counter stood the Master, the proprietor and chef. From his round belly on up, every feature had been drawn with a curve. Rounded arms ballooned up to overstuffed shoulders, on which a wonderfully rounded head rolled from side to side and up and down. Lips came to a rest in a circle, eyes as amusing as a puppet's.

Below the wood-paneled ceiling, ink handprints of sumo wrestlers hung on the grimy walls. A CD player perched on a shelf, and suspended from a beam was a blowfish, dried, hardened, puffed—as big as the Master's head.

Short, wobbly chairs squeezed round the only table.

Elliot was sitting in the chair farthest away from the counter.

That evening two women worked with the Master. One was his sister.

She had been drawn with bold, straight strokes. Her thick eyebrows and thin slit eyes were fixed on parallel lines, as were her lips. The corners of her mouth only extended sideways, even when she smiled.

And since the teachers often went to the robatayaki, the Master's sister had become as direct and generous as a favorite relative.

She brought Elliot a moist hand towel and set down a pair of chopsticks on a ceramic rest, the shape of a flatfish. Elliot pointed his finger to the tip of his nose, raised his other hand, four fingers up, and said, "Five."

The line of her mouth stretched like a piece of elastic. She went to the counter and brought back five dishes filled with sweet hijiki seaweed.

Elliot always ordered for the teachers at the robatayaki. The Japanese words he knew were those for pleasurable sustenance.

Tonight he began with teriyaki yellowtail and buttered grilled potato.

The teachers and Meryl joined him. After Meryl admired the flatfish chopstick rests and answered yes when Fiona asked if she thought the hijiki seaweed looked like shiny black worms, the Master's sister brought a dish that Elliot hadn't ordered.

"The Master is giving us this for free." Jo put her hands together in the customary prayer. "Itadakimasu."

"He is?" Meryl asked.

Fiona told her to say itadakimasu—

"E-ta-ba-key...ma."

And was impressed; it had taken her five days to try to say it.

Darryl said, "Say ookini."

"That's easy." Meryl looked over to the Master. "Oh-key-knee."

Puppet eyes glittered. Circle lips opened wide. Laughter exploded like balls of fireworks at a summer festival.

"A delectable delight," Elliot said. "Grilled lotus root stuffed with ground pork. Your son's favorite dish. Put a little of that mustard on it."

"Byron's favorite? No, Byron's favorite is *my* potato salad."

"That was before he came to Japan." But Fiona really had no idea. "Try the lotus root. It's nice."

"I didn't even know you could eat lotus root."

Fiona gripped one of her chopsticks as if it were a dagger, stabbed a slice of lotus root, and waved it under Meryl's nose. "Eat anything you like. Even live shrimp if you want. Called dancing shrimp."

"Their legs," Darryl said, "wiggle as they go down."

"That's here?"

"Relax," Elliot told Meryl. "That fish bait is at a sushi bar. We're at a robatayaki. Take a whiff. Everything's grilled. Goes well with the beer. There's also chilled sake."

Meryl said she didn't drink alcoholic beverages.

"Whaaawt? Byron always does." Fiona took great satisfaction at the surprise and uncertainty in Meryl's eyes.

Elliot passed Meryl a cup of sake. "Your son's favorite, nice and cold."

"No, thank you. But I'd like some water, please."

Fiona drank Meryl's sake. "You crossed the ocean for water? Next thing you'll want a cheeseburger."

Elliot ordered shochu and water on ice for Meryl.

The best shochu came from the island of Kyushu.

The shochu served at the robatayaki was distilled from the Satsuma sweet potato and had little flavor when the Master mixed it with water and ice. It tasted how water from the best mountain spring in the world should taste. The teachers named it H_2Sho. After a blissful night of indulgence, each of them had woken up as fresh as a daisy...H_2Sho never leaves behind the reminder of a merrymaker's guilt—the hangover.

Elliot's crescent smile hid his motives.

What a splendid favor he was bestowing on Meryl. The H_2Sho would relax her. She'd sleep well. Plus when Byron got back, he'd be able to crow, "Saw your mom shitfaced." Uninspired. Sophomoric. Nevertheless, to see blondie become dreamy eyed and loosened up was an easy temptation to give in to.

The Master's sister brought more delectable delights.

Conversation topics included the mummified blowfish, why sake cups were so small.

And when Meryl unbuttoned the top three buttons of her blouse and said it was hot, Elliot ordered a fourth glass of H_2Sho for her.

Jo leaned to Meryl. "Do you often travel halfway around the world to visit the city where your son lives when he's not there?"

Meryl focused on why she was there in the first place. "I brought something."

Elliot stood up. "Pardon me while I miss the unveiling."

"But the excitement's starting," Darryl said.

"Whiz time."

Meryl moved the dishes. The teachers stacked. Then the Master's sister came and—with a nod of thanks and a straight line of a smile—the dishes disappeared.

"It's a wartime flag." Meryl's dreamy eyes blinked a few times. "Something my cousin's...neighbor's...father had. We want to find the family it belongs to. So does Byron's professor."

She fumbled with the flag and the envelope, until Fiona took them.

"Please, look at it. I'm going out to stretch my legs."

It Doesn't Make Sense

JO spread the flag across their table.

The teachers thought the brown stains on it were soy sauce and the soldier a sloppy eater. Their minds had stalled and then...

No bullet holes. No slashes from shrapnel. Only the old bloodstains the color of spilled soy sauce.

Darryl asked Fiona if the flag was silk.

"Too expensive for all those soldiers. It's cotton, tightly woven cotton." Her work with theater costumes was coming in handy, in a way she had never imagined.

"It looks like someone wrote on it yesterday." Darryl turned to their black-ink expert. "Jo, why hasn't the ink faded? Jo?"

The pink glow on Jo's cheeks was gone.

Fiona put her cigarette case on the table. "For God's sake, tell us."

Jo looked away—

Shamisen music played from the CD player.

Then she said, "It's sumi, charcoal."

"Like for a barbecue?" Darryl asked.

"No. It's hard like a stick of polished marble. You grind it on a stone tray that's shaped at one end to hold a little water. Depending on the quality of the sumi...how much of it you grind...how much water, you get the intensity of black you want."

Fiona took out a cigarette. And in her heart, she thanked the infinite universe Jo didn't start bawling because of some dead bloke's dried up old blood on his flag. Fiona certainly wasn't going to get emotional. It didn't have anything to do with her. It was a long time ago. Why waste her time caring about what happened to dead people when she could barely keep up with the living? Fiona almost stopped liking Meryl for ruining their happy time with this macabre jolt from the past.

But after another swig of sake, Fiona changed her mind. How could she ever not like the woman who had brought Byron into the world, the man who she adored to pester, poke in the stomach, and whack on the shoulder?

"So you grind a charcoal stick every time you paint?" Fiona asked. "I thought the ink was out of a bottle."

"I thought it was powder," Darryl said. "Add water. Instant ink."

Rosiness returned to Jo.

"For these flags, while they were grinding the sumi, they counted to a hundred and eight...It prepared their hearts."

Jo talked about the ritual on New Year's Eve when priests ring temple bells 108 times "...to take away all that sticky, undeniably gooey stuff that makes us human. Obsessions, fears, hopes, character traits, and temperaments. All those conflicting opposites, love, hate, honor, deceit. The brave, the cowardly, the naive, the worldly, the virtuous, the villainous. And everything sexy. It makes our hearts or souls new for the New Year, as sweet as a baby's bottom."

"I thought they rang the bell," Darryl said, "because it sounds great. Gooooongggg!" His dark mane shook as if the inside of his skull echoed. "Added bonus. Cleans my soul."

"Your soul doesn't need a bath," Fiona said, then to Jo, "How do you know all that?"

"My sumi-e sensei told me."

"What does it say?"

"It's in the handwriting of that generation. Too difficult for me."

"Whaaawt?"

"I can't read enough of it to get any meaning." Jo pointed to a kanji character on the flag. "This is 'cherry blossoms.' "

Elliot was back. "Meryl brought war booty? Haven't seen one of these in a long time."

"Elliot," Fiona said, "someone wrote 'cherry blossoms.' Why do you suppose?"

"Can't say. But it was a motif for the Imperial Army."

"Maybe the petals are the soldiers," Darryl said. "Flowers in full bloom. That's when they're marching in a parade. Then the wind, rain come. That's the battle. The petals fall one by one like the soldiers."

Elliot fingered a place on the flag without a bloodstain. "The suckers were doomed from the start."

Darryl asked why someone would have taken the flag.

"Collecting ghoulish goodies, souvenirs. Props to brag about. Pick up a little cash. Some lowlifes buy or sell anything."

"But it doesn't make any sense," Jo said.

Elliot lifted his sake cup. She filled it. And after a sip, he began.

"You innocents don't realize that sometimes war booty has as many layers of meaning as a stanza of good poetry."

Fiona lit her cigarette.

Elliot poured sake into Jo's cup. His eyes followed it to her sweet sake lips.

"I was around twelve when my friend's brother came back from the War with a gunnysack of German coins. Man, did we want to get our hands on those coins. Count 'em. See whose faces were on 'em. The coins had to be gold. We *knew* it. But he wouldn't show us. We sneaked into his room...found the sack...got caught red-handed. I thought we were dead. My friend was always bragging about how his brother had bazookaed a tank full of Krauts a day—"

"Elliot, we can see he didn't kill you." Fiona flicked her cigarette. "What happened?"

"He calmly took back the coins."

"That's it?" Another flick.

"No. My friend grew the dick to say something." Elliot imitated the boy, demanding and disrespectful. " 'Tell 'us. How many did you kill?' His older brother answered in a voice you don't toss anything smartass back to. 'Never ask a soldier what he did. He's not going to tell you. If he does, it'll never let you go.' "

Fiona sighed.

That evening was getting rather heavy.

The Master's sister was at their table with more sake.

And the straight line of her lips became even thinner.

Darryl nudged Jo. "Ask her if an address is on it."

There was a place name, perhaps a village, but the Master's sister had never heard of it. Tears made her narrow eyes glint. She brought her hands together, bowed to the flag, then spoke slowly while Jo translated.

" 'This is sad. A war can never happen again. Now young people wouldn't go. They only know...only want peace. If we don't have peace we can't do anything fun. We can't eat good food...drink sake.' "

Elliot asked the Master's sister for one more sake cup. It was poor business etiquette for her to drink with the customers, and Elliot hoped she wouldn't say no.

She didn't.

Elliot stood up, poured sake for her. The group lifted their cups to the flag when he said, "To peace."

Then the Master's sister went back behind the counter and wiped it with broad strokes. Her father had lost his flag on a battlefield, had made a new one by cutting his finger and smearing his blood into the center of a white handkerchief, had brought that home.

The stained flag still covered the table.

Darryl started quietly. "A tragedy. But it was war. Anything could've happened. Where do you think he was?" A sense of mystery took hold. An underlying thrill electrified his voice. "Wouldn't it be great to find someone who knew him?"

Jo agreed.

Fiona blew her smoke away from them. "It would be miserably sad."

Darryl's eyebrows lifted. "But great. Sad and great."

"Right," Fiona murmured and put out her cigarette. "Now how are we going to solve this mystery?"

Jo put the flag in its envelope and handed it to Fiona who put it in Meryl's bag. Elliot ordered another H_2Sho for Meryl and another decanter of sake for the rest of them.

Meryl was back. "So many people are outside. They all look a little tipsy. Is it always like this?"

"No," Elliot said.

Meryl didn't know Elliot well enough to hear the sorrow and underlying bitterness in his voice, but the others did.

Meryl only saw what Namba had recently become.

Evening business had slowed down by about 90%. The first blow came with the earthquake that January...then the terrorist attack in the Tokyo Subway that March, and some time later an attempted terrorist attack—a poisonous gas bomb was found by chance at Kintetsu Namba Station, a seven-minute walk from the robatayaki.

"Who do you think can find his family?" Darryl asked no one in particular.

Elliot was tickled by the teachers' feather-light fall into a happy-ending fantasy. He sent them on their merry way.

"You need someone with a keen sense of deduction, a wannabe mystery writer. And newspaper reporter. You need Mr. O—"

Darryl, Jo, and Fiona cried, "OH! NOOOO!"

"Mr. Ono," Jo said, "he's our man."

Meryl asked, "You know a newspaper reporter?"

"We teach him," Elliot said. "We teach everyone. Doctors, lawyers—"

Fiona added, "Indian chiefs," with smashing ennui.

"English! Get your English! For tax consultants, standup comedians, rock musicians, politicians, nuclear power PR reps, all kinds of engineers. Anyone with money, Honey."

Fiona's chin lowered and her fiery emerald eyes skipped back and forth across the table faster than a blackjack dealer's. "Mr. Ono will do anything we ask." Her power over Mr. Ono was palpable. "He takes English lessons when he's sup-posed to be working. Not that we'd ever tell his boss."

"Once we wanted to go to a pro baseball game," Darryl said. "He got us great seats."

Jo batted her eyelashes. "Free for sumo."

"Oh! No!" Meryl almost tipped over her glass of H_2Sho. "You're not coercing him like they do in gangster movies...are you?"

Elliot took his last sip of sake for the evening. "He's not even here and he gets someone who's never met him to cry 'Oh! No!' If he can find the family of the poor soul, what a boon of a feature article it'll make. It's good timing."

"Fifty years," Jo said, "from Hiroshima and Nagasaki."

Elliot pushed his chair away from the table. "My train's a-comin'. Meryl, a pleasure."

She was about to get up, but Elliot told her to stay as she was. They shook hands, said good-bye, and when he turned, he got an unwitting peek down her blouse and Jo's.

Fiona was half a step behind Elliot.

"You leaving too?" Elliot asked Fiona.

"No. I'm calling Mr. Ono."

"You carry Ono's number?"

"I carry everyone's number. Don't make anything out of it."

At the cash register, Elliot kept his eyes on a sumo's handprint hung on the wall. A smile teased the edge of his lips.

"I find it amusing that you feel the need to tell me to"—he turned to Fiona—"*not* make anything out of it."

"Good night, Elliot."

"Good night, Fiona. Be nice to Ono."

Elliot paid his portion of the bill, waved good-bye to the Master and his sister, slid open the door, stepped out of the way of two businessmen who were coming into the robata-yaki...and wondered if Ono would ever have the balls to get it on with Fiona.

having met again
and again I would see her
how my desire grows—
this it seems is the reason
she hates familiarity
—Anonymous, *Kokinshuu*

Mr. Ono

EACH NIGHT before getting into his bathtub, Mr. Ono—the newspaper reporter and wannabe mystery novelist—squatted on a stool, showered the city exhaust from his face, then washed his hair, a stubborn mix of oily and dry. No matter the shampoo, his roots looked greasy every morning and his ends stuck straight down, each distinctly separate, like the teeth of his wooden comb from Kyoto.

A sales clerk had suggested the comb, the kushi, when Mr. Ono said he wanted a souvenir for his sister. Later on the phone, he told his Okan (a South Osaka word for "mother") about the kushi. But..."Only buy your own kushi. Never give a kushi!" The sound "ku" brings to mind agony; "shi," death. Did he *want* to give his sister agony and death wrapped in a gift box? At first, Mr. Ono was disappointed in the clerk, who sported the same sleek bob as his secret love Fiona O'Shea. But his disappointment soon faded. And once again he told himself that few could win a match of manners pitted against Okan. His sister never heard about his trip to Kyoto, and he used the wooden kushi every morning and after his bath.

Mr. Ono's bathroom encased him in beige plastic—walls, floor, the low ceiling, his small bathtub, even the door.

"To shower and bathe inside a beige bento lunchbox," Mr. Ono often sighed.

He had to squeeze in his bento tub by sitting with his knees bent, nearly pressing against his hairless, somewhat sunken chest. At times he separated his ankles, letting those almost twin parts of his body he seldom shared to hang low and roll along the bottom of the tub.

He didn't understand why he did this, except perhaps to remind himself that his kintama were still there. He loved the literal English translation, "golden balls"...hated the English word "testicles," reminded him too much of the word "test" and the connotations of that were hardly uplifting. Sometimes he thought about why they were called only "balls" in English and not "golden balls."

Sometimes he asked himself if Fiona knew the word "kintama."

No matter the answer, relaxing in the bath, rolling away the minutes, was by far the best part of Mr. Ono's long days of headlines and deadlines.

Except when he saw Fiona.

And on that muggy July night, Mr. Ono was home earlier than usual, squatting on his stool under his beige showerhead.

He felt blessed. He wasn't at a media stakeout...melting into an iridescent puddle, like a chunk of lard in a hot cast-iron pot.

He washed, rinsed off the lather, picked up the bar of soap again, and turned it over and over. Then in the bubbles, he tenderly coddled what he loved most, washing each fold and follicle of his *son*—a euphemism of his countrymen—and golden twin companions.

At times his boy grew up, immensely pleasing him. Since meeting Fiona that happened more often.

But tonight, the poor lad remained unfazed.

"Already asleep?" he asked, like a father to his drowsy, young son leaning heavily against him before bedtime.

Mr. Ono rinsed off, stood up, and turned off the shower. From his rinsing bucket, he poured bathwater over his legs and shoulders, then sat down in the bathtub, knees forced to bend to the hilt.

His twins were ready to roll when the phone rang. He counted the rings. Experience had taught him, twenty meant either his boss or his mother, Okan.

At the calling end in the robatayaki, Fiona was about to light a cigarette.

"Mr. Ono," she whispered, also counting the rings. "Pretending not to hear this? I'm guessing you didn't go home with anyone. You're alone, and you want to come out, you gallant and proper man. Your only desire is to do whatever I ask. Come out, come out, wherever you are."

She lit her cigarette, sucked in slowly, exhaled as slowly.

Smoke lingered between her lips, then eased toward the hazy wreath above the counter where the businessmen sat, casting their eyes at the shimmering woman.

Fiona grew annoyed and glanced around.

The Master stretched out his robust arms and proclaimed her beauty, as he did whenever she was at the robatayaki. "Beppinsan ya ne!"

She waved her cigarette at him.

Another drag...exhaling into the receiver...Fiona liked the skin-color pink of indoor public phones, circa 1950. Unobtrusive, yet easy to spot, sensible. She talked to her cigarette.

"Mr. Ono, please answer before this runs out."

Back in the bath, at twenty-one rings—boss or Okan. After thirty meant Okan—no one was more single-minded than Mr. Ono's mother.

Someday, Mr. Ono mused, wouldn't it be great fun to get a place with a bathtub big enough to stretch his legs and deep enough for the bath water to cover his shoulders? And a bathroom window. He longed to gaze out at the new leaves of a mountain maple in springtime—green, like Fiona's eyes—and the bright, contemplative ones in autumn—red, like Fiona's lips...lipstick.

At twenty-seven rings, Mr. Ono stood dripping next to his refrigerator.

He squeezed his eyes shut. Natto fermented soybeans and a sip of chilled sake. How tasty and refreshing after the phone conversation with, almost no doubt, his mother.

Mr. Ono's phone had a dial and was shiny black like freshwater clamshells in miso soup. He didn't have an answering machine and kept his cell phone off during bath time.

Mr. Ono still counted.

So did Fiona.

"Twenty-nine? Mr. Ono, this is ridiculous. Pick up!"

She flicked her cigarette ash out of a grimy window.

And that made it thirty.

The ring broke. "Mr. Ono?" Eyes mantis wide, Fiona pounced. "You weren't sleeping this early, were you?"

He shook water from his ear. The words came to a place in his mind he hadn't known was there...where his mother spoke perfect English with a splendid British accent and called him Mr. Ono.

Fiona put the receiver nearer her mouth. "This is your English teacher, Fiona O'Shea."

Still silence.

"Mr. Ono? Say something."

He gurgled, "Ms. O'Shea."

Thank God!

She stretched her arm to where the businessmen were sitting, tapped the closest shoulder, waved her ciggie gesturing for an ashtray, got one, crushed her ciggie, and stirred her butt like a spoon in a cup of her beloved instant coffee.

She told herself, Be pleasant...Asking Mr. Ono for his help, a student contributing to my salary and therefore, general well-being. Not to mention, that bloody Japanese flag. Really, a bloodied flag! Seeing that would make even a moral degenerate with a heart the size of a caterpillar's show some consideration towards Mr. Ono.

Fiona wasn't that bad.

For a split second she wondered if caterpillars even had hearts. And cringed. She told herself, I don't mind being nice to Mr. Ono. It's just...he's so *not* manly, so *not* powerfully built, and *not at all* as swarthy as a pirate. There's no cool recklessness in his eyes, nor humorous cynicism on his lips. He's so...NOT. Oh, bollocks!

"Yes, it's me, Ms. O'Shea." Without thinking twice, she asked, "Were you in the bath?" Fiona covered the receiver and gasped.

So did Mr. Ono. He was ecstatic. Fiona, often invited into his imagination, had imagined what he'd been doing.

His *son* rose to the occasion—

"We have someone we want you to meet."

We?

Then sank.

"Mr. King, Ms. Hurley, and me. We're going to that coffee shop in the underground."

He told her he was on his way. Out flew his summer underwear—cotton briefs, undershirt of crepe cotton, and to go over his briefs, long crepe cotton undershorts, falling below his knees.

Most men Mr. Ono's age didn't wear the comfortable, yet expensive, crepe underwear. But Okan had the underwear sent to him from a department store. The package also had white summer dress shirts, dark blue summer socks, pastel handkerchiefs, and a shiny silk tie—its green, gray, and yellow reminded Mr. Ono of saltwater clams steamed in sake, one of his favorite dishes.

If the women Mr. Ono worked with knew what was under his trousers, they would snicker, "Grandpa." If Fiona hadn't told him the other teachers were joining them, he wouldn't have put on his crepe underwear in case there was an infinitesimal chance to stroll Fiona to the nearest love hotel, where he would gladly show her the meaning of "kintama." He sighed.

Clark Kent glasses on, wooden comb twice through his wet hair, clam-colored tie knotted, Mr. Ono tapped the tip of his shoe on the floor, forcing his stockinged, damp toes into it, then headed to the coffee shop. Its facade looked like a design from Tudor, England. Inside were stuffed teddy bears, some holding tiny union jacks, a few dressed as beef-eaters. He sat down at a table with a view of the entrance, wiped his face with a baby-blue handkerchief.

Then the door flew open.

Mixed Juice

Mr. Ono stood up the second Fiona walked in.

If only dashing men treated me with chivalry, Fiona felt about to whine...not ones with complexions like Mr. Ono's.

He had wiped his face and was stuffing his soggy handkerchief in his trousers pocket.

Nevertheless, with the graceful air of a hostess at a tea party, she gritted her teeth and smiled dutifully. "So nice of you to join us, Mr. Ono." A moment later, still-tipsy Meryl was at her side and Jo and Darryl were sitting at the table. "This is Meryl, Byron's mother."

As Fiona had guessed, Meryl's long legs rendered Mr. Ono speechless.

Fiona asked him to order mixed juice for them, a blend of tangy citrus, banana, soda water, gum syrup, and crushed ice with a dollop of cream on top. "Coffee will keep us up all night. We want Meryl to get her beauty sleep. Meryl, every year Mr. Ono gets high marks on English proficiency tests."

Meryl announced that she had drunk a gallon of water at the robatayaki. Jo pointed to the ladies' room.

"Mr. Ono, Meryl brought this." Fiona took the envelope from Meryl's bag and passed it to Darryl to give to Jo, who was next to Mr. Ono. Jo unfolded part of the flag.

To Fiona's utter surprise, a change came over Mr. Ono's annoying demeanor. His face looked different as well, almost mystical and otherworldly dashing, but only for an instant.

As the Master's sister had done at the robatayaki, he put his hands together, closed his eyes, and bowed his head.

The flag was much more than a piece of cloth to Mr. Ono. The flag was the soldier. The soldier had come back the only way he could—in the words written for him, in his bloodstains, in the memories of those who knew about the flags.

"An uncommon family name. Not from Kansai."

Fiona glanced at her watch. "Not from around here? You know that by only the name?" She told Mr. Ono he was brilliant.

He lowered his head, then looked up.

Fiona thought Mr. Ono looked like a pet turtle waiting for someone to toss a food pellet.

"If his name was Tanaka or Toyota, it's impossible to know where he was from. But this kanji means 'kuzu.' It's a kind of plant. This one is 'west'—'nishi.' Have you ever taught anyone with the name Kuzunishi?"

The teachers said no.

"I don't think Kuzunishi is a name. There's another pronunciation for kuzu I don't know and then nishi turns to sai."

Meryl plopped back down into her chair and leaned over the table to Darryl. "What's he talking about?"

Darryl leaned over too, his shiny nose almost touching hers. "The reason I quit studying Japanese. Kanji characters usually have lots of ways to say them. You have to memorize...all the possibilities."

Meryl leaned back, eyes distant and dreamy.

A waitress brought a tray of tall glasses on saucers with white paper doilies. Soda fountain spoons jingled against the glasses.

"Doilies!" Meryl's eyes lit up. "I haven't seen these since Byron was in elementary school. We made the most precious Valentines." She lifted her glass. The doily was still dry.

"Here, take mine," Fiona said.

Everyone passed Meryl a paper doily, and she promised each a Valentine.

"My first!" Mr. Ono did the turtle thing again.

And in his heart, Mr. Ono asked the soldier of the flag to laugh along with them.

"Can you find the family the flag belongs to?"

Mr. Ono was deeply moved. Fiona had thought of him for help.

He told her that his friend worked for the national government.

Mr. Ono's father also had government connections. The War Department no longer existed, but there were records on the troops.

"Once we know where the soldier was from, we can contact the local government office. Family records are kept there."

Fiona scooped up a tiny cloud of cream in her soda fountain spoon. "Meryl wants to take the flag to the family. She's here for a week. Can they be found soon?"

Mr. Ono couldn't answer. Finding the family depended on someone else.

Jo passed Darryl the flag.

"She'll go anywhere with you," Fiona said, even though Meryl hadn't said a word about this. "Please make the arrangements."

"I'll call my friend tomorrow morning."

"Mr. Ono, you're magnificent. Tell your boss that your English teachers think so." Fiona slurped her drink, then dug into her shopping bag for a fancy paper bag she had bought for 100-yen earlier that day.

Jo talked to Mr. Ono in Japanese.

Fiona took the flag from Darryl and put it in the fancy bag—Successful shopping day. Not nice to be in only an old envelope. Will hand to Mr. Ono later.

Jo still rattled out Japanese.

Fiona was about to stretch her leg and knock Jo's anklebone when at last Mr. Ono said something.

"Anyone who has passed away is 'nakunarareta hito.' But the word 'senshi' honors soldiers...because they died for the country and the emperor. 'Sen' is 'war' and 'shi' is 'death.' "

Jo bowed her head. "Senshi."

Fiona nudged Darryl into Jo. "Quit the morbid stuff."

"Sorry to bore you. Saying the obvious to Mr. Ono. War is a miserable way to become a hotokesama."

"What's a hotokesama?" Darryl asked Jo.

"What we become after we die. Isn't that right, Mr. Ono? It's a spirit, like an angel."

"Who says everyone gets to be an angel?" Fiona glanced at Meryl and found a goofy, silly, undeniably adorable look on her dreamy face. She wasn't listening at all.

"If the soldier was Buddhist, he became a hotokesama," Mr. Ono said. "And because he died in the War, he also became a Shinto kamisama. In those days, people thought a kamisama was at a higher level in paradise than a hotokesama."

Darryl knew what a kamisama was. He told Fiona, "It's a god."

"Like you."

"Only I'm still alive."

Making Plans

AFTER leaving the coffee shop, they strolled through the underground shopping street and headed to Meryl's hotel, the Nankai South Tower. Years earlier, Mr. Ono and the teachers had stood at the windows of the language school when the hotel was being built and had figured out that if it toppled over in a massive earthquake, it would hit them.

THE TEACHERS lagged behind Meryl and Mr. Ono—their topic of discussion: Tomorrow with Meryl. They couldn't leave her adrift in the city without a plan.

Jo suggested Shinsaibashi, a bustling district of shops and restaurants, a random blend—densely packed and undefined. Meryl's eyes would fill with an enormous mechanical crab waving its legs across a restaurant facade...a life-size mechanical clown in Mr. Magoo glasses rat-a-tat-tatting on a snare drum...the diamonds at Tiffany's. There was also a shop selling only seaweed: dried—powered, flaked, or in sheets, some paper thin—or slimy fresh.

Jo gazed ahead to Mr. Ono tagging alongside Meryl. The fancy bag looked like a lunchbox and Meryl, a mother walking her young son home from school.

"But maybe that's stimulus overload."

"So where can we take Mother Meryl?" Fiona asked.

"Why not Princess Meryl?" Darryl's eyebrows angled upward. "And the castle?"

"With her feet? Even I had trouble on those stairs."

About one-third of Fiona's foot had hung over the steps of the stairs in Osaka Castle...shoe size 6.

"We don't want to go there anyway," Jo said. "The tents. Remember?"

After the earthquake a tent settlement had sprung up in Osaka Castle Park.

"Oh, yeah," Fiona said. "Superb. Come to Japan and see what the government is *not* doing for the earthquake victims. What a tourist attraction. It's a scene out of *The Grapes of Wrath*—only tidy. The washing is hung out perfectly."

"I read that in high school." Darryl rubbed his swarthy forehead. "Couldn't get the grape part in the title."

"Rather have strawberries or mangoes?" Fiona tried to remember if she had bought a Hello Kitty eye mask that afternoon and dug through her shopping bag. The eye mask would look dazzling on Meryl during her flight home.

Jo put her dewy arm through Darryl's, his biceps as thick around as an anaconda. Fiona always said.

Darryl glanced over Mr. Ono, then over Fiona. "How about an HCS?"

Human Copulation Show.

A student, a spyware specialist, had recently taken Darryl. Buns flapped on stage. Tassels spun from tits. Darryl's 007 martini was lounging on a low table near the daiquiri and bare legs of a samba dancer...in a spangled dress...an action-packed hemline full of suspense. A tassel torpedoed the air. Darryl jumped for it. So did the dancer. And in the scuffle, under the spangles, an intrigue rose, rivaling the size of Darryl's anaconda biceps...the sight of it toppled Darryl into their cocktails. He beat a hasty retreat to a backroom stage—ran into the HCS performers with a bang. But even after a standing ovation, Darryl's top secrets had stayed secret.

He glanced over Fiona again, waiting for her to say something, but she was admiring her Hello Kitty, especially its gleaming bronze lamé.

"Nara Park is always nice," Jo cooed.

On its spacious lawns and in its ancient cedar forest, sika deer roamed, mingling with tourists, like at a petting zoo.

Almost a millennium had passed since the deer were protected from being hunted on what had been sacred ground.

The teachers picnicked in Nara Park once and Elliot had taught Fiona some history:

"This is how it was. Morning, noon, night, venison in the miso soup. Venison in the sushi. Even served cold on tofu. What's a Shinto pope to do? The only sensible thing. Good as gold. A vision of a god—riding a white stag in these very same woods. Who can kill 'em after that? At last, his holiness got some pickled mackerel."

There were sprawling shrine and temple complexes in the park and also a garden with slopes of wisteria trellises. But after a visit, most tourists only remembered the deer crackers at kiosks and how those crackers had been nibbled and pulled from their hands.

"Yeah," Fiona said. "Let's go to Bambi Land. That's about Mama Meryl speed."

Ahead of the teachers, Mr. Ono and Meryl stepped onto the up escalator, heading out to the sidewalk. They were also enjoying a pleasant conversation.

SINCE landing, Meryl had made obvious observations and she had one question she wanted answered.

"Mr. Ono, why do car license plates have neon lights?" She wondered if the Professor knew. "I mean the numbers and the characters. It's such a beautiful luminescent green. Stands out against the white plate."

Of all the questions a person could have, Mr. Ono was especially pleased with this one. Because of all the people Meryl could possibly meet, she met the person with the answer.

"My father's company makes those license plates."

"Your father?"

"Yes. It's not neon. It's a kind of paint. Looks black in the daytime, looks like neon at night."

A tiny voice called out from the back of Meryl's mind—Things aren't always as they seem!

"Why?"

"What?"

"Why, Mr. Ono? Why would anyone want license plates with numbers that glow in the dark? Everyone can clearly see them."

"When my father started his company, there were few streetlights outside the cities. It gives more light for other drivers to see."

"That's so nice! People in the United States want to hide license plate numbers"—Meryl nodded deliberately, then winked—"from the coppers."

Mr. Ono nodded and winked too and wished he knew what she was talking about.

Meryl put her hand on Mr. Ono's shoulder. She felt great and strangely different. Here she was in OSAKA (the day before—Arizona, Freckles, and the Professor) talking to a real live newspaper reporter in a business suit with so much information about JAPAN!

Meryl tapped Mr. Ono's shoulder. "I love the color."

"You love dark blue?"

"No. Yes. I mean. Do you? What's your favorite color? Mine is the glow...the luminous green on Japanese license plates."

"Okan, my mother, chose the color. It's the color of fireflies."

"I've never seen fireflies." Meryl thought there was something romantic and Japanese and mysterious about license plates glowing like fireflies.

"Maybe you'll see fireflies in Japan."

How she would love to see fireflies! "Tell me, Mr. Ono. Do you like being a newspaper reporter?"

"No. I want to be a bestselling mystery writer. Then I can hire my own private English teacher."

He had estimated how much Fiona would charge him per lesson. Only a series of bestsellers leading to a string of Hollywood blockbusters would bring her to him.

"I love mysteries." Meryl called out to the starless patch of night sky. "Everyone does. Are you writing a mystery that's solved at the end? Or in the beginning, like Peter Falk solves his? I like those the best. I can never figure out who the killer is. I can't spot the clues."

"Peter Falk. Funny man. On TV whisky commercials. I solve my mysteries in the middle."

"The middle? Now that's a new one."

"Yes."

"Then what happens?"

MR. ONO'S mystery novels had a detective, a female Sherlock Holmes...Fiona. After she solves a twisted and bizarre mystery—combing scenic areas in Japan to catch the deranged, yet sharp-witted, criminal—aided by levelheaded, loyal Dr. Watson-Ono, the plot turns softly sensual. Draped in a kimono minus the obi, Fiona ravishes Ono for, depending on the author's fertile imagination, Hours! Days! Weeks! with occasional refreshment times for them to savor scrumptious food and seductive sake of the locale. Then when Fiona is about to feel the universe break open and the entirety of her womanhood unleashed the telephone rings, there's another mystery to solve, and on to the sequel.

Mr. Ono was positive there was an untapped international audience for this type of genre, but they reached the hotel before he told Meryl that.

THE TEACHERS caught up with Meryl in the lobby.

"Jo and I are taking you to Nara Park tomorrow," Fiona said. "We don't have to work till evening. See you here around ten."

Meryl told them that her room had two double beds.

"The people at the front desk must think I need an extra one for my legs. Game for a sleepover?"

Jo couldn't resist.

Nor could Fiona. "I absolutely love staying in a hotel. Makes me feel posh, like the Queen."

Darryl slipped his arm away from Jo's and was about to ask if he could join them, but what would Mr. Ono do? Feel bad and think he wasn't included? Or ask to stay the night too? Fiona would be livid. He'd have to keep his hand glued to her mouth the entire night so nothing rude about Mr. Ono escaped.

But somehow Darryl's heart had become set on sleeping next to Meryl.

Fiona turned to him. "Good night, sweet prince."

Then to the surprise of everyone in their party, Meryl exuberantly hugged Darryl and Mr. Ono...like a small child on the best day of her life.

Jo followed Meryl's lead.

Fiona lopped to the elevator and pressed the up button.

Mr. Ono bowed to the girls, and the doors shut.

"Americans like much skinship."

"You mean physical contact, my man." Darryl put his hand on Mr. Ono's shoulder. "Women from London hate it."

Mr. Ono left the hotel, undaunted. Then later, in the draft of his first mystery, he used the insight he'd gotten from skinship with Meryl and Jo and wrote, in the softly sensual portion, a bestseller of a scene.

Day 2 in Japan

since this is a life
that cannot pass just as my
heart might wish it to
I'll make no promises in
this inconstant world of ours
—Fujiwara no Atsutada, *Shinkokinshuu*

Nara Park

THE TRAIN got to Nara Station before noon. Outside, a taxi door opened. Fiona scooted across the backseat. "Meryl, squeeze your legs in someplace and stop looking for your wallet."

"Taxi custom," Jo added. "First one in pays."

They headed to the most talked about hotel in Nara City, passing through Nara Park, famous for tame sika deer. Pine trees lined the path between the street and the lawns. No sika in sight.

At last, Meryl spotted her first one near a maple tree along the hotel's private drive. A doe stood as still as a statue.

"Look at that deer."

Fiona opened the window. "It's mechanical."

"But it looks so real."

"It'll turn this way when I wave."

It did.

"People think of everything." Meryl was going to take a picture of it on their way back.

"Someone might move it by then."

"Meryl, that's Fiona fiction." Jo swung her dewy legs out of the cab. "It's a real live deer."

"But it looks so mechanical."

Fiona told Meryl they would see more deer robots that afternoon. "You can even feed them. They'll bow their heads and say arigatou."

Meryl gazed at the curves of the hotel's tiered roof and asked Fiona if she made everything up as she went along.

"Not really."

The exterior was what one expected a hotel designed in retro-Momoyama-period-residence style would be. Lots of windows, white plaster walls, ornate bronze metalwork, fanciful eaves, cypress and stone, only two floors.

Meryl later read in her guidebook that members of the Imperial Family still stay at the Nara Hotel whenever they visit Nara Prefecture. Charlie Chaplin had slept there before the War, Richard Nixon during the Cold War. And Audrey Hepburn graced its hallways in 1983.

Pictures of them were on display in a room off the lobby, but Jo and Fiona didn't bother taking Meryl there.

Instead, the three passed the gift shop, headed to the cafe at the back of the hotel, and got the table on the glass-enclosed verandah with a view of a garden and a pond and the surrounding woods.

The cafe was a blend of what Meryl had read about in mystery novels and seen in her husband's books on architecture.

Meryl found herself in the cluttered coziness of a European sitting room and the simplicity of a Japanese tearoom that had invited the garden to come indoors and join them, elegant, welcoming. There was a melt-in-the-mouth sweetness about the place. Had it seeped into the woodwork from generations of families, friends, and lovers who had found comfort and joy there? Everything glowed with warm memories.

They ordered sandwiches and tall glasses of fancy iced tea filled with blueberries and raspberries.

Jo and Fiona chatted about all sorts of interesting news. But Meryl didn't have any topics to add. They didn't know her dog Freckles. Her close cousin had insisted that, as much as possible, the topic of Byron stay off-limits. It was her adventure. Meryl knew she wasn't thrilling or complex like a character in a mystery. She hadn't gone to college...but now she knew the Professor...or worked full-time, hadn't traveled abroad...until Japan. At home, when Byron had brought his friends over to get something to eat, she'd asked them what they were up to, but their mouths were always full, forcing them to use gestures, like some kind of sign language.

Meryl fell back on an old habit from when Byron was a toddler. She looked inside her bag for something to show.

Out came a folded piece of paper.

"I've got a poem."

Fiona asked Meryl if she'd written it.

"I can't write poetry. I'd love to study literature. When I'm reading, I know I'm missing something. Sometimes I'm not sure what I'm suppose to feel."

"If you like it, that's enough," Fiona said. "There's no point in analyzing a book to death."

Jo asked if Byron had written it.

"The girl next door did—for Byron. She's about seven years younger...he never paid much attention to her. She talked with my dad one day. He's retired from the army. Then she gave this to Byron."

"But why do you have it?" Fiona asked.

"Byron gave it to me."

"Let's see it then."

Fiona moved her glass of tea aside.

"Memorial Day. What's that?"

Jo told her it was the national holiday to remember those who lost their lives serving their country.

The poem was about the Gulf War.

Fiona began reading. " 'When I was a child at play, what was Memorial Day?' Good. It rhymes. 'Desert Storm...early morn.' No one but a teenage girl would write this—'A million tears in these few short little years.' I like 'little years.' The last verse is about that memorial for the Vietnam War veterans—that wall of black marble. 'Whispers from far away, think of me on Memorial Day.' Well, now that our poetry reading is finished, let's get started."

From the moment Fiona laid eyes on Meryl, she knew that Meryl had a temperament like her own mother's, not an enigmatic bone in her. Fiona was certain beyond a doubt that she could get away with asking anything. Meryl would be as gentle as a butterfly and answer all her questions.

The only scolding she was going to get would be Jo's.

"Meryl, there are so many things I want to know about you. You see, I trained in the theater. Human behavior and emotions enthrall me. But we only have this week. We'll have even less time if Mr. Ono finds where the flag belongs and takes you away. We've got to cram everything I don't know about you into the next few hours."

As expected, Jo scolded her and said, "Meryl's our guest."

"Meryl isn't a complete stranger. We've shared the same hotel room. And we've seen her son almost every day these last few years..."

Fiona kept talking, but Meryl had stopped listening. Since the flag arrived, her emotions had churned around inside her like laundry in a washing machine, twisted and knotted and confused. She felt things about her husband and about herself that she had never faced before. Everything that had happened those last few days added up to the answer. But who could she talk to about it? Not her cousin. Not her father. Everyone thought she still loved her husband. And she did. But—

She took a deep breath and felt she was about to dive into a black pool.

"I hate my husband. There it is. I said it. I love my husband, but I hate him."

"Can you do that?" Fiona glanced at Jo, but Jo was staring at the berries in her glass of tea. "Can you love and hate? Don't the two cancel each other out...you end up feeling absolutely nothing?" Fiona hadn't imagined Meryl hated her husband. It was distressing.

"No. I feel something, like I'm sick to my stomach, but my whole body has it...My husband's dead."

"Meryl..." Fiona glanced at Jo again—still staring at berries. "I didn't know. Please don't think I'm insensitive wanting to know about you. Well, it's all right to think I'm insensitive. Don't hold that against me."

Meryl told them it was difficult to know what part of the past to talk about.

"We've been having so much fun even though I brought that flag with me. It's not something I wanted you to see, but I needed your help. You both should know only joy. Please forgive me for blurting out my feelings."

"All's forgiven."

And thoughts multiplied in Fiona's mind—How did Meryl's husband die? It was tragic to be sure. It could've been anything, from a bee sting to a rattlesnake bite. Was it an accident? Someone's fault? A victim of crime?

Fiona felt as she did speeding through the pages of a suspense to get to the end...Oh, why hadn't Byron told them?

"My past...well..." Meryl twisted her wedding band around her finger. The old sorrow was taking hold, strangling her soul.

"It's...I...I killed my husband."

But she hadn't killed Peter. She had held him tight...and kissed him...said she loved him...watched him get into a taxi. Waved good-bye.

"Whaaawt?" Fiona lowered her voice. "This isn't something Mr. Ono would write about, is it? Don't confess to anything."

"Thank you, Fiona. But I will confess."

"Oh, Good Lord!" Fiona grabbed Meryl's arm.

"I let my husband go. He died in Vietnam. He was an air force pilot. His bombs must have killed many people, many children. I hate him for that. I hate myself for letting him go. I should've tied him up and kept him home."

"Thank God! No jail!"

Jo asked Meryl how she could have possibly stopped him. "You couldn't have."

Fiona started on about her favorite historic romance and the American Civil War. "Even that conniving, unscrupulous vixen with the hornet-sized waist couldn't keep her men from going."

"Who *are* you talking about?" Jo asked.

"Not nice to name names."

Meryl told Fiona she loved that novel too.

"Fiona, please," Jo said, "be serious. Meryl, it was his job to drop bombs. Most everyone goes off to war when they have to. You couldn't stop what was happening in Vietnam or what our government was doing."

Meryl looked out the window. A carp broke the surface of the pond and a few lazy ripples spread over the water. She turned back to them.

"But someone could've. A mother. A wife. Someone in charge. All the time I was watching Byron grow up...you know...there are children who aren't in this world because of my husband. They'll never fall in love or have a child, like I did. I'm alive when I think maybe I shouldn't be...It's not right...I'm here and they aren't."

She told them that Peter's life insurance had paid for her house and she got a monthly widow's pension—both from the military, both from what her husband had done.

"I'm such a hypocrite. Thinking about it takes the wind out of my sails."

Jo murmured, "The uttermost depths of despondency."

Fiona slumped in her chair. She had almost had enough of Meryl feeling bad. "Until everyone stops loving tyrants, nothing's going to change. About the children in Vietnam and your husband...it's not your fault. I'm sorry, Meryl. Perhaps you can bring them back, in a dream or something. You know what I mean, don't you? About you being alive...well, if everyone who thought they shouldn't be here stopped living, the human race would've petered out eons ago, and then where would we be? Meryl, maybe no one has told you this before, but you don't have to have a reason to be alive. About the pension, millions if not billions of women and children throughout history never got a tuppence from governments when their husbands and fathers were killed in a war. For you and Byron to get support somehow makes this world a little better. Stop thinking about it. You used the money to bring up a child who didn't go to war. Every mother in history is proud of you for that."

Fiona was sure her mother would be.

Meryl thanked Fiona. "And there's something else. I don't know where...my husband is."

Fiona asked if his body was somewhere in Vietnam.

"No. They brought him home."

"This isn't going to get philosophical or religious, is it?" Fiona whined.

"Didn't you think"—Jo sipped her tea—"about philosophy or religion when you acted?"

"Most characters are as superficial as I am."

Jo asked Meryl if she was wondering whether or not her husband was in heaven.

"He killed children. If there's a heaven, I'm almost sure he's not."

Fiona kept quiet. Meryl had a point.

"And I don't think there's a place for me either because..."

"You let him go," Jo said.

Fiona hadn't thought of that either. Oh Lord. If you don't end up in heaven, religion's only good for holidays and presents.

Then Jo said, "Let's be like Fiona. Superficial. We'll never know what happens after we die. Isn't it enough to be alive? And feel? And love?"

"That's not superficial, is it?" Fiona stirred more sugar into her tea.

"It's only my fluffy opinion, but if everyone was loving or loved, no one would think about war or eternity. Meryl, start dating. Promise."

"I loved my husband so much I don't know if I can."

Fiona asked Meryl if she was being irrationally faithful.

"Sometimes I feel I'm going out of my mind. I think Peter will get out of a taxi in front of our house and walk in the front door. I'll have everything I thought I wanted...but now I don't know if...I want him anymore."

"The man who dropped bombs," Jo said.

Meryl nodded.

"You haven't stopped grieving for him...and for what he did."

"No, I don't think I can."

Fiona told them about her mother.

"Sometimes I think she's still here. I'll never get over her being gone. But I have moved beyond it."

"Meryl, you've got to get out there and love again," Jo said.

Meryl promised to go on a date if anyone asked her.

"Have you ever fallen in love, Fiona?"

"Me? Good Lord, no! It's too risky. Perfect for you and most everyone, but not for me. I don't trust fate. I'll choose who I love. My decision."

"Jo, how about you?"

"Jo hunts sexual animals and keeps them like trophies."

"In this modern age"—Jo beamed—"men and women have everything. We don't need to get married. So I asked myself, for my pampered generation, what's marriage?

"Everyone has their own answer. Mine's S-E-X. The toe-curling kind. The kind that will lead to fidelity and lifetime commitment. But the only way I can find that is if I test drive...them."

"Sex can do that?" Fiona asked.

What Jo said sounded familiar to Meryl...a line from her cousin...something about the importance of experience and becoming worldly-wise before marriage...something Meryl hadn't been.

"Jo, you're careful...right?"

"Play adult games, follow adult rules." She took three condoms from her wallet and stacked them like poker chips in front of Meryl. "For when you start thinking about sex. Then you'll fall in love."

"What kind of nonsensical drivel is that?" Fiona asked. "Think of sex, fall in love?"

"Worked for me."

"You're not in love. Never have been. Never will be."

"The first time I was in love, I was sixteen. But my man didn't die, almost though, in a car accident. I wasn't with him...Maybe if I had been...maybe it wouldn't have happened. Like Meryl, it took the wind out of my sails."

"What's that supposed to mean? The man you loved almost died and because you almost lost him forever, you couldn't bear it. You chucked him out of your life so you wouldn't have to bother with your emotions of fear and possible loss. Since then, you've found it easier to conquer men than to love any of them. You and your fear took *the wind out of your sails*—it's as simple as that."

Meryl took Jo's hand. "You're still not afraid to stay with someone you love are you, Jo? Love splashes a different color on the world. You should have that color. And keep it. Promise me you'll stay with that man, you and your toes. Fiona, promise me you won't wait too long to choose who you love."

Jo promised.

Fiona snatched up a sandwich and gulped it down.

Meryl asked herself what Freckles was doing with the Professor.

The waitress brought the smallest and prettiest servings of cake Meryl had ever seen, even prettier than pieces of a wedding cake.

"By the way, do you happen to know who Byron's going to marry?" Meryl asked.

"Do I look like I've got a crystal ball?" Fiona was about to push half of her cake into her mouth.

"You don't know his girlfriend?"

"Byron doesn't have a girlfriend. You've been misinformed."

"I want you two to be in love. But my son...I want him to stay home with me, not fall in love with someone who may keep him in Japan."

"Meryl," Jo said, "perhaps you need to loosen those apron strings a little more."

Fiona took a swig of her tea and caught an ice cube between her teeth. "Didn't your mother ever tell you, it's no good worrying about something that hasn't happened and probably never will?"

"Byron sent a letter to his professor saying he'll be married by the time he gets back home. But he hasn't told me. I thought you knew."

Fiona choked on her ice, sputtered, "Who would marry Byron?" ordered another round of cakes, then asked Meryl what other mysteries she had to solve.

THEY ran out of time for sightseeing and took a taxi back to the train station. On the way, Fiona and Jo waved like tour guides.

"Big Buddha over there. Same shoe size as Byron's. Farther off is a temple built on a hillside. Has a view of deer on a lawn. Not like the view we have at the school."

Fiona added, "Meryl, you can see it tonight if you sit in on our classes and promise to behave yourself. No slouching in your seat."

Meryl promised.

The taxi stopped near a kiosk where children were pulling thin cords tied to inflatable Bambi toys, pink, orange, and blue. Meryl bought a pink one for Freckles.

Nearby a young man was feeding crackers to a few deer. They bowed their heads before nibbling from his hand as if to say arigatou.

Meryl got back into the taxi and didn't mind that she hadn't seen some of the most glorious and well-known sights in Japan.

She was with Fiona and Jo.

Shopping with Fiona

LATE that afternoon, the three got back to Meryl's hotel room, took showers, and dressed in new outfits they'd found in the underground shopping street. Jo went to the language school; her first class started earlier than Fiona's did. Fiona took Meryl to Takashimaya Department Store; Meryl wanted a decorative box for the flag. She had spotted some at the gift shop in the Nara Hotel, but they'd been too small.

"No dawdling, Meryl."

Fiona leapt onto the escalator and climbed up on the left side.

"What floor are we headed to?"

"The sixth. Keep moving."

They made good time.

The other shoppers stood on the right side of the escalator.

"Did everyone move over for us?"

"No, Meryl, this is Osaka style."

"Efficient. Arizona department stores have only two floors. How do people remember where everything is?"

Fiona stopped, turned round, and looked down.

"This is why people in Japan are so smart. They build astronomical department stores, and everyone memorizes where everything is. It stimulates children's minds and keeps older members of society from unscrewing their heads and leaving them on train seats. We also have enormous department stores in London."

"I feel so left out."

"Never you mind, Ms. Desert Flower of the barren suburbs. This escalator fends off dementia and increases your IQ by five points."

At the display for lacquered plates, tea containers, and round trays, Fiona found a case the right size for the flag.

"What about this one, Meryl."

"Can a box be more beautiful?"

Moments later Fiona said, "I'm famished." She took Meryl for summertime soba, served in a shallow bamboo basket.

Meryl's noodles slipped off her chopsticks. "This is going to take forever and a day."

Fiona mimed to the waitress.

"Here's a fork, Meryl." Fiona's noodles were already twirled around hers, and she was dipping them into a cup of chilled dashi. "No time for chopsticks. Class is in fifteen minutes."

Mrs. Quist's Maiden Name

IN the elevator going up to the language school, Meryl asked Fiona to introduce her by her first name or by her maiden name, Cunningham.

"Don't want everyone to know you're Byron's mum?"

"My cousin thinks I have to detach from Byron. Says this is my adventure in Japan. If the students don't know my married name, they won't ask me about Byron and they won't talk about him."

How intolerably horrid!

Fiona would be appalled if her mum thought her own personality suffered because she was *attached* to her daughter.

Americans were flakier than Fiona had ever imagined. How would she bear it if her mother had traveled halfway round the world and hadn't talked about her to everyone she met?

It was Fiona's duty as a fellow adult-child to act on Byron's account.

It's Tuesday, Fiona thought. That means—Mr. Baba. He likes Byron and won't mind talking about him.

Oh, to see Meryl's face when Mr. Baba tells her the ridiculous stories her son has told him—

Fiona was positive the stories would be ridiculous because they were Byron's.

No! Meryl won't escape.

Mothers are never allowed to escape from their children or detach. Where do Americans come up with these bogus ideas? Mum would never think of something so stupid...

Fiona felt jealousy sneaking up on her. Byron's mother was there when her own mother never would be. Melancholy was also encroaching, but Fiona's honey-coated smile kept it at bay.

"Anything you wish, Ms. Cunningham."

A Crane Waits

MERYL and Fiona walked into the lobby minutes before Fiona's lesson with Mr. Baba.

In the hallway, they bumped into another English student, Fusako Kawanishi.

She captured summer in her tailored dress of creamy-yellow batik—a high collar, straight sleeves coming down to her elbows, a narrow, closely pleated frill along all the edges...in her hand, a wickerwork bag...a curious shade of dark brown. Her shoes, about half the length of Meryl's, were the same color. Platinum loop earrings hung from her earlobes, pulling them down but not making them nearly as long as the Buddha's. Dior red brightened her tiny fingernails.

"Ms. Kawanishi, good evening."

She greeted them with a mixture of breathless excitement and aged charm in the demure lilt all her own.

"I'm fine. Thank you and you?"

Her head bent back quite far to see the tall woman's face. But the view was the underside of the woman's chin and the nostrils of her nose.

Isn't this so reminiscent of days gone by? Ms. Kawanishi thought. A skip back through time to childhood...holding Mother's hand. She looks nothing like Mother, but what magic.

Ms. Kawanishi never imagined that women grew so tall—not even foreign ones. Once she asked her teacher Byron why he was so tall. His answer: Lots of water and sunshine.

Fiona replied, "I'm fine too, thank you. This is my friend, Meryl."

Ms. Kawanishi brought her head back to its usual position and tried saying Meryl's name but soon gave up, smiling in exasperation at simply being unable to say a person's name. The *r* and *l* sounds were her weak points.

She again looked up and up at Meryl.

"Tall...almost same like teacher, By-lon. Sometime get on train...hit head? Have you...herumetto?"

She patted the top of her own head, expecting Meryl to laugh as Byron did.

"No, Ms. Kawanishi," Fiona said, "she doesn't have a helmet," and turned to Meryl. "Probably someone *taaaall* taught her that."

Ms. Kawanishi then asked Meryl a question she had asked each of the teachers—careful of the rising inflection, "Where are you...come from?"

"The United States, Ms. Kawanishi." Fiona nudged Meryl along. "We've got to go teach."

Ms. Kawanishi, however, nimbly blocked Fiona's pretty friend and stuck out her hand, skin delicate with age, muscles strong and agile from a lifetime of constant use.

"It is nice...meet you."

Meryl wrapped her hand around the softest hand she had ever held.

"Thank you. You too."

Long, silver hair loosely circled the top of the student's petite head. "I understand...you speak." Her hand covered her giggles as the handles of her wicker bag slid down to the crook of her elbow. "You like Japan?"

"Everyone loves Japan, Ms. Kawanishi." Fiona took a step away. "See you next week at your exhibition."

Ms. Kawanishi had invited her English teachers to an ikebana exhibition she was putting on.

Excitement overwhelmed her and out poured some amusing sounding Japanese to play with.

"Tsuru kubi, tsuru kubi, tsuru kubi de matte imasu."

Fiona shifted her voice to teacher mode. "English please."

"Do know you tsuru?" Ms. Kawanishi stretched her neck up, like a child trying to gain height.

"What on earth are you doing?"

"Tsuru...bird...kind of bird."

"A bird, you say? What does it look like?"

"Big."

"Big Bird?"

"No...Yes...Big! With long."

Above the pleated frill of her collar, Ms. Kawanishi petted her throat in short strokes as she would a kitten.

"An ostrich? The big running bird?"

"No. Japan New Year's big bird."

"Does she mean crane?"

The two looked up at Meryl.

"Crane?" Ms. Kawanishi flicked her wrist down, her hand comically clawlike, then mimed the movement of a building crane. "Crane?" An instant later, she touched her neck.

"That's it!" Fiona puckered her lips, wondering how Meryl figured that out.

"So...I am wait you like crane—tsuru—big bird. You understand?"

"In anticipation of my arrival at your ikebana exhibition, you'll be waiting and watching for me, your neck stretched like a crane's. Yes, I understand."

Fiona patted Ms. Kawanishi's shoulder and felt the texture of the batik. She loved Ms. Kawanishi's outfits, though she knew she wouldn't look good in them. They were tasteful and elegant.

"You're a good teacher, Ms. Kawanishi."

"I am student. Will write *crane* in diary."

Ms. Kawanishi kept an English diary and wrote down what her teachers taught her.

Fiona nodded. Always hope for English students.

"At exhibition," Ms. Kawanishi said. "You see. I'm kimono."

"I'd love to see a kimono," Meryl said. "Wish I had one."

Ms. Kawanishi turned away.

Fiona twisted her neck up to Meryl. "Are building cranes called cranes because they look like a crane, I mean the bird?"

"I never thought of that until now."

Mr. Baba

IN the teachers' room with Meryl, moments before the lesson, Fiona talked about the fashionable and consistently grammatically incorrect Ms. Kawanishi.

"She does everything...Japanese dance, the tea ceremony, calligraphy. The ideal all men wish to marry, except they don't know they've missed the boat by a few decades. Our secretaries—the recent remake—can't hold a candle to her. I mean, they look lovely, but...And Ms. Kawanishi is so modern." Fiona spoke the last bit with a speck of envy. "She still runs her late husband's insurance business. Plus, invested profits from her stock holdings into real estate, then sold most of her real estate before the price bubble burst."

If Fiona had a few more minutes, she would've added—Ms. Kawanishi loves being around young men...She always wants her lessons with your son.

Instead—"Makes me look prehistoric."

"You're not at all prehistoric. I am!"

"If you insist, Meryl." Fiona checked her teeth in a compact mirror and touched up her lipstick. "I wish Ms. Kawanishi spoke better English. She must know so much about life."

"I would love to find out about her too. I guess I never will." Meryl's wistful eyes took on a serious slant. "I think Ms. Kawanishi is near my father's age."

"Early seventies."

"So she experienced the War. And then that earthquake this year."

The week after the earthquake, Fiona had asked Ms. Kawanishi if everyone she knew was all right. She had brought her hands together in prayer and said, "Some to heaven in War...some to heaven in earthquake."
Fiona got a pad of paper and a pen from her locker.
"Time to go."
"I hope I don't say anything I shouldn't."
"Don't worry. I'll be sitting next to you and pinch you if you do."

MR. BABA'S classroom had a view of Osaka that extended south into an urban haze, which hid the flowing lines of the Izumi Mountain Range. Fiona stood at that window every now and then, in fantasy, proud, anonymous monarch overlooking her domain, her Camelot. Under the sun, a stormy wave of buildings. Under the moon, a multitude of illuminated points, city stars scattered before her.
Awe...reverence...inspiration...the power of humanity.
She adored the view, buildings cramped together and stuffed full of...consumers! With so many of them spending so much. Food and entertainment and shopping options had reached nearly epic proportions.
Fiona wanted Meryl to relish that part of the city in lights. All those lights for all that spending money.

MR. BABA stood up when the women came in.
Fiona introduced Ms. Meryl Cunningham. But Fiona was determined to get Mr. Baba to talk about Byron. It didn't matter that Meryl's cousin had told Meryl not to talk about him.
What do cousins know about mothers anyway?
Fiona sat down, glanced at her watch, and wished for the impossible...her mother in Japan.
Never mind, onwards and upwards.

THE TEACHERS didn't have to use their textbook or explain fussy grammar rules or practice trance-inducing language drills with Mr. Baba.

He read novels in English. Hardy's Tess defined the true woman. Fiona's opinion on her favorite American historic romance and "the man to fall in love with" sounded like his daughter's. He took notes during his lessons.

Mr. Baba wasn't a salaryman in a dark suit, a company emblem pinned to his lapel. His uniform was a pair of pale green slacks and a matching short jacket with his family name embroidered in English lettering above the front left pocket—the uniform for managers in factories. He commuted to Namba for his lessons from Higashi Osaka City, home to the best factories in the world for machine parts.

Mr. Baba was ten years old when he had first heard American enlisted men speaking English. Long noses and big ears stuck out from their heads. Children squealed, "ozoosan mitai," even though the only elephants they had ever seen were in picture books.

Young women stood on rubble-lined streets. Homegrown proprieties had been defeated by fleeting smiles and flimsy promises. The victors offered chewing gum and Hershey's chocolate...an easy penitence or a simple act of forgiveness, a kind gesture or payment for an open door. Had he put out his hands, he could've gotten as much as he liked.

But he never did.

He wanted rice, soft and sticky —in the shape of Mt. Fuji—rising above the rim of his bowl.

He didn't trust them.

They had burned Osaka to a wasteland.

He knew about Hiroshima and Nagasaki. The summer sky over Osaka had turned a threatening and sickening gray the day the Americans dropped their atomic bomb on Hiroshima. A flash of light. Everyone dead. No escape.

Not like the cluster bombs. If the B29s dropped them right over you, the wind carried them away to fall on others. If the planes were coming toward you when the bombs dropped, then you ran for your life...for your arms and legs...your flesh. The bombers brazenly lit up the night sky, came casually in the light of day. No need to be clandestine. Osaka was defenseless, and the enemy knew it. No artillery powerful enough to hit the planes. Even on the last day of the War an inferno came hurling down on them.

He hated the enemy.

But he listened to the Americans' loud voices and chortle as they got their boots shined by skinny boys, then strolled away with women whose husbands, fathers, and brothers were never coming home.

He gnashed his teeth to keep from screaming, "Give back my father! Give back—our men! I'll slaughter you...Laugh in hell!"

His mother told him to respect the Americans. They were going to make Japan good and bring peace. Everything wonderful would happen.

He wanted the Americans to know his mother was starving. Each time he emptied his bowl, she gave him hers, filled with boiled vegetables—the vegetables vendors had tossed away. He wanted the Americans to know he was slowly killing his mother because of what they had done to his country.

But he couldn't speak a word of English.

When Mr. Baba was able to go back to school, he had an English class. Later, he studied on his own. And then when the bubble economy brought customers from abroad to where he worked, the company president asked if any of his staff spoke good English. Someone said, "Baba's kick-ass." Mr. Baba was handed an attaché case filled with stacks of 10,000-yen bills, sent to the language school, and for years on every Tuesday after work, had stepped onto the train for Namba, sat down on a cushioned bench, shut his eyes, and thought of what he was going to talk about during his lesson.

Mr. Baba hadn't, however, shut his eyes on the train those last few months. Instead he peered down the aisle searching for anyone carrying an umbrella with a tip sharp enough to split open a plastic bag filled with poison.

A terrorist cult had forced the change in Mr. Baba's routine. Followers carried out the poison gas attacks throughout the Tokyo Subway System four months earlier, and the year before, the target was Matsumoto City, Nagano.

No one Mr. Baba knew had heard of the poison called sarin before Matsumoto. There was no law banning the production or possession of sarin. The cult's leaders had planned to kill every person on the face of the planet with it. But terrorism hadn't changed everything.

Mr. Baba still gazed out the windows as the train pulled into Tsuruhashi Station, three stations from Namba, for the view of a row of two-story buildings and their muddy-brown roof tiles not quite straight and their corrugated steel and their thin planks—all stubbornly holding off the encroachment of sleek, modern architecture.

His train stopped in Tsuruhashi during the best time...when savory aromas blew out from grease-laden fans at nearby Korean beef-barbecue restaurants...turning the passengers into a pack of Pavlov's dogs. Expectation squeezed their stomachs and filled their mouths with saliva.

Mr. Baba had lived partly on the smell of food when he was a child...He had believed so. The browned sweetness of roasted yams wafting throughout the streets grabbed him at his ankles, holding him and his empty stomach captive. He devoured the smell with each deep breath. Somehow that encouraged him until a morsel he could chew came along.

He scavenged at the black market in Umeda. Stabbings were common. Women selling bread kept it under their clothes until money was in their fists. Makeshift barbecues were built on top of metal roofs. Grilled meat, out of sight, out of reach...Whiffs of it drifted down—rat, rabbit, boar, deer. Who knew?

Mr. Baba had also done business on the black market.

He and some older boys crossed a canal to get to a munition factory near Morinomiya after an air raid, hauled out a boatful of wreckage, sold it as scrap metal. Then later, when he heard the tall tales about the "Apache raid" on the bombed-out ruins, he felt a kinship with the warring tribe in Hollywood motion pictures. His father had taken him and his friends to a cowboy flick during the easy days before the War. Outside the theater, the boys cried war whoops, then ambushed and scalped each other all the way home.

And around that time, his mother had warned him, "Telling a lie leads you down the path of the thief."

Even when he was starving, he never lied.

Mr. Baba's favorite restaurant finally reopened when he was a young man...the one serving freshwater eel, skewered and steamed—as soft as tofu—repeatedly dipped into a pot of mirin, sake, and soy sauce and grilled to the color of a red fox basking in the sun. Mr. Baba stood outside the restaurant, shut his eyes, took deep breaths through his nose, and saw himself with enough money someday to buy all the rice topped with eel he would ever want.

That someday had come true.

He no longer had to make-believe the whiffs of roasted yams and grilled eel filled his stomach. But even so, at Tsuruhashi Station the whiffs of barbecued beef held him through his English conversation lesson till dinner.

Mr. Baba would meet Meryl on an evening when the steamy air—brimming with the smells of fried garlic, onions, and spicy barbecued beef—fed an idea that had found a seat in his mind the night before. At dinner, his grown children didn't touch the dish his wife had made with freeze-dried tofu.

"It's like eating the kitchen sponge."

They had no respect for food, no idea what hunger was. They never believed him when he told them how long he had gone hungry or what hunger could do to someone, how it consumed the soul. His son and daughter thought he was making up stories, was trying to drill an outdated manner in them—the one that went "Eat everything you're served."

Yes, that night during his English lesson he was going to talk about respecting food.

The English Lesson

BUT when Fiona walked into Mr. Baba's classroom and introduced Meryl Cunningham—eyes as blue as the sky after a summer storm—he changed his mind and began.
"Ms. O'Shea is an excellent teacher."
"Please, tell that to my boss."
Mr. Baba dismissed Fiona's remark as if it were his own daughter's, turned to Meryl, guessed that her father had been in the War, and found something in her eyes he had once seen in his mother's.
He shut his English notebook and asked her, "Do you mind if I tell you a story about my mother?"
"I'm honored."
Fiona was twirling her pen between her fingers.
And for the first time, she really looked at Mr. Baba. Droopy eyes, flat, unimpressive nose, thin lizard lips, wide forehead with straight lines running across it, equal distance apart, like strings on a musical instrument...like a shamisen. His ears stuck out far from his head.
Fiona kept her thoughts to herself...Whaaawt? And the Japanese girls think foreign guys have big ears. Especially Byron! Well, Byron does. Bozo-the-Clown-size. But these are nearly Dumbo-size. Ears only a mother could love!
Then Mr. Baba said, "I was ten years old when the Americans firebombed Tokyo."
Fiona put her pen down—
"Everyone was sure Osaka was next."
And bit her bottom lip.

"Parents had to send their small children out of the city. My mother handed me over to the officials. Her face, streaked with tears. The other mothers didn't cry. I looked. We children boarded the train for Okayama Prefecture."

Fiona had once heard Jo say Okayama bordered Hyogo, and Hyogo bordered Osaka to the west.

"We got there. So many children, sad...lonely...quiet. We did what we were told. Those officials...strangers, grabbed us...hit us for no reason. They made the younger children cry. I couldn't stand that, but I was too small to fight them. I made up my mind to leave that night."

"Alone?" Meryl asked.

And Fiona, "So you took the train back?"

"I followed the road to the station, then the train tracks to the Yodo River...made my way to a small boat. You don't see them anymore. It had a narrow pipe sticking up like a chimney...made the sound *po, po, po* when the exhaust blew out."

Fiona never failed to look out the train window from the bridge spanning the Yodo River when she went into the northern part of the city.

"It must have taken you forever."

Her comment sounded casual. But she stirred in her seat.

"It took all night and the following day, into that night. There in front of me Osaka blazed. The sky, a terrible red. People running past me, running away from the city. I couldn't understand completely. Osaka was under attack, the noise tremendous, like thunder...thunderclouds raining fire.

"I wasn't afraid. I already lost everything when I left, would do anything to get it back. Then morning came. The air still choking. Buildings burned down."

He didn't tell them of the bodies a shade of black he had never seen before. A black that had stopped time.

"Everything I knew was gone. My mother couldn't be alive. This was why she had sent me away. If she was dead, I wanted to be dead with her. That was how my mind worked."

The shamisen lines on his brow deepened.

"Behind me came my mother's voice calling out my name. Calling me from heaven. I shut my eyes. Her hands were on my arms...holding tight. I was happy. She was going to take me with her. I opened my eyes. And kneeling before me was my mother. Alive! She pulled me to her...never sent me away again."

Mr. Baba waited for Meryl to say something.

But she didn't.

If Peter hadn't gone to war but had died in an accident or of illness in a peaceful country, wouldn't she think deeply about souls taking loved ones to heaven? It was a beautiful idea. Instead, she was left with what Peter had done in Vietnam—to cities, to mothers, to children. But...she had let him go.

And Fiona thought...I *can't* believe it. Mr. Baba *would have* to tell this gut-wrenching story *today* in front of Meryl! Oh, why didn't I ask him something about Byron from the start? Why didn't I stop him? How could I? Even a buffoon with a pinhead of sensitivity wouldn't stop Mr. Baba from talking about this experience of his during the War. I could never stop Mum from going on and on about the suffering that had been in London.

Fiona knew full well her next comment would sound completely inane.

"Mr. Baba, I'm glad you and your mother made it out all right."

"I can't tell my children. You know, they don't believe me. I'm their father."

Fiona asked him to tell a story, one that he'd heard during an English lesson.

Mr. Baba looked through his notes. "Mr. Quist always has a story."

Thank God! Fiona said under her breath. A diversion from the talk of war and little boys and mothers and death.

As Fiona had planned—Meryl will hear what the students think about her son, no matter that her cousin doesn't want her to.

At the mention of Mr. Quist, Meryl's eyes opened wide and she put on a pleasant smile.

Mr. Baba turned to her.

"An intelligent and charming young man. He has manners, good posture. Never looks at his watch."

Fiona acted on cue, slouched even more in her chair, and yawned.

Manners are overrated.

"Yes, Mr. Baba, but what did he talk about?"

"He told me a story I'll never forget. Not about himself—about crime and punishment. But not from a court of law. Mr. Quist told me a fellow shot a cactus."

Fiona's face became the stage for the monologue in her heart—What daft idiot shoots a cactus? And Byron's just as daft to have told this to Mr. Baba!

Even so, she was positive it was going to be only another mundane story Byron had thought was funny, perfect for his mother. At a glance, Fiona saw that Meryl was warmly interested in what Mr. Baba was saying.

"The fellow practiced his aim—using a cactus. A saguaro. Mr. Quist said they're protected by law."

Fiona asked why.

Mr. Baba read his notes. "He said they're only found in Arizona, California, Mexico, and they grow slowly. Mr. Quist emphasized that point—fifty to seventy years to mature enough to flower."

"What does it look like?"

Mr. Baba told them it was tall and had big arms.

"As tall as Ms. Cunningham?"

"Mr. Quist said up to twelve, thirteen meters."

"It's the cactus," Meryl said, "everyone thinks of when they think of a cactus. May I?"

With Fiona's pen, she sketched a saguaro in Mr. Baba's notebook.

"He shot *that?*" Fiona boomed.

Sparks of merriment lit up Mr. Baba's eyes.

"He shot it many times, then walked away. But the cactus fell—"

"You mean fell over like a tree falls over? A cactus can do that?"

Mr. Baba tilted his head to Meryl, and she nodded yes.

"So the man ran to escape the cactus." Boring, boring, major boring. Excruciating, mundane stories. Can always depend on Byron for that.

"The cactus fell on him," Mr. Baba said.

"And that makes it about crime and punishment? An attack cactus?"

Fiona laughed in the most delightful way, emerald eyes glancing from one corner of the room to another. She gave up all hope of understanding whatever in the world Byron had been thinking.

"Mr. Quist told me a saguaro is heavy, up to ten tons."

For an instant, Fiona didn't understand what Mr. Baba was saying, rolled her eyes, and then...

Dear God! Not someone flattened like a pancake in the desert sand!

"Ten tons? A ten-ton cactus?"

Fiona looked to Meryl for some sign that this was a tall tale Americans find hilarious. Byron often exaggerated, immensely annoying her.

But Meryl didn't bat an eye.

Nor did Mr. Baba.

He was pleased with Fiona's animated response. Her usual clipped comments lacked such colorful emotion. He had opened a little door in her ad libbed insolence and was able to peek in.

"Mr. Quist said that many people thought this story shows the vengeance of nature. But nature has no punishment or vengeance or thought. It was the laws of physics. We talked about that. And poet justice."

"That's *poetic* justice," Fiona said.

"Mr. Quist said there's only poetic justice in literature—but not in life."

Mr. Baba's listeners were quiet.

Fiona was puzzled and irritated and wondered if Byron's absurdly tragic story hid some meaning.

And Meryl...Her father had told Byron about Peter's death. It was a mechanical failure. His jet fell. *The laws of physics.*

"I'll always remember what Mr. Quist taught me about corn meal." Mr. Baba's hands hovered over the table like a magician's. "Do you eat corn bread, Ms. Cunningham?"

Meryl didn't answer.

Fiona pushed her knee against Meryl's. "Mr. Baba, I eat corn bread. They have it at the bakery in Takashimaya. I'll bring you some."

She pinched Meryl's thigh. "You eat corn bread too, don't you, Ms. Cunningham?"

Meryl found Fiona's hand and held it. "I make it in the winter."

"Wonderful," Mr. Baba said. "Ms. O'Shea doesn't talk about cooking...like my daughter."

Before he began his next story, Mr. Baba shut his droopy eyes and envisioned US Occupied Osaka...and once again, his mother. She would've been a little older than Fiona then. He was happy Fiona and his children lived in a time of prosperity and peace...though tainted with the recent events of the earthquake and the poison gas attacks in Matsumoto and the Tokyo Subway...was worried they were too pampered to face any hardship.

He hoped with all his heart they never would.

He pursed his lips and nodded. His eyes met Fiona's, then settled on Meryl's.

"Mr. Quist told me Americans eat corn bread."

WHEN Mr. Baba said the title, Byron asked, "You read *The Grapes of Wrath*...in English?"

"Yes. Such a great loss. The children so pitiful. Have you read it?"

"Required in high school. My grandfather saw it on my desk and told me it was about the kind of life he had—when he was a child."

"Your grandfather?"

"He grew up in Oklahoma. Said Steinbeck wrote about the lucky ones. He was too poor to leave."

Mr. Baba's teacher was the grandson of a once starving boy.

"I pity your grandfather."

Byron had never pitied his grandfather, had never thought that *pity* and *grandfather* belonged in the same sentence. Whenever he was at his grandfather's house, the refrigerator was packed and second or third servings were being finished off his grandfather's plate.

The Dust Bowl was only a short chapter in a history book, a setting for a novel.

"My grandfather is all right."

Mr. Baba's children felt the same about him.

"But he wasn't...all right." Mr. Baba waited a moment. "Do you eat everything on your plate?"

"How do you think I got this tall?"

"Even Japanese food? Sashimi? Natto?"

Byron told Mr. Baba that he loved both raw fish and fermented, slimy soybeans.

"There isn't anything you don't eat?"

"Well, there's a combination I don't like. I like buttermilk. That's milk, but a little sour and thick. And I like corn bread. My grandfather sometimes pours buttermilk over corn bread. It's pretty disgusting."

"Did you say 'corn bread'?" Mr. Baba's voice was low.

"Yes. It's made from cornmeal. My mom bakes it in the winter."

"Only *pigs* eat cornmeal in America." Mr. Baba had known that since childhood.

"Pigs eat anything in America."

Deep in Mr. Baba's heart a memory smoldered.

"Corn bread is common in the States. My grandfather ate it when he was a boy. I think you mean corn cobs."

"Cobs?"

"Pigs are fed corn cobs." Byron sketched an ear of corn, a kernel of corn, a cob without kernels.

"That's not what I...after the War. Americans." Mr. Baba strained under the weight of his emotions. "Sometimes in our neighborhood my mother got cornmeal from the Americans. But my mother didn't know how to cook it. She mixed it with water. Fried it. It was terrible."

The muscles in his throat tightened.

"It eased our hunger pangs...a little."

The palms of his hands had become sticky cold.

"Everyone said, 'It's food for pigs.' I thought the Americans gave us cornmeal because...because they thought we were," Mr. Baba gasped, "pigs! Animals!"

"I'm sorry you misunderstood."

"The Americans didn't think we were pigs?"

"No, they didn't."

Mr. Baba looked again at Byron's sketches, then reached into his back pocket for his handkerchief and pressed it to his eyes.

NIGHT embraced the evening. From the endless myriad of lights sparkling across south Osaka, a magical enchantment rose.

But Fiona and Meryl weren't looking at the view from their classroom window while Mr. Baba told that story or when he ended it at the time the bell rang, signaling the end of his lesson.

The curve of Fiona's face showed a depth of emotion that caught Mr. Baba off guard.

The visitor thanked him more than necessary.

And then the women left.

For a while, Meryl put aside her thoughts of her husband in Vietnam.

Mr. Baba had believed something that wasn't true...all those years. But her son changed that. She only knew this because she came to Japan.

She was glad her cousin had sent her the flag, thankful for the Professor encouraging her and watching over her sweetheart dog. She imagined the Professor and Freckles going on walks together in the evening and wondered what time it was in Arizona. What would the Professor say when she told him about the lesson with Mr. Baba? She could hardly wait for what was next, for any news from Mr. Ono. How she hoped Mr. Ono had found the family. How she wished to meet them.

Fiona loved the corn bread story. It was a splendid story, a three-cheers-for-English-teachers story. And thank God, nobody had died.

Ms. Kawanishi

On the Way Home

AFTER talking with Fiona and Meryl at the language school, Ms. Kawanishi stopped by Takashimaya Department Store for a small box of summertime confection, kuzu mochi. The clerk put it in a paper bag, printed with an illustration of dark pink roses.

The week before, Ms. Kawanishi had given Fiona a box of kuzu mochi. "People in London would never eat this!" Fiona poked a bamboo fork into a jiggling, sticky blob, drizzled with a sauce the color of coffee, sprinkled with roasted soybean powder, and as opaque as a frosted cocktail glass. When her lips curled up in wonder at its texture and delicately blended flavors, Ms. Kawanishi had asked, "Is good?"

Ms. Kawanishi paid for the kuzu mochi, left the department store, then went to Namba Nankai Train Station where she got on the train heading south toward Sakai City.

She knew some Sakai trivia.

Long ago it was famous for ironwork. The largest tomb in the world had been dug there with locally-forged shovels. Later there were katana sword smiths. And with the age of flintlock muskets came large-scale manufacture of firearms. On a different note, the Chinese shamisen had first arrived at Sakai's port.

Ms. Kawanishi spotted a seat next to a young man in an unbuttoned, plaid cotton shirt; under it was a light gray T-shirt printed with a monkey holding a yellow hat.

She wondered why the man wore a T-shirt that would look so much sweeter on a child.

Ms. Kawanishi bowed slightly, sat down, and put her bags on her dainty lap.

Usually when Ms. Kawanishi was on the train, she thought of everything she had to do.

But that evening Fiona's tall friend came to mind. She wished she had asked the question she knew in English, "How do you each other know?"

She envied their freedom—to be able to call someone from a different generation a friend.

For Ms. Kawanishi, everyone older or younger was pasted with some kind of label—a teacher, student, client, employee, or business acquaintance. Even the words she spoke changed depending on the social rank or age of the person she was talking with. She only had friends from her same school year. She had gone to an all-girls school.

At the language school, Fiona and Jo said the men teachers, even the oldest one, were friends.

Had she ever had a friend who was a man?

In her memories, she heard the strumming of the shamisen and saw her teacher sitting in front of her, watching her fingertips press down on the strings along the neck of her shamisen...her disobedient little finger wiggled about instead of resting near her palm.

She loved the shamisen. What fine sounds came from an instrument made of cat skin, elephant tusk, and the cocoons of silk worms. It didn't seem right.

Ms. Kawanishi put her hands on the sides of her wickerwork bag. Her fingertips tapped almost unnoticeably.

Layers of age had made her once shy gestures as smooth as lacquer.

But during Ms. Kawanishi's childhood and youth, when she and her shamisen teacher had been in the same room, her quivering hand at her lips had hidden an uncontrollable smile. Her eyes danced about his face, flitting across his brow, along the line of his jaw. She stole glances...his thick hair at the collar of his kimono...the fall of his shoulders as he bowed...the knot of his obi...his taut tabi socks.

All those years she had studied with him—

ON the train taking her home, one stop north of Sakai City, Ms. Kawanishi once again remembered the days when she had played her shamisen. Then she had been Fusako.

Osshohan

FUSAKO MORIKAWA was an adorable child, the eldest of three.

She had straight black hair as shiny as moonlight on the still waters of a rice paddy in late spring. Every day her mother tied it up and complained, "You have too much hair! I can't hold it all in one hand." Fusako had a sweet mouth that everyone loved. Her lips were full, even as a baby. Her father loved them the most and often explained why. "Full lips mean you'll always be rich. I won't have to worry about you one bit!" And she had a round mole on the back of her neck. Her grandmother had told her, "A mole is like a little pouch that fills with wonderful things; one on the neck is for clothes. You'll always have something new to wear." Fusako also had earlobes that were a little longer than most everyone's. Whenever she said anything that sounded enlightened, her friends would say, "You and the Buddha!"

In 1929 and six years old, Fusako started studying the shamisen and never had but one teacher, her Osshohan. She called him in the Osakan way, a softer term for the standard "Oshishoosan," meaning a teacher for theatrical arts.

From her first lesson Osshohan captured her heart. It was in June when fuzzy green fruit dotted the plum tree in the garden. She wore what would become her favorite kimono...one the color of new willow leaves, with a pattern of bouncing balls striped red, white, and black. Her obi was tie dyed shades of purple wisteria and textured in tiny puckers, which looked like melting snowflakes. It was knotted behind her in the shape of a butterfly.

Fusako was sitting on the tatami floor when Osshohan came into the room. She didn't wait for him to sit down, as her father had told her to, but instead bowed her head, moved her hands to the proper place in front of her, and with the most polite words, asked him to teach her.

He smoothed his kimono, kneeled down, sat in front of her...and laughed.

"You sound like a grown-up lady!"

Fusako had wanted to sound exactly like a grown-up lady and had practiced what her mother said whenever she asked someone to do something for her. Osshohan noticed and said something.

From a melody of giggles came "I did it!"

"So you are a little girl after all."

She nodded yes, at the same moment felt bashful, and lowered her eyes. "I'm a little girl."

"Well then, I'll have to teach you the shamisen if you are a little girl."

He began by showing her how to hold it. But since her shamisen was too large to set on her lap, he put it at her side, leaning it against her. And when he saw how her obi had been tied, he made up a verse—

"*sway morning willow*
wisteria candy sweet
red butterflies dance"

Fusako had never been happier.

She was Osshohan's youngest student.

Fourteen years later, playing the shamisen was prohibited.

The War had been fought for about a year, then the news of military losses. How could anybody have fun after that? Dancing, playing instruments, reading mysteries, going to movies...banned. The government took over the theaters. No more gutsy Garbo or leggy Marlene. Only war propaganda films. Kabuki and bunraku performers were sent to battle.

Fusako felt the world was coming to an end.

Even so, she went to her shamisen lessons at Osshohan's home. But she didn't pluck the strings with her ivory pick any longer; the shamisen's impressive sound would've been heard throughout the busy neighborhood. In peacetime, people had stopped and listened to heart-moving melodies. But during that time of the War, they would've gone to the police. Fusako held the shamisen, softly voiced its sounds "*chin, chin, chin, rin, tsun, tsu-n, tsun, tsun, ten...,*" and lightly plucked the strings with her fingertips.

And when the air raids began, Fusako's father didn't keep her from her lessons, nor did her Osshohan. They thought everything would be fine if they went about their lives as usual.

There was one change, however, that the men insisted on. Osshohan would teach her at the Morikawa house. Fusako wouldn't have to be out at least on the day of her lesson.

Her father and Osshohan talked. Peace will come someday. Won't everyone want Fusako to play the shamisen then? Won't everyone want to see Fusako in kimonos? Won't everyone wear them again?

During most of the War, men's kimonos and suits were replaced with civilian uniforms—button-down shirts of a drab yellow-beige color, matching slacks with gaitered legs. No ties.

Women were forced to make monpe from their cotton or wool kimonos—pants gathered or tapered at the ankles and belted at the waist...sleeves gathered at the wrists...the front of the top still looked like a kimono.

The excitement of being a young woman raced in Fusako's heart, but she was forbidden from wearing anything colorful, gorgeous to touch and look at. Fashion was frivolous...extravagant. Traitorous. "Desire nothing! Not till victory!" Fusako heard it everywhere and saw it on posters.

Battles were lost. Men well over forty were drafted into service. Fusako was nearly hysterical at times worrying about her Osshohan. For her father—not a second thought; everyone believed he was safe since he worked for the government-subsidized electric power company. Summer of 1945 came, and Osshohan still hadn't received a draft notice. Why, she never knew.

Military leaders had no souls, her parents whispered. Those devils would net a songbird, the uguisu, silver green like dewy moss in the shadows of dawn, snap its wings, and toss it to a stray cat.

Fusako never forgot any of this.

THE YOUNG MAN in the T-shirt next to Fusako Kawanishi on the train fell asleep; his head dropped sideways and bobbed near her shoulder. In front of her, a businessman stood reading a neatly folded newspaper. Two high school girls dressed in school uniforms sat across from her, their pleated skirts rolled up at the waistband to shorten them, legs recklessly splayed apart.

Darwin

WHEN Ms. Kawanishi was a few years older than those girls, she had wanted to wear a red satin evening gown. She had most of her life but never did. The War and the Occupation, then marriage, then motherhood, then old age. A life without wearing the color she loved, the dawning sun of the Japanese flag. Her English teacher Byron had once said the flag looked like a pickled plum stuck on a bed of rice in a bento.

Byron was like the boys who had left for the War.

Most of the men who had stayed behind were weak in body or mind. The women of her generation called them kuzu since they were worth as much as pencil shavings and clumps of dust—the real meaning of 'kuzu' (屑). [This kanji character is different from the one for the kuzu (葛) vine, what kuzu mochi is made from.]

The DNA of those weak men would have been lost during peacetime—what families would let their daughters combine with it?—but had a chance after the War when few soldiers came back. Families were desperate for their daughters to marry. And the girls did marry and had sons who grew into small, soft-muscled fellows, lacking vitality and virility.

Women of Ms. Kawanishi's generation knew that those weak sons—who were nothing like the lively boys they had grown up with—wouldn't be there if it wasn't for the War.

Ms. Kawanishi recently said this to her thirty-four-year-old daughter.

"Mother! You're like a Nazi!"

No. She wasn't.

Ms. Kawanishi hated Hitler's eugenics as much as the next person. Not to mention that mustache, hardly dapper. And on Adolf Hitler, diabolical...but on Charlie Chaplin, each twitch amusing. How was that possible?

"I'm telling you what I know firsthand about evolution. Boys with the great DNA were killed."

It was the polar opposite of Darwin's notion about the survival of the fittest.

MS. KAWANISHI felt a bitter pity for the high school girls across from her. Perhaps they would never know what it was like to sit next to a man with a spirit and life force so powerful that a young woman could only give it a furtive sideways glance, impossible to look upon its face...a man who would give them joy.

No wonder young women studied English conversation with tall, good-looking men from abroad.

That was DNA you wanted to survive.

The drowsy, bobbing head of the young man next to her came to a rest on her shoulder. Fusako Kawanishi shifted in the seat, enough to get him to sit up straight—only for his head to start again on its slow descent.

She thought he must be comfortable.

Like Heaven

WHEN Fusako was a child, a comfortable chair the color of pale green china arrived from England. Her father proudly put it in their European-style parlor.

That chair took on a silvery glow after each of Fusako's shamisen lessons while Osshohan talked about how well she played.

But whenever he was alone with her father during those last months of the War, his voice lowered to a whisper.

In the second week of July, her father asked Osshohan to their house. Osshohan sat in the chair from England and held a cap-like hat the men wore. It matched his civilian uniform.

Her father's voice rose to an urgent pitch.

"We're leaving for my wife's country home—"

Eighty kilometers away, Soni Village in Nara Prefecture. Her little brother was already there.

"Leave the city with us! Please!"

Fusako was stunned.

That was why her father had asked Osshohan to visit...why he had asked her to stay home...why he had stayed home!

What? More air raids? More bombs setting the city on fire? Wooden buildings—fuel for an inferno. More people killed!

Their shoes were set in a row in the entrance hall, each pair worn thin, brushed clean. Osshohan stepped down into his. The smooth stone floor was black, as shiny as shoe polish. Osshohan stood there in his drab outfit and made a striking picture.

Fusako's younger sister pulled at his sleeve as Fusako and her mother bowed deeply, imploring him to join them.

They left the house, and from the corner of her eye, Fusako caught a glimpse of the plum tree in their garden. In the next instant, they were on the trolley car.

Her Osshohan was fleeing with them!

She had been so frightened for him when he wasn't at their home. She imagined her Osshohan alone, in flames. Those thoughts had torn through her soul every minute since the first air strike hit the city a few months earlier in March.

For Fusako, that lovely month had changed forever.

KA-E-RO-U

MARCH had once been a festive time. Homes with daughters held court to displays of prince and princess dolls specially made for the celebration of Girls' Day. Each year more dolls were added to the displays with a prayer that the little girl grows into a healthy young woman and marries into a good family.

When Fusako was little, her father had lifted her to the branches of their plum tree. Her nose brushed against soft petals, the first warm fragrance of spring.

A few springtimes later, Fusako pulled down on the stiff branches, jutting out at odd angles...blossoms and buds running up and down. Their centers were magical—like tiny starbursts!

How Fusako loved their plum tree.

It hadn't changed during the War when everything else around her had.

But after the first air raid, the plum tree couldn't take her mind away from what might happen to them and her Osshohan.

FUSAKO stood next to Osshohan in the trolley car, and she did something she hadn't done for a long time...let her mind wander into the world of dreams...

They'll be together in Nara. Like heaven.

She'll serve him tea, help cook his meals, lay out and put away his futon. Oh, and her grandmother's dairy cow, chickens...all the white rice they could possibly eat. Break an egg into a bowl for Osshohan, add a splash of soy sauce, beat it, and pour over steaming rice. And the storehouse with its barrels of pickles. She'll be able to sneak in anytime, day or night.

No air raids. No bombs. No fires—

The trolley car passed by wary, haggard people, souls frayed and worn out like the clothes on their backs.

Fusako's eyes filled with tears. The window blurred as she imagined her grandparents' home in Nara. Her mother's old shamisen was there.

She'll take Osshohan into the mountains and play the songs she had practiced in her mind, had only fingered on her shamisen over and over again those past three long years...notes riding on a breeze, sounding like music in a faraway dream.
She's going to be with her Osshohan. Nothing else matters.
Fusako glanced at his face, then looked down, frantic.
What?
Another glance.
Something had happened in his heart. A melancholy regret had taken hold. The lines around his eyes, forlorn...his jaw, set tight.
The trolley car came to a slow stop. They stepped down into the street.
Osshohan moved in front of Fusako's father and thanked him, then told him that he wasn't going to leave his shamisen to the bombs. Osshohan bowed more deeply than Fusako had ever seen and said he would join them in Nara late that night.
But before her father could speak, Osshohan was across the street, boarding a trolley car headed in the opposite direction.
Fusako started after him...her father grabbed her from behind. Her sister and mother gathered round, and they swept her away.
"We'll wait for him at your grandfather's house," her father whispered at her cheek.

MS. FUSAKO KAWANISHI wondered why she was thinking about that day so long ago at her father's home when her Osshohan had sat in the pale green chair from England. Then her mind skipped to her English teacher, Fiona—the one who really was English. Did Fiona have the same kind of chair at her father's home in London?

The Sumitomo Building

MS. KAWANISHI'S father was the eighth son in the Morikawa family of Takamatsu, Shikoku Island. Kihachiro grew up on a farm—a large parcel of flat land for rice and wheat, plus a few terraced hills for mandarin orange, sweet plum, and apricot.

Since Kihachiro wasn't the eldest son, he had the freedom to live away from his parents. His father loved him well enough and had money enough for his education in engineering. Kihachiro's ability and manner secured him a position at the electric power company. An executive there knew a family whose hired girl was the daughter of a well-to-do rice farmer in Nara Prefecture. Nao Matsumoto was learning firsthand how to run a household in the city.

Introductions were made. Intermediaries talked. The two met for the first time at their wedding ceremony.

Fusako was born ten months later.

Kihachiro was like most fathers. He thought a daughter should study to become a good wife. From when Fusako was six, each evening after school, he sent her to private lessons. Flower arranging, calligraphy, tea ceremony, Japanese dance, and the shamisen. There were also years of lessons for sewing and Japanese style embroidery and for mastering the abacus.

Like all girls, Fusako was seldom unchaperoned during her school years. Kihachiro went with her to Osshohan's home in Sakai City for her shamisen lessons, then waited to take her back home to Abeno, a district in southeastern Osaka City. Her father told Fusako the manner—do *not* look around on the trolley car and train. Other passengers would see.

"Best not to encourage people to think about you."

Each time he told her this, she wanted to ask, "Why would they see me looking at them if they're following manners and *not* looking at me?" But she never did. Her father sounded so sure.

Most of her friends' schooling finished when they were fourteen or fifteen. But Fusako went on to study advanced science and mathematics and a few months before her eighteenth birthday, graduated in March 1941.

Osshohan made a new schedule for her shamisen lessons. Her weeks alternated: one week studying with her Osshohan, all day, every day except Sunday; the following week, practicing what she had learned. She still went to her other private lessons in the evenings and started going to new ones—for cooking and baking.

The military was advancing deeper into China, winning its battles...had even invaded French Indochina.

Newspapers boasted that Japan was making those countries better for everyone. Fusako didn't see how that was possible, but she didn't pay much attention to the news.

She was too busy enjoying her lessons, especially those with Osshohan.

And then, nine months after Fusako graduated from school, the political and military leaders ordered the bombing of Pearl Harbor, a naval base in Hawaii.

To Fusako, everything changed overnight. Her country and the United States of America were at war.

All dependent, unemployed, teenage girls and single women had to become nurses for the troops or workers in munition factories.

The government sent orders to neighborhoods.

The Morikawas' front door slid open.

"Mrs. Morikawa. Sorry to bother you."

The neighbors were in monpe and white aprons. Banners across their chests announced them: Women's Committee for National Defense.

Fusako heard her mother chirping hello in the entrance hall.

"Mrs. Morikawa, you look lovely even in a monpe!"

There was a rush of panic in Mrs. Toudou's voice.

"Munition factories! Where's the fun in that? Your pretty doll has got to get a job someplace that's doing something for the military. Even sewing uniforms is enough. My husband says those munition factories will be hit first if the Americans attack. But they'll settle this before too long."

Mrs. Toudou's voice sounded woefully unconvincing, at odds with the rest of what she said.

"Why did this all start anyway? Look at us. These monpe! You look cute, but what about me? It's too cold to wear by itself so I've got a kimono on underneath. It bunches up—"

Mrs. Toudou pointed to her lumpy behind.

"As big as those on Hollywood movie stars."

The more she said something lighthearted, the more Fusako sensed the gravity of the situation.

"Now all my husband does is grab me here—every time he sees me."

They started laughing a strange, unhappy laugh and pressed their fingers onto their tears.

The neighbors told Nao that if Fusako couldn't find a job for the War Effort in ten days, she had to go to a munition factory in Shikanjima.

Nao followed them out and thanked them. They laughed fretfully again when Nao spanked Mrs. Toudou's pillowy bottom.

Fusako ran to the entrance hall with her coat.

Nao's hands were trembling as she wrapped a shawl around Fusako's shoulders.

"Don't worry, Mother. I have an idea."

At her former school, Fusako met with the headmaster, who remembered her well. He asked her to come back in two days. When she did, he had a letter for her.

A manufacturer of large cranes, which move cargo on and off ships, had hired her. Its office was in the business district of Kitahama, a twenty-minute commute.

Fusako could still go to her shamisen lessons all day on Sundays—Osshohan decided.

She became one of the women assistants to the men in the office.

Then those men began being drafted.

Each draftee brought a national flag on his last day at work, the flag he would carry into battle.

The office manager would take out his calligraphy brush and ink. The staff members waited their turn to write a message on the flag. Fusako was the last because she was the youngest.

Exquisite and strong and passionate...Fusako's colleagues admired her writing, embarrassed by their own calligraphy skills. Someone never failed to say—

"She's the baby here, but can she ever hold a brush!"

Then they wished their new draftee well—

"We'll be waiting for you. You *will* come back!"

Months later, a government announcement came to Fusako's boss. The women staff members were ordered to work at a munition factory in Nagoya Prefecture.

The factory's name—Yashima No. 801.

Fusako had foiled fate only to be sent away, far away to Nagoya.

She told her parents the news but would wait till Sunday to tell her Osshohan.

The next morning at her office, there was a flag spread across the desk of the fellow in charge of machine parts.

"Time to sign mine," he said.

Fusako had never seen a smile look so sad.

Her boss took Fusako aside.

"From tomorrow, you're in charge of machine parts."

He couldn't stop every woman in his office from going, but he had somehow found a way to keep one—the one whose shiny hair and full lips reminded him of his own daughter's. Though *his* daughter wouldn't have known...a nut from a bolt.

DECADES later, Fusako saw a TV documentary on what had happened to Yashima No. 801 and the other munition factories in Nagoya.

They had been firebombed the day after the Americans had dropped an atomic bomb on Hiroshima, the day before their atomic bomb dropped on Nagasaki. From the thousands of young women and teenage girls, only two had escaped the flames.

AND so...Fusako became in charge of orders and deliveries for machine parts.

Nobody believed it. Fusako, an Osaka businesswoman! Her office was on the fifth floor in the most famous stone and concrete building in Osaka, the Sumitomo Building. Its architect was well known, a foreigner. Her father often mentioned that point. "If American bombs ever fall on Osaka, the building the German designed will be the one left standing."

Not even a window cracked in the Sumitomo Building.

Most of her father's office building was also spared. A bomb plummeted through it but didn't explode. No one was maimed or killed.

Fusako stopped by, and some of her father's staff talked about the Americans who had built it. "Those bozos—clumsy, dumb shits." Undeniably, they felt a bit lucky. The work of the Americans had been so perfectly slipshod.

But in Fusako's heart it wasn't American incompetence that had kept the bomb from exploding.

She imagined a munition assembly line and a young woman—no lipstick, wavy hair tied with a scarf.

In the woman's childhood, she had been given a gift, something from Japan, something she treasured...a set of lacquered prince and princess dolls small enough to set on her hand...or perhaps a paper fan, painted with a kingfisher perched above a brushstroke of watery blue. Deep down the woman must have known that not everyone in Japan wanted war. Some had always longed for peace. It was the only thing for the munition worker to do. Make a bomb that wouldn't explode.

And she did.

Gravestones

MS. KAWANISHI had many memories of her youth under attack in Osaka. She did her best to keep them buried.

Sometimes on the train home from her English lesson she thought about what style of clothes her teachers had worn or what funny faces they'd made during pronunciation drills.
But not that evening.
That evening she told herself the War was over. She was alive with her arms and legs and unscarred face. Her fate hadn't tossed her into one of the mass graves she knew of. There was even one under the building for public waterworks. That building was a kind of gravestone.
Most all the buildings in Osaka were gravestones.
The voices of the high school girls sitting across from Ms. Kawanishi interrupted her thoughts.
They were a few years younger than she had been when the trucks stopped.

THE STREET Fusako took to work was lined with rubble. The trucks bumped along at a slow speed. Bare-chested men jumped down off flatbeds.
Fusako wondered if they had come to start rebuilding. They worked in pairs, heaving with great effort, each man grabbing onto one end of...what? Bags of garbage?
She walked toward them. The trucks grew monstrous. It all took shape—wretched faces she didn't think she knew, arms and legs in unnatural angles. No candles. No incense. No gentle touch of good-bye. No chants to follow into paradise. Souls gone without prayers.
There were so many.
Why hadn't she seen them yesterday? Or the day before?
Those manners her father had taught her when she was a little girl...keep to yourself...don't look aimlessly around. Had they twisted into a defense against truth, until now...now when there were so many torn, rigid, dead bodies filling the trucks?

THE BUSINESSMAN standing in front of Ms. Kawanishi swayed with the movement of the train. His briefcase was on the rack above her and his belt buckle not far from her face.

She turned her head and looked out the window. The sun was setting, and above the buildings the sky hung heavy.

Her hands became still.

At moments when Ms. Kawanishi's mind wasn't busy with something in her hands—sketching an idea for a flower arrangement...or sewing a hair ribbon for her granddaughter from a kimono remnant...or writing in her English diary—when the evening sky grew a desolate color her imagination couldn't brighten, she remembered the day she had stood at a window in the Sumitomo Building.

The window had been opened wide as the day was fine.

On the train home, Fusako Kawanishi closed her eyes and saw the sky...a small American warplane came out of nowhere and slashed down low over the business district of Kitahama.

FUSAKO shouldn't have been at the window.

The old men she worked with were face down on the marble floor. The men who had left for the War, the handsome ones, those with children, those everyone loved, hadn't come back, not even one.

"Get down!" the old men cried.

But the window frame had trapped her. The street below cleared...On cue, the players on stage exited. Everyone ran for cover—except one man.

From his neat appearance, his sprightly step, Fusako knew he was an ordinary businessman, exact, predictable, and dependable, like her father—one of those who kept the city from hurling into madness.

No, he wasn't her father. But he was someone's.

She screamed in a voice not her own, wild, demanding—in her heart, a rising horror.

"Run! Hurry! Get inside! Someone pull him inside!"

She beat down on the stone windowsill.

"What's he thinking? Is he thinking?"

Her father would sit and think regardless of any ruckus around him. His mind silenced the world.

Panic fueled her screams until the pilot marked his target and was gone.

ON the train bound for Sakai City, Ms. Kawanishi wondered if somewhere in America the pilot of that warplane ever thought of the morning, that bright, clear morning in Osaka when only one man had been outside, walking with a sprightly step.

And then...Ms. Kawanishi took a deep breath and blinked her eyes again and again and bit the inside of her lip. But it didn't do any good.

A memory fell into her heart...like a drop that had stayed on the tip of a limestone dagger in a chilly underground chamber until natural laws forced it to fall.

That evening in July, the day Fiona introduced Meryl, Fusako Kawanishi also remembered the firebombing of Sakai City. It was on the day she had taken the trolley car with her shamisen teacher. They were going to flee Osaka together. Osshohan never came to her grandfather's home in Nara.

She took her handkerchief and held it to her lips.

One of the high school girls, across the aisle, was fingering a few strands of her bangs. A makeup pouch spilled open on her lap.

Ms. Kawanishi tried hard to think of something or someone and who she thought of was the woman with hardly any makeup on at the language school...the one whose name was difficult to say, who was ten or fifteen years older than Fiona.

Perhaps her father had been in the War? Or the Postwar Occupation Forces? Had he been one of the officers who passed her on the stairs in the Sumitomo Building?

Chocolate

AFTER the War, the First Corps of the Sixth Army made the Sumitomo Building its General Headquarters.

The staircases were segregated: one for the Japanese office workers and one for the US military—many junior officers, trained in civil affairs and military government, ready for peace and an Osaka smile.

Every now and then, a few of the officers slipped over to the staircase for the Japanese. They said, "Good morning" or "Nice day, isn't it?" as if Fusako was a next-door neighbor.

People warned, "Never look an American in the eye. They'll shoot you!"

But the officers at the Sumitomo Building were pleasant and dressed so nice, shoes as shiny as a sumo wrestler's oiled hair, the creases in their slacks, sharp. They laughed with children who had learned to say "chocolate" and "please."

The officers weren't at all like the American soldiers in the wartime newsreels—each with the same hateful face.

Fusako was ashamed of the ragged soldiers who had come back. They howled at the children for no reason, like hell-bound devils being punished with a glimpse of heaven and what should've been.

She didn't want to see them, but every day she did. And she thought about them.

That's what happened to some who had gone off to the War. There had been little chance of coming home and only when the War ended. And what was waiting for them? The same landscape where they had fought. Everything in ruins. And...their loved ones dead.

Fusako would have gone insane. She knew it.

But the men had to go. Those speaking against the War disappeared. There was hearsay of executions, of dying in prisons.

She never thought about what the soldiers did on the battlefields...Oh, during the War, she had wanted each one to run and run...around the world until they came back home, like marathon runners to a finish line. She was foolish, but perhaps many girls and young women had thought something as ridiculous.

It had been too difficult...no, impossible to think about the truth.

ON the train, one of the high school girls put on lipgloss as the other one whispered into her ear, then they burst out laughing.

Ms. Kawanishi had also whispered to friends.

Maki

BEFORE any American soldiers could rape and kill them, most of Fusako's friends had vowed to use chopsticks to grip their own tongues, bite them off, and bleed to death.

A few of those friends later married American officers. One moved to Alaska and sent Fusako a coin purse of baby seal fur with a silver clasp, a little difficult to open, forcing the comment—

They don't make things as nicely as they do in Japan.

Fusako had never thought of marrying one of the officers who had smiled at her in the Sumitomo Building. Her parents would never have allowed it, and she had never thought of going against her parents' wishes. Too much had happened during and after the War. They had kept her safe and fed, had stayed alive for her. She wasn't alone and unprotected and forced to go to the brothels for the American soldiers. How she hated her government for sanctioning those brothels.

How could she go against her parents' wishes?

Her best childhood friend Maki never married anyone, Japanese or American, and probably wouldn't have married even if there hadn't been the War and there had been plenty of men.

A pity, but her nose was flat and her jawbones slanted outward, like gills of a fish. Her head was attached to her shoulders, it seemed, without the graceful support of a neck. And when she wore a kimono, the collar stopped short at her earlobes. Her hair wasn't lacquer black but had strains of copper mixed throughout, giving her the look of a country cousin.

A few months after the War started, when Maki and Fusako were almost nineteen, every girl from around age fifteen on up had to start training with a bamboo pole. The pole would've been sharpened into a spear if the Americans invaded.

Drills were held in neighborhoods, and on the first day, Maki started off with her right leg instead of her left, so her bamboo pole somehow ended up hitting the pole of the girl next to her...Fusako.

Their instructor—a rickety war veteran from a battle Fusako had never even heard of—blew a gasket, and at the decibel of a steam engine's whistle, told them that if indeed the Americans invaded Japan, it would be because of Maki's disobedient right leg. Maki was about to burst into tears, which was highly unusual. She was used to being yelled at and couldn't care less why men got angry. Her five brothers were angry at her all the time.

Fusako didn't understand why the instructor was making a big stink out of which leg to start with. After all, if an American were charging at her, she wouldn't bother thinking about which leg to start from before she skewered him. She knew *skewer* wasn't exactly the right word...though it sounded oddly amusing...One shouldn't, however, be oddly amusing with a bamboo pole...but she was almost out of her mind with fear...and at the wrong times something inappropriate popped into her head. Skewer an American! Oh, the thought of it was terrifying. She was positive she would ditch her stupid pole, hightail it in the opposite direction, and pray the American had forgotten to load his gun!

Fusako couldn't bear watching her friend being tormented any longer.

Maki's nose had filled and was ready to run. She was too petrified to breathe; her face was as red as a sea bream's—Fusako's favorite kind of fish for sashimi—and she looked about to suffocate.

Fusako let go of her bamboo pole, and it landed on the feet of the girls standing next to her.

She expected the old tyrant to whack both her and Maki, but he only scowled, ranted and raved, spewing out words fast and curt, sounding like a grunting and snorting wild boar, albeit wizened and with some teeth missing.

The other women and girls went home.

Maki's and Fusako's punishment? Practicing with their bamboo poles until sundown.

"EEECHI!" Left foot, one step back. They were told they had to step back so they could see the angle the American was advancing. (The Japanese word for "one" is "ichi," but in this exercise they said eeechi. Fusako never figured out why and no one ever told her.)

"NI!" Right foot, one step back.

"SAN!" Left foot, one more step back.

"SHI!" Left foot, one step forward.

"GO!" Right foot, one step forward.

"ROKU!" Raise the bamboo pole over your head.

"SHICHI!" Lower the bamboo pole.

Scream "*EEEEE*!" and SKEWER!

Fusako knew they didn't stand a chance. With all that stepping and screaming the Americans could enjoy a cup of coffee and still shoot them before they got their bamboo poles anywhere near the Americans, especially since they were supposed to spear the soft spot at the bottom of the throat. Even she knew that was impossible. The Americans were too tall. They should try for the center of their wide chests and maybe they would hit their hearts. But she forced those thoughts out of her mind and pretended she and Maki would be all right.

On their way home, out of earshot, Fusako couldn't hold back her laughter any longer.

"Did you see how high those girls jerked their knees up when my pole hit their feet? Were they doing that to get me into more trouble?"

Fusako thought Maki would laugh too and maybe imitate how the girls had squatted down and rubbed their toes.

But she didn't.

"I'm going to practice and be the best. No one will ever hurt you."

And so, Maki practiced with her bamboo pole every day, believing she would spear the evil American hearts—Fusako later told her to aim for the heart—and keep Fusako safe. Fusako sometimes practiced with her, even though she had promised herself to bite off her tongue at the hour the Americans invaded Osaka.

It wasn't until after the War when *even* Maki figured out a bamboo pole was no match for a soldier.

"Was I ever the dimwit! Bamboo against machine guns and flamethrowers? Talk about a noodle head!"

They giggled through their tears at Maki's naivete.

"But everyone thought the same," Fusako said.

The giggles stopped.

"Why did the government do that to us? The military? Expecting women and girls to die for them! Why were we at war anyway? Only for the Americans to kill everyone in Japan?"

Fusako and Maki promised each other never to trust their government. Ever. If someday they had sons, they promised never to send them to war.

After the Surrender, Maki did come face to face with the American enemy. But instead of being raped or riddled with bullets or burned alive, she got DDT powder dusted on top of her wide head, behind her almost nonexistent neck, and down her monpe—for lice and flea control.

The bombed-out city had become infested. American soldiers stood at the subway exits and Maki and Fusako had to pass by them on their way to work. Maki was dusted along with everyone else.

But Fusako wasn't.

For her, the soldiers pointed their DDT dust guns away, smiled gallantly, and let her pass, unpowdered, her thick hair left luminous black. Maki tried walking behind Fusako, then to her right side, then left. But Maki was always caught in a cloud of bug spray; Fusako, in the warm glow of American grins.

Maki walked arm in arm with Fusako and said, "Beauties get all the breaks," with the resigned and wry humor of someone who had figured that out at the age of six.

Fusako could never understand why one so pleasant had such an unlucky face.

THESE DAYS one can do so much with such a face.

Ms. Kawanishi glanced at the girls across the aisle and thought how happy they must be with their makeup pouches.

She and Maki had promised to grow very old together. Maki wanted to live a long life...live it for her five brothers. Each to the War, each a god.

Maki ended up with a career at a crystal manufacturing company and had often sent Ms. Kawanishi sets of bowls, plates, sake cups.

But then there was the Great Hanshin Awaji earthquake—almost six months had passed.

The crystal from Maki had jingled on Ms. Kawanishi's shelves.

Sometimes life doesn't turn out as one hopes.

The voice in Ms. Kawanishi's head sounded like her mother's.

The train came to a stop. Ms. Kawanishi got up from her seat next to the drowsy young man, bowed slightly, then stepped away.

He caught her profile as she stood on the platform.

The sudden heat gave her a radiant blush, which the fluorescent lighting overhead didn't fade. She took a step and joined the flow of people passing by.

The young man glanced at the two high school girls—all the sloppiness of unkempt youth—stringy hair, rumpled blouses, rebellious legs apart, fast-talking voices conveying a roller coaster of emotions, clamorous and conspicuous.

Then he nodded his head and shut his eyes.

MS. KAWANISHI walked a few minutes from the station to the apartment building she owned.

In the entrance hall was a German clock, a gift from her husband. He had admired objects from abroad, as her father had.

The Insurance Man

THE MILITARY had turned up its nose at Jiro Kawanishi even when it was gobbling up boys of thirteen and sixty-year-old men.

Yet Fusako's parents asked her to marry Jiro.

The War had been over for five years. Fusako was nearly twenty-eight, and her younger sister wanted to start a family. A younger sister never married before an older sister.

But Fusako wasn't interested. She was too busy dancing.

A few years earlier, her former dance teacher had visited their home.

A traditional dance troupe would put on performances for the American military. The Kabuki Theater had been destroyed, but not the old Senpukan Building. Granite pillars ran along its veranda and chandeliers hung in its dazzling ballroom. The wooden floor was painted to look like tiles.

Fusako's teacher chattered. "The soldiers must be homesick." Her hands flitted like songbirds between stalks of bamboo. "Everything different here. Not nice. Not like it was."

Fusako excused herself.

"But we'll show them what Japan should be, what Japan is. Won't that be something?"

Fusako's father fumed. A year hadn't passed since the air raids. Osaka citizens still starving, food still being rationed...money wasted on the Occupation, the black market out of control. But Kihachiro stopped his outburst at the words "forced abortions." Government policy. There wasn't enough food.

He was thankful his children weren't married, thankful his parents and in-laws grew rice.

In her room, Fusako changed into one of her old silk kimonos. She wasn't as good at dancing as she had been at playing the shamisen, though she'd studied dance from the time she was six years old until it was banned, when she was twenty. But she was good enough for Americans.

In the parlor, she tilted her head like a young girl gazing at flowers.

Her father puffed up. "If Fusako doesn't win over the Americans, no one ever will!"

Fusako quit her job at the Sumitomo Building and started practicing and performing.

In the dazzling ballroom, with a folding fan, she danced the emotions that fill the human heart—pleasure, anger, love, happiness—and pretended her Osshohan was playing his shamisen on a cushion on the painted wooden floor.

Some Americans spoke to her. "A Japanese doll come to life!"

It was true what her father and her Osshohan had said during the War—When peace comes, everyone will want to see Fusako in kimonos. Her father and her Osshohan hadn't known they were talking about the enemy.

Her father knew, however, her career in dance would be short lived. Better dancers would perform for Japanese audiences after the Americans went home.

Besides, he thought a woman could only be happy if she was a good wife.

And so a few years later when his drinking buddies got on the subject of a match for his daughter, he listened as the sake turned his ears red.

JIRO KAWANISHI looked like a tame ogre made of apple jelly but had been blessed with a keen sense of business. He was fair, trustworthy, good humored and had relatives and acquaintances with business connections spanning generations. He knew Osaka City and the families who ran it like the back of his pulpy hand.

Jiro opened his insurance office when insurance companies weren't regulated closely. After he married Fusako, he took out several policies on himself. And then years later, at the start of the economic boom, he made a fortune on the stock and commodities exchange. He was frail, for sure. He often confessed it hee-hawing, "A wimp"—his apple-jelly frame jiggled—"but no numbskull!"

He knew his body couldn't keep his soul in this world long, and he wanted his wife to have money to spend after he was gone.

Fusako thought it was natural that she had been left with a comfortable estate.

Then one evening, in the lobby of the language school, a few weeks after the Great Hanshin-Awaji earthquake, she began to reassess the man she had been asked to marry.

Fiona and Jo were talking about the families left with nothing from the earthquake and the fires that had followed. Some had to keep paying on loans for condominiums in high-rise buildings that had crumbled into gigantic mounds of concrete and twisted steel. Only the air was left...They were paying a loan on what was, in fact, empty space.

If Ms. Kawanishi's apartment building ever burned to the ground, she would have another built. She told Fiona and Jo, "My husband was kuzu. Small. Not handsome. Not strong." But he had left her a heap of money.

"He loved you," they said.

She didn't think so.

Jo insisted. "It's one way he showed his love. He made sure you were all right after he was gone."

Ms. Kawanishi thought the girls incorrigibly romantic, but she wrote down what they had said in her English diary and read it again and again.

Then a few months later, the old wooden marker at her husband's family grave was replaced with a speckled granite gravestone, beautifully carved and of the highest quality.

Ms. Kawanishi even invited the priest to the cemetery to chant prayers and generously paid him.

MS. KAWANISHI put her handbag on her dressing table, then walked past the tatami room that held the family altar. A carpet from Istanbul was spread across the mats. Her husband had given it to her.

WHEN the deliverymen rolled out the carpet, it looked like a flower garden had sprouted and bloomed in shades of golden yellow, the shades of tatami at varying years of age. Fusako's happiness graced her smile.

Jiro knew a woman of her beauty would never have married him or perhaps, even been in the same room with him had it not been for the staggering loss of men during the War—men like his former classmates, those dandies who had captivated Osaka City, Venice of the East.

Drunk at a farewell party, he had wished he could join them.

"Jiro-chan,"—they'd called him since boyhood—"you've got to protect Osaka. Keep it as it is for us. No matter what happens...save Osaka!"

Jiro's friends in the Eighth Regiment were the men who flourish in times of peace. They were the sons of long lines of merchants and thrived on sake, irresistible food, luxurious apparel, humorous entertainment, lively music, and lovely women adoring and pampering them. Each of them epitomized the saying, "Merchants can't get through the night without burning a hole in their pockets."

They had believed their government could achieve international prominence by doing business and engaging in cultural trade in other countries instead of destroying and ransacking them. Jiro could barely bring himself to think of his friends' misery and pain, of the bitter anguish they must have felt for their country where they had grown into gentlemen...only to be sent off to war. They were expected to become violent, heartless brutes.

But those fun-loving Osaka dandies Jiro wished he could become couldn't be anything other than what they were.

Some people sneered, "The Eighth Infantry Regiment! What's going to happen if you lose *again*? Bunch of spoiled, silver-spooned brats!"

But Jiro imagined this...Instead of killing the other poor bastards on the side of the enemy, his friends had written haiku in their hearts before their souls were ripped from their bodies. How he prayed for their eternal peace.

He had done his best to keep his promise to them.

By the time he was granted permission to marry Fusako, he had enough spending money for his bride's kimonos and tailored suits and beaded gowns. Later, he sent their children to piano lessons and the same private after-school lessons that his wife had when she was a child. He spent on his family as much as he saved and invested, knowing—as all Osakans do—money has a life of its own and must move constantly or else suffer atrophy, like most living things.

Jiro never expected his wife's admiration. He knew she must have dreamed of someone godlike who would have done the same.

The War had given Jiro the unattainable.

He never forgot that.

WHENEVER Ms. Kawanishi had chosen a present for her husband—a coin purse, cuff links, tiepin...the simple things of men—she pretended that it was for her shamisen teacher, her Osshohan.

But she never bought her husband a kimono. She had wanted to give a kimono only to her Osshohan, to thank him for everything he had taught her.

She thought of him more than she had of any man in her life.

The Kawanishis had two children. Ms. Kawanishi imagined it would be better to have one or two...to keep her mind on something, her hands busy.

At the Altar

EVERY YEAR during the weeks leading up to the anniversary marking the end of the War in August, documentaries with interviews of veterans were televised.

THE DAY before Ms. Kawanishi met Meryl, she watched a war documentary.

Some of the old men tried to talk, but what they saw in their minds came out as tears. Some, however, did tell of the horrors they had seen and had done with searing clarity. Ms. Kawanishi saw herself in a city in China and on a battlefield in Burma and in a cave on Palau.

But she still didn't understand how anyone from Japan did those things. The men she had known who went to the War, the men who she knew now...No, not them.

What part of Japan had those cruel, merciless soldiers come from? Had they never known love?

Then Ms. Kawanishi thought something she had never thought before.

Had those soldiers known love and fought savagely to get it back? Could love do that?

What if she had been a soldier? To live, to be able to come back to her family, to her Osshohan...what would she have done? What would she have become? She had always thought she would've killed herself if the Americans invaded her city. But then she wondered. Would she have gnashed through her own tongue...taste her life gushing over her lips, gushing down her throat...choking her?

It would take untold courage to bleed yourself into eternity because maybe there was nothing after death. Had the soldiers killed because it was easier than facing an eternity of emptiness and no one to love?

The end of yourself...of love...

Even after thinking this, Ms. Kawanishi still didn't want to believe what had happened.

But she knew it had.

She still didn't understand any of it. Why had they dropped bombs? Why had the soldiers killed each other, massacred women and children?

It was a simple thought, she knew. The world didn't need soldiers.

Oh, how much time throughout her life had she spent battling back her war memories?

She couldn't reconcile the men in her life with those soldiers in the documentaries.

And the Americans in the newsreels at the theaters...those faces of hate. But after the War, the officers in the Sumitomo

Building had on the same friendly faces of the boys she had known—except for their light-colored hair and their large, blue eyes.
Were they, each one of them, a Dr. Jekyll and Mr. Hyde? Was she?
If only she could know. What would her life be like if there hadn't been a war?

THAT EVENING, after the pleasant conversation with the teachers and a stop at the department store, Ms. Kawanishi was in her kitchen.

She put ice in a crystal bowl, set a small bamboo basket on the ice, and from her shopping bag, took out the summertime confection...the kind she enjoyed the most—kuzu mochi. The confection box was lined with bamboo leaves. She lifted them, along with two small packets and the soft, opaque kuzu mochi, then put them in the basket. She opened the rich kuromitsu, the color of fine coffee, and drizzled it over the kuzu mochi. Then she sprinkled on the roasted soybean powder, the color of a dusty, late summer moon on a night before a rainy day.

Kuzu mochi had been Osshohan's favorite confection too.

She crossed the carpet in the tatami room and put the kuzu mochi and a cup of green tea in front of a brass bowl. It was filled with ash from burned incense and stood between candleholders.

She kneeled at the family altar and imagined she was with her Osshohan in the department store. He was about to pay for a box of kuzu mochi...was asking for extra soybean powder, the stuff of a dusty moon. He had on a white linen yukata. Its pattern, the color of roasted tea, looked like an uncountable number of plus signs (+) colliding into each other but was a kanji character in the word "ido" (井戸), meaning "water well."

Low on his hips was a wide obi the color of green tea leaves...the bits at the bottom of a teacup...long after a guest had sipped and said good-bye. The ends of his obi hung from a knot, bunched on his back. The thin straps of his geta matched the color of his obi. So did the ribbon above the flat brim of his finely woven straw hat.

Like most Osaka men, her Osshohan had been stylish.

He would have been ninety-five years old that year.

Ms. Kawanishi imagined them strolling together. If he became a little tired, without a word she would take hold of his sleeve. His back and shoulders smaller with age, his posture still perfect.

People would think what a fine couple. His young wife kept him healthy. Since there were few men her age to marry after the War, people would think her parents had no choice but to accept an arranged marriage with a much older man.

In this dream, the War gave him to her.

A twenty-four karat gold bell rested on a silk cushion in her husband's altar. Jiro had bought it, thinking the price of gold would be up when his daughters inherited it. But Ms. Kawanishi knew that would mean a war had started somewhere. Strange how the price of gold goes up as governments spend on their wars. She wished with all her heart for a gold bell that had no value.

Every morning and evening, she lit two candles and three sticks of sweet sandalwood incense. One stick was for her husband, one was for all those in his family line, and one was for those souls who no one knew of, who had died without anyone to pray for them or give them offerings. Then she would ring the bell twice.

But that night she added one more incense stick...for her Osshohan.

She didn't think her husband minded and wondered if his ancestors or relatives did. But no one was there to tell her it was sacrilegious or impious or some other word she didn't care for. They were souls too, hotokesamas, in paradise. Surely, they got along together...all hotokesamas do.

Between the flickering candles, in front of the burning incense, cradled in crystal—was the basket of kuzu mochi. She brought her hands together and spoke to her Osshohan:

It has already been fifty years since we've been apart. Thank you for watching over me. Osshohan, even now, how

I wish you were alive. Talking to you in front of the family altar is perhaps inappropriate, isn't it? If once, when we were together...Oh, how happy I would've been saying this then. Osshohan, I so wanted to tell you...I love you—

Ms. Kawanishi cupped the crystal bowl.

Osshohan, here is an offering, the kuzu mochi you liked so much. Please enjoy it.

She bowed her head. The incense wafted about her. The candles flickered out.

After dinner, she had some of the kuzu mochi with a cup of weak green tea.

That night she wrote in her English diary—

Today meet nice American lady.
Tall as teacher Byron.

To Meryl, to Akita

The French Teacher from Algiers

AFTER Mr. Baba's lesson, Meryl went to the vending machine in the lobby at the language school.

Fiona joined Elliot on the sofa in the teachers' room. Darryl was clearing off a table for his ikebana arrangement.

In sashayed Jo. She slipped out of her high heels, the tips of her toes mouthwatering pink. Her hem caressed her thighs as she sat down near Fiona.

"Mr. Mazouzi's here."

MR. MAZOUZI was from Algiers and held a black belt in karate. That was all anyone knew about him.

He had the winning air of an aristocrat, making him a bit unapproachable. Jo and Fiona longed to whisper their life stories to him, but they could only bring themselves to utter ho-hum niceties.

He spoke English with a French accent, making his creamy voice creamier.

Jo was positive—Mr. Mazouzi, an African fertility god incarnate.

He was, in his entirety, every romantic ideal for a man—from that mysterious continent. He had a presence as eternal as the pharaohs, a physique as taut as a Masai tribesman, and the savoir-faire of a double agent in Casablanca. He moved like a satiated savanna cat...his skin, the color of shadows stealing across dunes at dawn. The shiny, dark locks framing his brow, not surprisingly, harbored a moonlit Tunisian night.

It was a cinch to imagine him surrounded by belly dancers adorned in scarves as brilliant as a sunset...or mounted on the hump of a camel—his body covered from head to toe in heavy cloth, gathered and draped in crevices and folds, only his eyes showing.

And what eyes! They held the secrets of the cosmos.

Mr. Mazouzi's hands were divine, long and slender, those that would strum a love song on a woman as masterfully as on a lute. He spoke in whispers and at times it was difficult to hear what he said. But no one minded. He was the epitome of sensual, mysterious desire.

And the most mysterious aspect of Mr. Mazouzi was the power he had over the dreams of a person he met for the first time.

Or so Jo wanted Fiona to believe.

FIONA feigned indifference. "Mr. Mazouzi's here? So what?"

"We have to introduce Meryl," Jo said. "That's all we need."

"Need? For what?"

"Don't lag behind. We want Meryl to fall in love, right?"

"Yes. But she can't fall in love with Mr. Mazouzi. She's flying home in a few days."

"Have you no imagination? Before people fall in love they have to start thinking about...the big S-E-X."

"No romance?" Darryl asked. "No candlelight or roses?" His abundant hair tumbled around his shoulders. "No ice cream?"

Elliot looked up from his teacher's book. He and Darryl had agreed to play along with Jo.

"First comes the thinking." Jo tapped her pretty foot against Fiona's sensible shoe. "What did you dream about the first night after you met Mr. Mazouzi?"

Fiona had dreamed a wildly amazing dream of herself with Mr. Mazouzi—one she was never going to forget.

Jo had been with Fiona the second time Fiona saw Mr. Mazouzi. Fiona had been in a fluster, her neck blotchy.

And once again, Fiona felt a flush of blotchy, pale red overtaking her neck...because of Mr. Mazouzi!

"How should I know?" She sprang from her seat in a beeline to her locker.

"You *do* know," Jo purred, "otherwise you wouldn't be running away. Because you're an oversensitive, asexual Virgo, I'll say it."

"I am not!"

Everyone knew Fiona hated being called oversensitive.

"Let's not quibble. Let's talk of love for Meryl. Here's what happened to *me* the night after *I* first met Mr. Mazouzi. The fuck dream of the century...with him!"

Fiona couldn't believe her ears. Or how hot they felt.

"But the spectacular details were nothing compared to the feeling that came right afterward. Mr. Mazouzi held me in his arms, like we were in heaven."

NO! That was Fiona's dream! How she cherished it, cherished that moment in the arms of her Mr. Mazouzi and wished for the dream again.

Fiona almost blurted out—That dream's mine!

But Jo couldn't possibly have stolen her dream. How perfectly implausible. Or was it? How could Jo have dreamed her dream?

"You had the same dream, right?"

Fiona silence.

"Confess."

"But that's so unfair. How did you have it, too?"

"Everyone does...then everyone falls in love."

"How can you possibly know that?"

"I asked."

"And everyone told you the same?"

Jo gazed at Elliot, then at Darryl.

Darryl's eyebrows rose and fell in a private rhythm.

"But..." Fiona was confounded.

"The Mazouzi Dream." Elliot named it.

Darryl told them that Byron said Mr. Mazouzi was a love machine in his Mazouzi Dream...state-of-the-art.

Jo said, "I'm positive in a previous life Mr. Mazouzi was a god of love. And so he still has the power to make everyone he meets feel...you know...with him...in a dream."

Fiona wasn't 100% incredulous. "Mr. Mazouzi, a god of love? How can you be sure?"

"It makes sense."

Fiona thought about that for a moment. "So you mean in our dreams we've...been...with Mr. Mazouzi? All of us? I don't know if I like that."

"I do." Darryl smiled like an angel.

"Oh, you would," Fiona said. "What's this about anyway?"

"We're trying to get Meryl to fall in love!" Jo said.

"Right. Introduce Meryl to Mr. Mazouzi. Tonight she'll have the Mazouzi Dream."

"That's the plan."

"And then she'll fall in love. But with who?"

"Written in the stars." Jo told Fiona to make sure she said Mr. Mazouzi's name to Meryl when she wished her pleasant dreams that night.

"Why don't you?"

"Got to rush home. Expecting a call."

An instant later—"I didn't fall in love after my Mazouzi Dream."

"Yes, you did."

And then Meryl walked in with cans of green tea for everyone, an unexpected blush on her neck.

"I met a gentleman from Algiers who speaks English with a creamy French accent!"

The teachers glanced at one another—

"When I told him I was your friend, he took my hand! Then kissed both sides of my face!"

And were struck with wonder...during that inconsequential moment when everything seemed right with the world.

heard at just the right
moment these too after all
arouse deep feelings
evening voices of the frogs
calling in the little fields
—Fujiwara no Tadayoshi, *Shinkokinshuu*

A Goldfish in the Ikebana

FIONA was in the lobby when Jo rushed past her on the way out.

"Remember—tell Meryl sweet dreams. Say Mr. Mazouzi!"

Then the telephone rang.

Fiona had a hunch who it was.

"Hello, Mr. Ono."

"Ms. O'Shea, Kouichiro's family has been found."

Fiona was more pleased than she thought she would be. If anyone could readily find the family the flag belonged to, it was the capable Mr. Ono.

He asked Fiona to ask Meryl to meet him in the lobby of her hotel in the morning with an overnight bag. They would fly to his favorite place (besides Osaka City and anywhere Fiona was)...Akita Prefecture, rent a car, stay the night at his friends' hot spring ryokan, and visit the family the next morning. Mr. Ono thought it was a great coincidence that the family was a one-hour drive from his friends' ryokan.

"It has a hot spring, you say?"

"Yes. On the way there, I'll take Meryl for a drive in the countryside. To see another face of Japan."

A question rose in Fiona's mind. Why not go straight to the family's house and fly back the same day?

Mr. Ono didn't believe in telepathy, only in good timing. Just then he had some.

He told her that important events—and returning a flag is one—take place in the morning. It was a custom Okan had taught him. Okan hadn't known, however, why that custom was a custom.

"In any case, we won't be able to reach the house before noon."

The part about before noon was a teeny-weeny lie.

Mr. Ono had told his boss that he needed two days to cover the story because why would he let a chance—to stay at his friends' ryokan, feast on their meals with flavorful Akita rice, sip chilled Akita sake, go on a drive in the countryside, and dream of Fiona while he soaked in a hot spring—pass him by?

But he hadn't planned on fibbing to Fiona. In his heart he said sorry.

And in Fiona's mind, no matter how fast the ideas whirled, none led to a reason for her to tag along. Her entire body switched on to irrationally-irritable mode. She hung up after a curt thank you.

Then in the teachers' room, Fiona found Meryl and Darryl sitting in front of his ikebana arrangement.

"Darryl, you never made one of these for me."

Meryl said the hydrangea looked like a waterfall on a cliff of reeds. She could imagine forest fairies dancing among the water lilies and lily pads—which floated near the reeds. It was the most exquisite flower arrangement she'd ever seen.

Fiona patted Meryl's shoulder. "Proves you've never been anywhere."

Darryl said, "It's not like Ms. Kawanishi's. She arranges masterpieces. If only they could last forever. I've been studying ten years. In the world of ikebana I'm a high school student. Ms. Kawanishi's been arranging flowers for over sixty years."

"No." Fiona looked at the back of the arrangement and then the straight row of reeds and hydrangea branches. "Ms. Kawanishi's been doing it since three lifetimes ago. Everyone in Japan has been doing something since three lifetimes ago. That's why they're so good at everything."

"Darryl says the flowers tell him where to put them."

"Conversing with flowers are we, Darryl?" Fiona's eyes narrowed. "Asked one out for dinner tonight?"

"Darryl held the hydrangea stems at different angles to show how the feeling of the arrangement changed. It wasn't as harmonious. The stems seemed to tell him 'Turn me a little more this way.' "

Meryl's imitation of a talking hydrangea impressed Fiona.

"It's amazing," Meryl said, "how beauty can change so much by a small movement."

"It's all relative, bit like an earthquake?" Fiona winced. What she said wasn't funny. Meryl will think she's insensitive. She felt like crying.

Fiona glanced at Meryl.

But the look on Meryl's face hadn't changed.

To Meryl, Fiona's remark sounded like something her father would say when he was sad or upset about something that had nothing to do with what he was talking about. Something was upsetting Fiona.

"Darryl told me an ikebana arrangement is like simple math. From each plant you have, you use three, five, or seven stems. You imagine lines that connect their tips. Those lines make triangles."

Fiona shrugged her shoulders. She no longer felt like crying.

"The height of the arrangement is in proportion to the width of the vase."

The vase was oblong and shallow.

Darryl had also divided the width into equal sections. The reeds and the hydrangea were one-fifth away from the left edge of the vase. To the right were the floating water lilies and lily pads, none touching, for a feeling of cool, open space.

But Darryl hadn't told this to Meryl. Instead, he had flirted.

Fiona counted.

"Darryl, your lily pads and water lilies *don't* add up to three, five, or seven."

"This one's for fun."

He took out the smallest lily.

The arrangement somehow looked lonesome, still beautiful and refreshing, but lonesome and serious.

Darryl put the lily back. Even Fiona smiled.

"Make everything mathematically perfect"—those brows lifted—"then add some fun. After all, what's perfection without fun?"

"The reason our Creator added us to the world," Fiona said. "Humans. Imperfect fun."

"Darryl says the empty space between the flowers and leaves and reeds is important too. He had to cut some flowers off to make the arrangement as lovely as it was meant to be."

Then Meryl said something she hadn't expected to.

"Whenever I hear the words *empty space*, I think of what Peter left behind in my heart. What my mother left. Maybe that empty space will someday make the arrangement of me as peaceful as this is."

She told them that Peter had given her flowers to wear in her hair on their wedding day, then quickly asked Darryl if he ever put goldfish in the water of his ikebana. "It would really be a miniature pond then!"

"Darryl probably has a tree frog in the hydrangea. You never know what boys hide." Fiona's hand was on Byron's locker. "Mommy Meryl, what's your son hiding?"

She flung open the locker door.

"Whaaawt? Only books! No half bottle of whisky. Not even girlie pictures, just..."

Out came a newspaper article.

"Gorillas!—At a village near a wilderness in Cameroon!"

Fiona started reading. " 'Hunters had trapped a baby lowland gorilla to sell to a zoo.' Don't zoos grow their own? Says here, 'As night fell, over sixty gorillas invaded the village in single file.' That baby's got jungle savvy! It must've dropped banana crumbs along the way. Listen to this. 'Gunshots didn't scare the gorillas. The next night, the gorillas beat on doors and windows.' That baby's loved. Oh! Happy ending. The goodwill hunters let the baby go. A corny last line—'Victory was the gorillas'.' But memorable."

Meryl took the article from Fiona. "I wonder why Byron keeps this."

"I came across it," Darryl said, "and told Byron when I was little, the news on TV talked about guerillas in Vietnam. This is going to sound dumb...I thought they were talking about the animals...I think I was six or seven. I wondered why the army was fighting them. It was unfair. Gorillas didn't have guns, and I wanted them to win the war. Byron told me he didn't remember seeing news of the war when he was little."

Meryl put the article back. Byron's father had been one of those who darling Darryl had thought killed gorillas.

"Next on the agenda," Fiona said. "Mr. Ono wants to take Meryl to Akita."

"Isn't Akita a kind of dog?"

"You know that?" Darryl asked.

"When Byron was a third grader, all he talked about was animals in Japan. Red-faced snow monkeys in hot springs. Short-eared Amami black bunnies. The mommy bunny buries her baby in a hole so habu pit vipers don't find it. Japan also has black scorpions."

Fiona put her hand on Meryl's arm.

"Mr. Ono isn't taking you to a dog show. He found the family the flag belongs to. They live in Akita Prefecture, wherever that is."

About Akita

LATER that night, Fiona and Darryl wished Meryl a safe journey, and Fiona kept her promise to Jo. "So nice that you met Mr. Mazouzi. Sweet dreams."

On the plane the next morning, Mr. Ono handed Fiona's fancy paper bag with the flag in it to Meryl.

"And here you go," she said, putting a bun—which Fiona had pointed to at a bakery the evening before—into his hand.

Chocolate cream filled Mr. Ono's mouth. The sounds he made as he ate brought to mind the word "ochichi," meaning "mother's milk." He concentrated on *not* glancing at the buttons on Meryl's blouse.

She was about to bite into a custard bun...excited about flying over Japan...staying the night at a hot spring inn...and most importantly, returning the flag.

Nevertheless in her mind she began playing back her Mazouzi Dream!

She couldn't let go of those powerful, sensual feelings that woke every nerve in her body—in her dream. She had never dreamed of making love. But sometime during the night, she melted into the cosmos of Mr. Mazouzi's eyes...felt his arms wrap around her...his body press against hers...heard his creamy voice, first in French then in English. "Yes, you understand what a woman can do."

Meryl fell into a trance, all the better to replay her dream. Thoughts of Peter moved to a channel without reception. Even the audible bites Mr. Ono took from his gooey bun didn't distract her.

Mr. Ono talked about the lake they were going to see, Lake Tazawa—breathtaking, dazzling, and deep.

The color of the lake changed in the sunlight, sometimes green like Fiona's eyes, sometimes blue like Meryl's.

He licked chocolate cream from his lips, then spoke about his favorite place in all Akita called Ani, a vast area of wooded mountain ranges and valleys. The younger sister of Kouichiro Kasai—the soldier of the flag—lived there.

Mr. Ono thought Meryl showed more interest in what he had to say than his Okan ever did. There was an eager smile on her face. If he paused, she nodded. She sighed pleasantly whenever he said something enjoyable. Meryl was like a traditional Japanese woman!

Then Mr. Ono droned on about Mt. Komagadake. The hot spring ryokan they were staying at was on its southwestern slope.

And his next topic?

"Kunimasu."

Meryl blinked her eyes and put her Mazouzi Dream replay on pause because...when Byron was a third grader, he had told her about kunimasu!

Mr. Ono sounded like a narrator on a TV documentary.

"In Lake Tazawa, a fish found nowhere else in the world had reigned, the elusive darling of fishermen—the kunimasu, the respected fish of the nation."

It looked ferocious, prehistoric. Bones pierced through its fins. It thrived in depths with temperatures as low as 4°C. Fishermen traveled far to catch the kunimasu in the days of dirt roads and steam engines.

But then a hydroelectric power plant was built at the lake, and the water level fell drastically. Nearby Tama River was diverted to it. A hot spring of acid, however, poured into that river.

"Strong, like acid in my stomach." Mr. Ono squinted his eyes and grinned.

The blue and green of Lake Tazawa turned more intense, otherworldly, unnatural. Then the news—the kunimasu was extinct.

MR. ONO was in fifth grade the day he opened his textbook and read about the fate of the kunimasu.

He cried, "How preposterous!" His country had a fish nobody else had, and it was killed! For electricity? What about the children who had romped along the lakeshore catching the kunimasu for their mothers? Kunimasu boiled in miso with carrots, onions, eggplant! His mouth watered at the thought of how delicious it must have tasted. Tears filled his eyes. In his entire life he was never going to taste kunimasu.

Then his teacher told the class something that wasn't in their textbooks—the government had built the power plant to operate munition factories for the War.

The shock was too great for Little Boy Ono.

At once his imagination took flight.

The kunimasu survived the War! In a mountain lake too treacherous to reach...Otters played there...Wolves frolicked in nearby fields...And fluffy white and pink ibises dotted trees like wads of cotton candy that sometimes stuck to his fingers.

The teacher had told the class that those animals had become extinct too or were on the brink.

"I THINK the kunimasu are OK," Meryl said.

"What?"

"You said fishermen traveled far to catch them. Someone probably released a few in a lake closer to home. Didn't want to bother with the long trip anymore."

"Yes!" Mr. Ono grasped this hope, like Little Boy Ono would have. "Someday, someone will find the kunimasu!"

Mr. Ono admired Meryl. She lived in fantasy better than he did.

He thanked her for his tasty bun at the moment she was about to finish off hers.

Meryl wished she could share it with her dog and wondered if the Professor was tossing Freckles a tidbit or a tennis ball.

And then.

Who did the Professor dream of?

Their plane landed.

And at the car rental counter, Mr. Ono looked through a list. His eyes stopped at a convertible...another of his boyhood fantasies...zooming along country roads with a movie star of a woman, scarf loosely wrapped around her hair, lipstick like raspberry sherbet. A color to lick off. If only he could live that dream with Fiona.

But the reason why he and Meryl were there chose the sedan.

They drove into the countryside...forests of leafy trees and bushy cedars, curtains of bamboo, rice paddies. Houses with red or blue metal roofs huddled near the edge of the road; in gardens, lilies and hollyhocks took their places next to rows of vegetables.

The day was warming and the colors passing by were hypnotizing. Meryl pointed to a large, white bird at the top of a tall cedar tree.

"A snowy heron," Mr. Ono told her.

She closed her eyes. She was in Japan taking the flag to where it belonged. The evening before she had met a man with a creamy French accent...who had swash-buckled into one of her dreams, had made her...his own.

Meryl leaned against the headrest. And before dozing off, she saw the Professor in her mind.

A Welcome Home Party

FORTY MINUTES from the turnoff to the ryokan was a field of highland flowers.

Lava had flowed there once upon a time. Volcanic rock kept trees from taking root. The place became a welcoming bed for wildflowers, grasses, and shrubbery...lots of sunshine...runoff from melting snow babbled along the course of the lava stone...the surrounding forest, its cradle.

Meryl was still dozing when they got to the curve in the road where the forest ended abruptly.

Mr. Ono pulled over.

A warm breeze carried the notes of a songbird, and Meryl awoke.

"Who planned the party?"

She had never seen flowers as festive and welcoming...clusters like large bouquets...towering stalks of tiny white flowers...orange-pink mountain azaleas bright in the sunlight. Lilies flitted like yellow butterflies against a backdrop of solid green forest and sky as blue as the one above the desert where she lived.

The breeze swept across the field and the flowers danced.

She leapt from the car. The road under her feet felt like one she wished she had known all her life.

"Happy colors for a party!" Meryl took a deep breath. How lovely the air, filled with unfamiliar scents and sounds. Yet for a reason she couldn't explain, she felt a familiar comfort.

Mr. Ono joined her. "Happy flowers. A welcome home party for Kouichiro."

"Mr. Ono, if only it was a welcome home party. I wish Kouichiro could see these flowers."

"Let's show him."

Show him?

A glance at Mr. Ono's face and they turned back to the car.

He took one end of the flag. She took the other.

They held it toward the field and started up the road.

Mr. Ono said Kouichiro must be pleased with this homecoming.

The flag caught the breeze like a sail and fluttered between them.

Meryl wondered if his spirit was there, if he knew what they were doing. Was Peter with Kouichiro? Did he see her?

Fuzzy, plump honeybees hummed among the flowers along the road.

"They're the biggest ones I've ever seen," Meryl said.

"Sumo honeybees."

"Really?"

"Joke."

Then the songbird sang again.

"I wish I could find it," Meryl said. "It must be beautiful with that voice...like a flute."

Mr. Ono told her it was an uguisu, the color of dewy moss in morning shadows, small enough to fit in the palm of her hand.

They held the flag in the direction of the trill and were answered with another.

On the way back to the car, Meryl waved good-bye to the party flowers and sumo bees and the forest where the uguisu was hiding.

And wondered how to show them to Peter.

"Beyond the Hill"
—Masao Koga

Long-legged Colts

MOVEMENT filled the landscape...branches swayed, leaves sparkled in the sunshine. Had Akita been painted with every shade of green? Meryl tried to remember each scene, but their car sped past and nothing stayed in her mind, and even if she asked Mr. Ono to slow down—how could she remember it all?

The road crisscrossed ravines and hugged mountains, one after another, no end to them...as endless as the buildings in Osaka. Sheets of corrugated steel jutted away from mountainsides, looking like storefront awnings—shelves to catch heavy snow.

Up and up the road went. A bridge they would cross was in the distance high above them and above that, a cloud of rising steam...in the air, malodorous sulfur.

"Mr. Ono, what's that smell?"

"Tama River Onsen. 'Onsen' means hot spring."

"That's the acid river you talked about, right?"

"Yes."

They passed a hospital, but the forest blocked it from view. "Home to the strongest acid bath in Japan. Some patients get better."

Meryl liked the idea of taking a bath to get well. But what an odor. "Have to get better fast or the smell will do you in."

"What?"

"Bad joke."

Meryl asked Mr. Ono if the hot spring at their ryokan smelled the same.

"No. Every onsen is different. We're staying at Komagadake Onsen. Minerals in the water are good for the skin. We say, 'bijin yuu'—hot water for beautiful women. Many beautiful women are in Akita. We say 'Akita bijin.' You are Arizona bijin."

Mr. Ono bobbed his head and laughed nervously. In his culture it was uncommon for men to compliment women. His father only grunted and nodded whenever his mother wore a new outfit. But Mr. Ono had heard Darryl and Byron compliment Jo. It was cool and looked like fun.

Because Meryl was Byron's mother, she would be good to practice saying compliments to—Faulty logic, but Mr. Ono hoped he was right.

"Thank you, Mr. Ono. Fiona is London be-gene and Jo is...I don't know where Jo is from. Do you?"

"She is everywhere bijin."

"Good answer. By the way Mr. Ono, where are you taking me?"

"Towada-Hachimantai National Park—to see a mountain view of Japan."

"You know, the roads we've been on aren't like roads in the Arizona desert...straight as arrows. I've never been on such curvy roads."

Mr. Ono slowed down and turned onto Aspite Line, a road through the park.

"Nothing straight in Akita." He asked her to get his shoulder bag from the backseat. "There's hard candy inside. Stops motion sickness. You're going to need some."

Each piece of candy was dark green and in its own wrapper. Meryl popped two into her mouth at the moment Mr. Ono asked for one.

She tried handing it to Mr. Ono, but he waited for her to do something more.

She couldn't believe that he couldn't open it while he was driving. Was opening a candy wrapper for someone a

Japanese manner? Well, now she knew what to do when her son brought his Japanese bride home.

She unwrapped the candy.

"Please, put it in my mouth."

That's a Japanese manner?

"Driving. Two hands on the wheel."

She'd taught Byron that!

Her timing wasn't graceful. She pushed the candy between his lips as the road curved. Her fingers pressed onto his chin.

"Um. Thank you." The candy rolled around in his mouth, knocking against his teeth.

Mr. Ono looked boyish in profile. When Byron was a toddler, Meryl had put bits of candy between his tiny, slurpy lips...his fists banged up and down through the air. Now her son was six feet four inches tall and those memories were stretching and pulling away from her like a piece of taffy in the fingers of a child.

"Good?" Mr. Ono asked.

"What?"

"Candy."

She puckered her lips and nodded yes. "The flavor is green tea."

Mr. Ono's candy moved to the pocket between his cheek and teeth. "From Kyushu, south island, Saga Prefecture. Famous for green tea. Okan—my mother—went there a few weeks ago. She always carries hard candy in her handbag. Osaka air is no good for the throat."

Meryl wondered if Byron talked about the things in her bag.

The road took them through a tunnel of trees and sparkles of sunshine—a romantic picture.

"Mr. Ono, may I ask? Do you have a girlfriend?"

"I'm too busy writing my mystery novels."

What? She hadn't yet asked the genius of an investigative reporter about her son's fiancée! Surely he must know something.

But he didn't.

He'd seen Byron go out with only the other teachers.

Meryl furrowed her brow. "This is becoming more and more of a mystery!"

The road climbed toward a plateau, passing by marshes, hiking trails, and hot springs. Clouds dotted the sky. The leafy trees began disappearing from the landscape.

And on the ridge, twisting up through a blanket of dwarf bamboo, were fir trees...ragged, wind sculptured. Limbs grew out from one side of the trunks; the other side, barren, gnarled, stunted. Half trees reaching out to one another, but none were touching.

Mr. Ono pulled into a lookout point. "Here is Japan's big sky."

Big sky?

Meryl got out of the car.

Her husband had grown up on a ranch in the Big Sky State—Montana. Byron had learned how to ride there...a mare the color of chestnut. It had been Peter's.

Mountain ranges spread out before her, one after the other, like a folding fan opening into the distance, each turning a lighter shade of purple. Meryl had never seen so many mountains in her life. Across from her on a slope was a forest. She murmured, "All those Christmas trees." She had decorated only one with Peter.

A mountainside curved into the canyon. The more she wondered what was beyond the bend, the more like a dream the surroundings became. Clouds billowed and boiled like dust and sand kicked up by galloping horses.

She closed her eyes.

Music that matched the wide-open grandeur of the place started playing. Mr. Ono had pressed a few buttons in the car.

The spirited strumming of mandolins ushered visions to Meryl's mind.

Peter, on the mare the color of chestnut, trotted toward her. And from the dusty, dreamy, impossible clouds surrounding him came children bouncing up and down on long-legged colts! He wasn't in Vietnam...nor were those children with everlasting laughter in their smiles. They were coming back from somewhere, eager to get back—as eager as the melody in the air—filled with the excitement of a welcome home.

"Nice view." Mr. Ono was at her side.

Meryl opened her eyes. The mountains still folded away from her—What was beyond the bend?

Mr. Ono told her that Byron had said the song reminded him of mountains in Montana.

"It reminds me of Byron's father...Mr. Ono, my son never knew his father. He died before Byron was born."

She gazed at the mountains.

Mr. Ono did too. "Very, very sad."

She lifted her hand toward the car. "Does this song have words?"

"It's about the fun of getting to the top of a hill and finding out what's beyond." Mr. Ono bowed his head. "Does Byron look like his father?"

"I have his picture." Had she found the way to show Akita to Peter? "Would you like to see it?"

Mr. Ono nodded.

"Except for his eyes," he told her, "Byron looks like his father. Byron has your eyes."

At the edge of the plateau, Mr. Ono held the flag. Meryl held Peter's picture.

Then on their way back, they stopped for Peter—at the field where the uguisu sang and the flowers danced in the breeze.

Okamisan, Fireflies, a Ruddy Kingfisher

A BRIDGE crossed a stream near the ryokan. Hydrangeas bloomed in shades of blue, looking like pieces of sky an angel had dropped.
Meryl's first glimpse of Okamisan was from the bridge.
"A kimono!"
"That's Shinobu," Mr. Ono said. "We call her Okamisan. It means 'wife.' But for us it means 'the woman innkeeper.' We call her husband Goshujin."
"Meaning 'husband,' but for us, 'the man innkeeper'?"
"You're a good student."
Okamisan and Goshujin welcomed them as if they had been looking forward to their visit for weeks.
The stone floor in the entrance hall was shiny black.
Mr. Ono stepped out of his loafers and up into slippers on the raised wood-plank floor of the lobby.
Goshujin excused himself, said he had to get back to making their tasty dinner, and shook his head at Mr. Ono's hearty mime of salivating and slobbering.
Meryl plopped down on the wood floor and took off her shoes. She knew no one wore shoes in Japanese homes, but slippers in the lobby at a ryokan, too? Was the Professor used to this kind of stuff?
She stood up and tried not to stare too much at Okamisan...and her kimono—a celadon-green, pointillist pattern of bamboo. Her purplish-brown obi had an embroidered scrollwork design in scarlet, golden yellow, and cream.

The outfit was beautiful. And so was Okamisan. She had a face like a doll, round and smooth, and a smile as playful as a child's—and yet, a face as understanding as a mother's. Her lips were the color of a red camellia under snowflakes, a color in a painting Meryl had seen shopping with Fiona. Okamisan's long hair loosely circled the top of her head as Ms. Kawanishi's had. And her motherly, dimpled hands looked as soft as Ms. Kawanishi's too.

Okamisan touched Meryl's arm.

"She says she's never seen anyone so pretty," Mr. Ono said.

"Please tell her she's the pretty one! I adore her kimono."

Mr. Ono told Meryl that Okamisan was apologizing. They didn't have a yukata long enough for her.

"What's a yukata?"

"At a ryokan, it's a cotton kimono we wear before and after bath time, like pajamas."

"I can wear a kimono?"

"She doesn't have one long enough."

"Please tell her my husband told me if I ever wore a kimono, it would come down to here."

Meryl bent over and touched her knees.

"Yes!"—one of the English words Okamisan knew.

She showed them up a wide staircase to a tatami room with floor cushions and a low table. The windows overlooked a shallow river, as wide as a country road, dwarf bamboo tumbled over its bank. Cedars grew on the slope descending away from them. Blue sky filled the space between the branches.

It was the only vacant room and Meryl didn't mind sharing.

Before she asked where the beds were, Mr. Ono told her. "Futons. They'll put them out while we're having dinner."

Okamisan poured two glasses of Mr. Ono's favorite summertime afternoon drink, Akita cider. And when she put the bottle down, Meryl poured a glass for Okamisan.

But Okamisan never drank with guests...a manner she gladly didn't follow for Meryl.

Meryl's eyes opened wide. "This tastes like my childhood."

It was fresh, bubbly sweet, a taste she didn't know. Yet it reminded her of playtime—reminiscent of wonderful surprises, simple discoveries. A taste a child couldn't imagine would be a taste, but was.

"But I wasn't a child in Akita. Or even in Japan!"

Mr. Ono said he wished he had grown up in Akita.

Okamisan told them her parents ran a ryokan in the hot spring town, Iizaka. The evenings of her childhood were filled with the sound of the shamisen while hundreds of geishas entertained businessmen from Tokyo. She could hardly wait to grow up because women were so beautiful.

Mr. Ono translated. "But now drinking cider together, it's fun being a child again."

"If I lived in Akita," Meryl said, "I could drink this every day. With one sip"—she lifted her glass to Okamisan—"me too. A child again."

Mr. Ono spoke some Japanese to Okamisan and told Meryl, "Asking about a florist."

After Okamisan left, Mr. Ono said, "There's a private onsen outside." A towel and yukata were under his arm. "Would you like to go?"

"Together?"

That wasn't what Mr. Ono had meant. Taking a bath with Meryl was tempting. But he wouldn't be able to fantasize about Fiona with Meryl in the same tub.

"I'm going to the big public bath for men."

He realized—only too late—no fantasizing there, either.

But for Meryl, bath time was going to be after dinner. She unpacked and put Kouichiro's flag into the lacquered box Fiona had picked out.

Mr. Ono came back, his wet hair pushed away from his face and his thick retro glasses off, confident in his yukata—not the clumsy, little boy he looked like in his business suit with its short lapels. A narrow obi was tied low on his hips.

Meryl wondered...If the Professor wore a yukata, would he look different too?

They went downstairs for Goshujin's dinner. Okamisan brought the dishes one by one, then bowls of Akita rice. Mr. Ono did his best translating a few ingredients. "A kind of horseradish, a type of mountain vegetable, one species of fish, an example of a mushroom, a bit of root from the plant kingdom, a sort of aquatic leafy grass."

Meryl discovered that the aquatic leafy grass looked like curled-up, miniscule lily pads and was slimy. She didn't ask Mr. Ono what other kingdom a bit of root could possibly be from.

Then Okamisan served Akita sake.

Mr. Ono said, "Long time ago, sake was medicine. It's good for you."

Okamisan told them the cups had been her grandparents'.

Meryl picked up hers. On the inside, the glazed pottery swirled into a smaller and smaller circle. Was it the spiral of a seashell or the circling of water? The cup felt as soft as satin on her lips. She couldn't make sense of it. Had she ever noticed how the rim of a cup felt against her lips?

It made no sense. The sake was the best medicine she'd ever tasted!

After dinner she went back to their room alone. Two futons had been laid out, a hand's width apart.

She slipped into her yukata, narrow obi around her waist three times...the hem, down to her knees. And with each step, the yukata's stiff cotton cloth sounded as if her legs were rubbing between clean sheets.

From a side door, a walkway made of planks took her to a shed.

It served as a dressing room and opened onto a deck with a shower and a square tub, about the size of a king-sized bed. The hot spring flowed into the tub from a bamboo spout. The overflow drained from a narrow slit in the plank at its edge and trickled into the river that she had seen from her window.

Meryl was under the open sky...had never been naked outside before.

The forest was in shadows.
She lathered up and wondered...
Were any bears across the river peeking?
She poured buckets of the hot spring water over herself—first legs then shoulders and back—to help her body get used to the temperature as Mr. Ono had told her to do, then she stepped into the bath, sat down, stretched out her legs, and sank into the water until it covered her shoulders.
"What a big tub! Big enough for two. If you're little like Mr. Ono, maybe five."
She twisted her waist, spread out her arms, watched herself move...and curled her toes.
"Pretty good for someone over forty."
If only she could show someone.
She floated to the side nearest the river and saw white frothy bubbles in the current swirling over rocks. The sound of rushing water filled her ears, relaxing her even more.
"This is the best bath I've ever had."
She closed her eyes, hoping to see Peter again and the smiling children. But she didn't.
Instead, above the river was a tiny dot of light.
A few blinks.
Tinkerbell?
"Iridescent green. My favorite color. The glowing license plates in Osaka...A firefly!"
The hovering dot sped off down the river, became smaller and smaller, then disappeared. She turned her head back to where it had been.
There was another! Following the first one!
Out of the tub, into yukata, obi...one...two...three times round her waist, wet feet on the planks—off to the side door.
Meryl spotted Okamisan.
Some made-up sign language...then to the main door...a flashlight passed between them.
Okamisan knelt down, glanced at Meryl's feet, put out a pair of wooden sandals for men, then pointed in the direction of the bridge.

Meryl's feet felt clumsy and heavy and her toes moved back and forth trying to grip the wooden slabs, but she was on her way!

At the bridge, Meryl turned off her flashlight.

A trace of evening light was still held captive in the sky. Cedars towered above leafy trees. Black on indigo. Each twig, each edge of leaf, sharp and distinct in a world of two colors.

She looked down at her hands and arms, pale in the deepening twilight.

Would eternal black wait for her to become indigo, then capture her and turn her into eternal night?

Meryl sighed—What *was* she thinking? Oh, how she wished for those tiny dots of light!

Her wish came true.

One by one from out of the forest they flew toward her, zipping and diving like fiery comets. Falling stars in a forest.

How they entranced her. If they had swarmed and flown in one direction she would have followed them, but they didn't. They performed their aerial acrobats right before her eyes.

Mr. Ono and Okamisan joined her.

"Mr. Ono, I can see the fireflies!" Two twinkled on a cluster of leaves high above Meryl. "You said maybe I would."

"There's a famous story about fireflies in Kyushu."

"The big south island?"

"Yes." He told her that thousands of kamikaze pilots had trained at military bases there. "Is a War story OK with you?"

Okamisan asked him if he was talking about a place called Chiran.

"Does everyone know the story?" Meryl asked.

"Most everyone."

"Please tell me."

IN CHIRAN, a woman ran an eatery for pilots. They called her Mom because she treated them like sons and they wanted to be home.

One particular squadron saw her trying to hide her sorrow on the last night of their lives. Their leader raised his voice. They would come back the next night...as fireflies! The others jumped up and cheered.

But Mom was about to bawl, her fist at her mouth.

The boys barely understood her.

"How will I know the fireflies are you...and not plain, old ordinary fireflies?"

As soon as the words were out, she wished she hadn't said them. But she couldn't keep quiet. Not that night. Not with those boys. She wanted to believe, really know they were coming back to her.

The pilots gathered round Mom and laughed and patted her shoulders.

One boy shouted, "We'll come inside!"

Another pointed to the rafters. "Light up the whole dining room."

And another made one more promise. "To prove it's us, we'll show up again the next night."

"Keep the door open."

"There now. Stop the gusher from your eyes."

"You'll see us again—as fireflies!"

She wiped her tears and put on a brave face, nodded and waved good-bye, promised not to be sad.

The next morning the boys took off.

That evening Mom kept the door to her eatery open. If anyone could come back as a firefly, it was those boys who had gulped down their suppers...and second helpings as if they would always have a tomorrow.

Mom got busy cooking.

She didn't notice the sun had set until someone said, "Is that a firefly?"

She looked up. And on one of the rafters was a glowing dot of green. She glanced at the open door and another flew in. And another! They lit up the room, all seventeen of them, the same number of boys who had promised to come back.

Mom laughed and cried and cried some more along with everyone there...on the next night too.

IN the story most everyone knew, there had been only one pilot, one firefly. For dramatic effect Mr. Ono exaggerated everything. Seventeen...Fiona's birthday.

It was the most beautiful story Meryl had ever heard. And she had heard it under an indigo sky in a black cutout forest bejeweled with fireflies.

Okamisan took hold of Meryl's little finger and pointed down.

Meryl smoothed her yukata.

On her knee was a firefly.

"No one's going to believe this."

When Meryl whispered, "Thank you, Peter," Mr. Ono shed a tear.

The three stayed out with the fireflies until the dot of light on Meryl's knee took off and disappeared into the forest.

MERYL went back to the stream of the fireflies the next morning. Beyond the bridge she followed a path lined with velvety moss and fanciful ferns. Vines beaded with flowers festooned the trees.

And right before her eyes a dusty, rusty-brown leaf flitted through the air. Even stranger—it brought a sliver of sky. Hadn't she seen a streak of blue? She blinked her eyes and in the stream a flutter of dusty brown...the sliver of sky...a splash of orange red. A bird! With a bright, festive beak and a patch of blue feathers on its back. Out it flew from under a rush of bubbles and landed on a shiny rock. It cocked its head, looking like it was about to start a conversation, but then flew away into the shadows.

Kyorororoo.

To Meryl, its song sounded like a telephone ringing.

"Come back. Don't you want to talk?"

ON the staircase Meryl stopped in front of a photo. "This was at the waterfall."

"A ruddy kingfisher," Mr. Ono said.

Okamisan told Meryl that something wonderful was going to happen to her and Mr. Ono that day. A guest had never spotted a ruddy kingfisher near their ryokan, nor had she or her husband.

Goshujin handed Mr. Ono two bunches of white and yellow chrysanthemums and deep green, thick-leaved branches of sakaki. Mr. Ono thanked him and Okamisan and paid her for them, happy that she had, as his mother would've done, saved him the bother of going to the florist.

When Meryl was about to get into the car, Okamisan put a small bag with two bottles of Akita cider into her hand. Her red-camellia lips blossomed into a smile.

"Children again."

Like an apple tree among the trees of the forest...
—Song of Solomon

To Ani Town

MR. ONO and Meryl stopped at a clearing on the slope of Mt. Komagadake to take pictures of Lake Tazawa, but a flat mist the color of slate hid it. Five minutes later they were at its shore.

The air was chilly and Meryl kept her window shut. It was hard for her to believe that nothing was alive in that lake.

They passed by rice paddies, a shrine, a few ryokans, then turned north onto Route 105.

Mr. Ono talked about Ani.

Meryl thought he sounded like a father reading a fairy tale. Wait. Where had she heard that before? In her living room...the Professor!

"Ani...a landscape filled with magic. Mountains curve softly...And in the spring, vines and leaves puff them up into zigzag dragons."

Would the Professor ever say zigzag dragons?

"Autumn bewitches them. Poof! Orange—red—purple—yellow. Sunlight shines through them...bright like gelatin desserts."

"The dragons morph into gelatin desserts?"

"The leaves on the trees."

Meryl looked out the window and thought, Yummy flavors.

Low-hanging gossamer clouds cast shadows on the wet trees, dark mysterious shades of green. There weren't any fences or concrete block walls marking property lines—only walls of stacked kindling and split logs.

"For long winters," Mr. Ono said.

In gardens the corn had grown higher than Meryl's knees.

Mr. Ono told Meryl he thought Ani was the real Akita of Akita, the heartland. It was his idyllic furusato...the place he wished was "his beautiful country home," where his roots had taken hold.

But why Ani? Even with his deductive and inductive reasoning skills that he had honed for writing his mystery novels, he couldn't put his finger on it. How could the colors of the sky or the leaves be different there than elsewhere? How was the air filled with more joy? But for him, Ani was like that.

Mr. Ono's favorite archeological artifact from Ani was a stone sculpture of a laughing face, robust lines grinning wider with more mirth than he had thought possible of a prehistoric fellow. It summed up his feelings for the place.

Ani had the best of everything that one imagined of country life. River fishing and crabbing, rice paddies, and lush forests. Honey from apple, acacia, horse chestnut, and mountain cherry. Flowers filled the air with a fragrance as sweet as youth.

Mr. Ono then talked about Ani's Matagi hunters.

Meryl asked him what Matagi meant.

"It's a name. Maybe from long ago. No one knows the meaning."

She didn't understand what the big deal was about Matagi hunters. "In the United States, about anyone can hunt with a license."

Mr. Ono answered with his interpretation of a piece of history.

He didn't bog her down with names of eras or social/political movements. Fiona once told him that the only history people want to know about is the one roosting in their family tree.

Mr. Ono summarized.

"This sounds unbelievable, but centuries ago there were more guns in Japan per person than in any other country in the world."

"I didn't know that."

"Civil wars were everywhere."

"Ditto."

"The armies were making a big mess of the place. Common people armed themselves. The soldiers didn't want to be shot at by everyone. So the leaders decided...no more guns, not even for soldiers. It was back to spears and the katana."

"What's a katana?"

"Samurai sword."

"Those are scary."

"Everyone went along with this idea—except the Matagi of Ani."

"I suppose it's easier to shoot a deer than chase it waving a katana."

Mr. Ono said those hunters had been a clever lot. Folklore told of ancestors from a defeated monarchy fleeing to the mountains of Ani. Perhaps they had learned how to trap and hunt from indigenous people. No one knew. Then guns came along. And after the government ordered the Matagi to give them up, they headed to the capital in Akita with a load of furs—monkey, fox, serow, tanuki, and tsukinowa black bear, a crescent moon of white at its neck. When the Matagi were asked how they had trapped the animals, they took out their guns.

The law changed again.

"They bribed government officials with fur coats!"

"The officials saw what they wouldn't be able to get because hunting would become too difficult."

"That's a nice way of putting it."

"Yes."

Mr. Ono told Meryl that the Matagi kept their guns and were given documents that permitted them to travel throughout Japan during a time when travel was restricted to most everyone.

The Matagi made their way as far south as the Yoshino Mountains in Nara Prefecture.

"I know Nara." Meryl said. "Jo and Fiona took me. You can catch a deer with a cracker there."

Mr. Ono kept a poker face but wished he had been with Fiona in Nara.

He talked about the medicines the Matagi made.

Monkey heads were used to treat high blood pressure; ferret, nervous temperaments.

He didn't say anything about the medicine from bear paws for men with sleepy *sons*.

Instead he told her the Matagi also farmed, made tools, worked in mines and in the timber industry, on the railroads...to eke out their scanty subsistence.

And then at the start of the twentieth century, people other than Matagi were able to get hunting licenses. Monkey and serow numbers dropped. This led to a ban on hunting. Furs were imported...animals commercially raised. Western medicine made inroads. Public education brought other opportunities to make a living.

The Matagi way of life has been slowly coming to an end.

Mr. Ono then switched topics to the mountain goddess of Ani—Yamanokami.

The Goddess Yamanokami was hideous.

"And she likes humor. The Matagi gave her an offering. The ugliest thing they could find. A dried okoze—a kind of fish."

The fish was repulsive, vile, and monstrously grotesque—words Mr. Ono picked up when Fiona had talked about prime ministers and presidents.

The fish was even uglier than Yamanokami. It made her laugh and for that, the Matagi were safe in her woods.

"In a way, the Matagi culture is like a fairytale," Mr. Ono said. "There's little written history about them—except for what I've told you. Even that is uncertain. Cultural anthropologists haven't been interested. But for a mystery novelist—"

"Such as yourself."

"They're perfect to write about because no one can say something is false—"

"Because no one knows what's true! Maybe there's a Matagi hunter in Kouichiro's family."

It would be a dream come true, thought Mr. Ono.

But they were returning Kouichiro's flag to his sister. How could he ask about the Matagi?

The road brought them to what looked like Main Street in old Western movies, except Ani's simple buildings had metal roofs.

Mr. Ono pulled up in front of a shop that had a window display of large knives with heavy-looking handles. When he got back in the car he told Meryl the Satos' place was across a narrow bridge over the Ani River.

What Mr. Ono didn't tell Meryl was...the man inside had said Mr. Sato was the Matagi turned apple grower.

Those buildings out of a Western disappeared, and the road ran through the forest. Meryl opened her window and was greeted with a fragrance, one as fresh as the colors surrounding them, as delightful as being in a bubble bath.

On her lap was Fiona's fancy bag—in it, the lacquered box with Kouichiro's flag. She lifted the lid for him.

The bridge came into view, then rice paddies, and then an orchard rising up a mountainside like a staircase to the edge of a cedar forest.

"Are those fruit trees?"

The Telephone Call

THE FIRST TIME Mr. Ono phoned Ayako Sato—Kouichiro Kasai's only surviving relative—she covered her mouth to keep from crying out.

But inviting Mr. Ono to bring her brother's flag into her home wasn't her decision to make.

Ayako didn't have a Buddhist altar.

It would have been customary for the flag to go to the blood relative who tended the family altar on her side of the family. None of her relatives, however, were alive. Her husband's family altar was at his older brother's home.

It was unheard of for a wife to bring a hotokesama—a spirit or angel—from her own family to the home of her husband, but Ayako was sure her husband wouldn't mind.

He knew she hadn't heard any news about her brother from the day he left home until years after the Surrender. Her husband had sat next to her while she read the letter from an old school friend whose cousin had fought alongside her brother during the last months of the War. That was when they learned about his death. Her husband had said how sad it must be for her.

Ayako told Mr. Ono she would call him back after she talked with her husband.

She filled his teacup and set it down in front of him.

He nodded thanks.

Her hands were trembling, but she looked so happy.

She told him about Mr. Ono.

"Someone from America has brought Older Brother's flag back."

"Older Brother's come home?"

"They'd like to bring us his flag."

"We'll be waiting."

She thanked him, then left the room, a small skip in her step.

Hiroshi Sato picked up his cup and peered into it as he would a deep hole in the ground.

By the happy hollow of a Tree.
—Shakespeare, *Lear*

Ayako Sato

AYAKO got ready for the visit.

She bought candleholders and several candles, a bell and a small cushion to set it on, a wand to ring the bell, a box of incense sticks, a vase to hold the sticks, and an incense burner.

The scent of the incense was aloeswood. Ayako was sure her brother would like its refreshing coolness.

She knew her brother had loved sake. His cheeks flushed as red as apples after a few sips. Their mother heated it up on snowy nights. He always reached for the bottle when it was too hot to hold, then his burning fingertips grabbed his earlobe.

"Whoa! Hot—how can this be so hot-hot-HOT?"

Her brother's laughing voice...

"It's an offering," she told the clerk at the sake shop. He wrapped two bottles in white paper and tied yellow and white cords around them.

At a fruit stand, there were cherries—smooth and shiny and dressed up, creamy yellow blushing into a party red. How many had she picked with her brother? Her bucket never filled to the top even when he had added his.

She spotted the bananas.

WHEN Ayako was four years old, her brother had brought home a banana.

In their garden, he squatted down and peeled it, first digging his thumbnail in at the stem, snapping it, then pulling a fourth of the peel halfway down. And in no time, the peel hung like petals of a flower with a center sticking out as long as Pinocchio's nose. The banana had been jungle green at the loading dock in Taiwan. On the voyage to Japan it had turned sunny yellow. He put it in both her hands and stood up.

Ayako's mouth was as wide as it could be when the banana hit her lower lip, broke off at where the peel was still in one piece, and tumbled away. Her brother made a daring dive, but it landed on a tuft of grass under droopy morning glories. Tears filled her eyes as her brother guffawed, picked up the banana, then rinsed it off in the bucket at the well.

She was still clutching the rest of the banana in its peel when she tried taking the wet piece from him. Right before her eyes...back on the tuft of grass.

Her brother keeled over, rapping his belly with the palm of his hand, like a chubby tanuki would after stumbling across a jug of sake. Then he rinsed the banana once again and held it to her lips. No need for another banana bath.

CHERRIES, bananas, grapes, a watermelon, and a pineapple—for Older Brother. Ayako bought them all. He had loved fruit.

APPLE BLOSSOMS perfumed their childhood. One grandfatherly tree had a hollow in its trunk, home to an owl family...the downy little ones sometimes peeked out. Her brother stayed nearby when they grew big enough to toddle onto the limbs. Mama and Papa Owl didn't mind.

Ayako had wanted to know why.

"Mutual guard duty. Keeping away the hawks."

The owls kept the field mice away from their apples.

After her brother left for the War, a series of good-byes followed—her parents died, their land was sold, and she went to live with relatives in Aomori City. A firebombing destroyed their home, her relatives killed.

KA-E-RO-U

The Surrender came. She managed to find work and lodging but longed for the peaceful orchards of her childhood. Months later, she heard a cute song on the radio about apples and remembered a faraway tale that her grandfather had told.

He had once taken apple saplings to a place called Ani and had never been anywhere more beautiful. The warm days and cool nights of summer perfectly suited apple growing.

Ayako made her way there. The families tending the orchards had known her grandfather and introduced her to the man who became her husband.

TRUMPET LILIES had been her brother's favorite flower...deep green, thick leaves, and a strong stem...white blossoms, aiming straight ahead as if sighting a target. He had taken her to a field of trumpet lilies, each standing at attention in full bloom, and asked, "Who sounded the order for that?"

AT the florist was a lovely fragrance Ayako didn't know. Flowers filled buckets...those of the season—bachelor buttons, sunflowers, gladioli; those sold year round—carnations, roses, chrysanthemums.

No trumpet lilies.

"How about these gorgeous ones?" The florist pulled out a bucket of Casablanca lilies.

The fragrance Ayako didn't know.

She also bought sunflowers and white and yellow chrysanthemums. Her brother would be pleased, she was sure.

While she was out, her husband had moved a low, round table into the tatami room they would use. She spread a tablecloth over it and arranged the candles, incense, and bell. Two vases of Casablanca lilies went behind the candles—in front, bottles of sake and baskets of fruit. She put a floor cushion near the table. Morning glories were embroidered on its cover.

Four more cushions went around a larger table in the center of the room.

She dusted and straightened, thankful for the miracle that had happened. She had prayed her brother would find her, had remembered everything she could about him, and waited. And now he was almost home. Exactly fifty years—the last year for a spirit to come back to this world before going on to the next birth. Her brother was coming back to her be-fore his new life began.

"He's as wonderful as I remember."

From the alcove, down came the scroll of an ink painting...the flower arrangement went to the entrance hall. In the empty space, up went a rack for the flag.

For her guests, Ayako put a bottle each of apple juice and honey from their trees into pretty paper bags. She wanted to give more, but more glass bottles would be too heavy and bulky to carry back on their flight.

Ayako wondered whether or not to invite the priest to chant a sutra—his voice as solemn as the ringing of the temple bell. But if the priest were there, he would take every bit of her attention. She wanted the newspaper reporter from Osaka and the woman from America all to herself when her brother came home. Ayako knew her husband would let her decide. And her brother would agree...another day for the priest.

She wished she could speak more English. It hadn't been taught because of the War. She had practiced the alphabet with her children years ago, used their Japanese/English dictionary...could say thank you.

But she felt so much more than a simple thank you. A woman from America—the enemy!—was bringing her brother home.

Did the woman know someone who had been in the War—father or brother or husband? Had he been the soldier who killed her brother? Small chance, but...

Ayako's mind took her to a place she hated.

Before her brother had been killed, had he killed someone? Someone who had been loved as much as she loved him?

Ayako went to the sink and washed her face.

Brave American woman—it must be sad for her too. If only Older Brother were alive. Did she think the same?

Then Ayako looked for a cassette that her daughter had given her from a trip to Okinawa. The day Ayako first heard one of the songs, she cried in their apple orchard...the only time she cried since her country went to War. During the War and afterward she couldn't cry. Everyone wanted to, but how could they when others had lost more?

She was going to play the song for the woman from America. The Okinawan jamisen may sound strange and she might not understand the words.

But the singer's voice was what Ayako wanted her to hear. It sounded like her brother's.

Blue as the Inland Sea

ACROSS the bridge, the road ran between terraced rice paddies; two snowy herons stood motionless, necks outstretched. Grapevines grew near the houses snuggled along the base of the mountain.

Mr. Ono backed their car into a small clearing. "It's the one by the apple trees."

Meryl's eyes moved from the orchard to the house.

"Mr. Ono. Please tell me what to do...what to say when I give Mrs. Sato the flag."

"You don't have to say anything. There are no words."

No words? Meryl thought. How can there be no words? Isn't there something? Something simple? All this way for no words?

She wished the Professor was there. He would say something.

"They'll light candles. If they follow Buddhist customs, they'll burn incense." Mr. Ono told her simply. "Candlelight and fragrance lead the soul to paradise. And when the soul comes back to the world during religious holidays or on the anniversary of one's death, the light and fragrance lead the soul home."

The serenity in his voice eased Meryl's mind...candlelight, the fragrance of incense...leading souls to heaven or home.

"There are offerings of flowers, food, green tea or water. Souls get thirsty along the way."

They finally got out of the car, and from the backseat, Mr. Ono took the offerings he had brought—a box of candles and the bunch of flowers and leafy branches.

They headed toward the Satos' house.

But Meryl's worry was back.

Mrs. Sato's brother wasn't coming home. They were bringing her an old flag—stained in his blood.

A question took hold of Meryl's heart.

If someone was bringing Peter's bloodied flag home, would she open her door?

In the entrance hall, Ayako had heard the car. And when she laid eyes on Meryl, nothing could keep her back. She rushed to her, took Meryl's arm in her hands, and spoke so quickly Mr. Ono didn't have time to translate.

Meryl had never had her worries disappear like they did then.

Ayako led them into the tatami room and put Mr. Ono's offerings next to the sake and fruit. Her husband followed them in, and they sat down on the cushions around the table.

"It's decorated so beautifully," Meryl murmured.

Mr. Ono translated what Ayako was saying—"A welcome for us and welcome home for her brother."

Meryl set the lacquered box in front of Ayako.

Its colors blended with the walls the color of sand and the worn tatami, dull golden yellow like a field of grass in late autumn.

"This is for you and your brother."

THE LID was painted with a design of the seven flowers of autumn. Fringed nadeshiko...kikyoo about to bloom its balloon flowers...red fujibakama...purple blossoms of the kuzu vine, and the tallest flower, a yellow ominaeshi. There was hagi—its tiny red-purple blossoms seemed to be floating in air. Susuki plume grass curved along one side...its lines as fine as those on the wings of a dragonfly. The background was the deep brown red of a sunset at harvest time...a design bountiful in beauty with a touch of wistful melancholy. Time will surely pass and take them into winter.

AYAKO'S brother had been born on a night when the brightest moon of the year paraded across the sky.

Her mother often said, "Everything good comes in September."

They reminded Ayako of her brother. Ripening rice, crisp apples...white, lacy fields of buckwheat...country paths lined with silvery-gold plume grass. In September, you could watch eagles teach their young to dive and land and then take off in the open fields. Across the sky, clouds rippled like the surface of a lazy river hit by a stone a child had tossed.

What made her think most of her brother was a flower. But it wasn't one of the seven flowers of autumn. It was the rindo—a shade of purple as deep as a moonlit night.

Her brother had found them...short, magical stalks...buds tight together, shaped and pointed like the scales of a serpent.

He told her, "Baby dragon tails." They'd fallen off for the little dragons to grow new ones, like the baby teeth she had lost.

AYAKO wondered how Meryl knew that the flowers on the box were for the month her brother was born.

Ayako spoke and Mr. Ono translated.

"Thank you. I am so happy. My brother is so happy too." Mr. Ono told Meryl, "She's talking to him...thanking him for watching over her and her family, telling him about us."

Ayako put her hands together and bowed to the box. The others did the same. She lifted the lid...slowly, as if something alive were inside...carefully, so sudden light and sound wouldn't startle it.

Her husband sat next to her.

Across from him, Meryl touched her wedding band.

Tears filled her eyes...eyes as blue as the Inland Sea on a clear winter day.

Mr. Sato took his prayer beads...moved to the cushion in front of the offerings and knelt...lit the candles and incense...rang the bell twice...put his hands together in front of his face...bowed, got up...patted Ayako's shoulder and left the room.

The front door opened as tears rolled down Meryl's face.

Ayako nodded to Mr. Ono.

He kneeled before the offerings with his prayer beads, lit incense, rang the bell twice. In his heart he welcomed Kouichiro home and asked him to comfort Ayako. And also Meryl.

He then joined Mr. Sato outside.

She's pretty like an apple that way...
—Hachiro Sato and Tadashi Manjome
"The Apple Song"

Children of the Matagi

AT the edge of the rice paddy in front of the Satos' house, irises and cosmos bloomed...purple and pink in the sunshine...the humming of bees in the still air.

Mr. Sato had a cigarette between his lips when Mr. Ono joined him. They were the same height, but the older man was as strong as an ox, his features as sharp as his eyes, and his thick hair was combed back away from his face, setting off his high forehead.

He held out the pack. "Quit years ago." And flicked a tarnished lighter for Mr. Ono. "Bought these when I heard Older Brother was coming home. Most all the boys had liked to smoke."

Mr. Ono took a puff. "I'll smoke this too...for Older Brother."

They headed to the apple orchard. The path taking them was a patchwork of clover.

"My wife thought she would never have anything of his. Yamanokami brought him back to her."

Mr. Ono knew something of Yamanokami. "The mountain goddess?"

"She brings us back home."

"You came back?"

Mr. Sato answered by turning away.

His flag had kept his belly warm in Manchuria, soaked up his sweat in the Philippines. Most families framed their flags and hung them in their homes.

But he had left his in a jungle. And only he knew.

Mr. Ono put his hand on the pocket that held his memo pad and asked himself, What newspaper reporter wouldn't grab this story? Mr. Sato—a Matagi hunter *and* a veteran of the Seventeenth Regiment from Akita.

MR. ONO knew more about the history of the War than most of his generation. Though his father hadn't seen combat—he had worked for the military at a Japanese bank in Indonesia—his father's boyhood friends were veterans. Mr. Ono had asked questions. Their hazy answers whetted his interest. He watched documentaries, read books, visited war museums. He memorized what prefectures the men came from to fill what regiments...all kinds of battles, land and sea...and the names of military leaders—as he would memorize rules of a board game. He studied the atrocities as impartially as any historian...slave labor, forced prostitution, the horrific treatment of POWs and of their own troops, the cannibalism of starving soldiers, the experiments and vivisection on humans. And like a philosopher, he mulled over the utilitarianism of a military that produced and trafficked illegal drugs to finance itself.

The demographics for Akita Prefecture changed in 1942. Most of its men filled the ranks of the Seventeenth Regiment. Boys as young as thirteen volunteered.

They were sent to Manchuria. Then when it looked like the decisive land battle in the Pacific would be fought in the Philippines, they joined the troops at Leyte Bay on the Island of Luzon.

MEN from the forests of Akita in the jungles of the Philippines...the thought made Mr. Ono wonder how any of them came back. Was Mr. Sato going to tell him?

What Matagi skills saved Mr. Sato's life? Did the Matagi hunters form a special sniper unit or assassination squad? Did they teach soldiers survival techniques?

Mr. Ono would write another feature story. And use the information in one of his mystery novels.

Mr. Sato turned back around to Mr. Ono.

"I was sure I was going to die there. The bay as red as red can be."

Mr. Ono adjusted his glasses on his nose.

"On the ship we heard about the boys from Yamagata."

Everyone in the regiment from Yamagata Prefecture had been killed in the Philippines.

"But the battle wasn't in northern Luzon when we docked. People were still going on about their business. Pretty girls danced. Played the piano."

Mr. Ono hadn't thought of girls dancing and playing the piano during the War.

"After a short while, the guerillas were picking us off."

The US military had supplied weapons—bounty paid for each dead Japanese soldier. The guerillas only had to give proof.

Mr. Sato stepped into the shade of an apple tree and patted a mossy branch.

"They could sure climb trees."

Mr. Sato's grandfather had taught him to look up into the trees...but he didn't tell Mr. Ono about that.

HIROSHI SATO'S grandfather had been a Matagi hunter, like all the men in his family from generations ago. Grandfather's old rifles proved it, a better collection than those at museums.

When Hiroshi was five years old, Grandfather told him about Yamanokami, then tied him onto his back and took him into the woods. Hiroshi peeked round Grandfather's whiskers at animal tracks, dens and nests, hiding places between rocks, claw marks on embankments.

In early spring, Grandfather put his hand out toward a wetland, smudged with slushy snow. "See those single white petals sticking up...hooded and pointy at the tip? That's mizubasho. Your grandmother says it looks like a Buddhist image. She's poetic that way. You remember this—bears chomp on it after their long winter snooze. Cleans out the poop and pee they've been keeping inside."

In early autumn, Grandfather turned his head upward to the trees and pointed out what looked like a leafy bird's nest. "That means a bear. It sat up there on that limb, broke off branches full of chestnuts, nibbled them from their spiny burs, then put the branches under its butt. Some kind of cushion!"

The summer Hiroshi was eight, Grandfather asked him if he wanted a dog or cat for a companion.

But Hiroshi reasoned a cow would walk by his side, not prance ahead or chase field mice.

Grandfather gave him one.

Hiroshi named her Bego, the local word for "cow." He fed Bego some watermelon rinds. She crunched into one—water sprayed, landing on Hiroshi's face and arms, like mist from a waterfall.

"Chowing down on the tastiest treat in the whole wide world!"

Bego's big eyes shined even brighter than usual.

A week later, Grandfather made up his mind...Hiroshi was ready for his first kill.

At the edge of a field, Grandfather flung a ring-shaped warada, made of straw. It whipped through the air, sounding like the wind against the feathers of an eagle in a dive for a kill. Hiroshi's eyes flashed. A rabbit raced to its hole. They were right behind. Grandfather got on his knees and pulled the rabbit out, hind legs kicking; then one weak cry and it went limp with fear. Grandfather supported its body on his bended knee, its head facing down.

Hiroshi had thought he was up to the task.

"Be fast about it. Don't want the little fellow scared any longer than it has to be."

Hiroshi's hand reached for the rabbit's back, warm and soft.

Grandfather's look was firm...*For any longer than it has to be.*

Afterward Hiroshi went home to Bego, but something had changed. And he couldn't put into words what that something was.

A few years later, Hiroshi spent weeks at a time in the woods with the other hunters. He got used to the sounds of wildlife and the rush of wind and water, the heavy thumps of melting snow hitting the ground...the sudden stillness. He learned what plants and mushrooms he could eat, where to find springs, how to track. And when they hunted bears, he knew which hunters made up the line to maneuver the bear into a clearing on a mountainside...who was on a ridge calling out their positions and what they should do...who shot. He learned how to rouse a bear from its den, how to tie up the carcass and drag it over the snow back to the village. He could spend all day in the wilderness with a few roasted beans in his pocket, which he'd gotten during a winter festival at a shrine.

Hiroshi Sato had more skill to help keep him alive in a jungle than the rest of his regiment had.

"Climb trees?"

"The guerillas. Snipers."

Before Mr. Ono asked how many there had been, Mr. Sato started.

"Don't blame the Filipinos for hating us. We had to fend for ourselves. Most of us took their food."

The army hadn't fed its troops.

Mr. Sato and a couple of buddies hunted, trapped, and fished.

"First time I ever ate lizard."

He put up his hands to show Mr. Ono how large it had been.

"The village men had gone off to fight. Only old folks and mothers and children were there."

His fingers pressed against his lips during a thoughtful drag on his cigarette.

"There was a river not too far from a village. Children would try to catch something for supper. We showed them how to make traps, where to set them. Good boys and girls. Laughed a lot when we juggled mangoes. Carried the younger ones on our backs and bounced them up and down like we were horses. They liked that, especially the youngest."

Mr. Sato took out his handkerchief and wiped his forehead.

"Didn't stay that way for long."

He unbuttoned his shirt collar.

"We were out...stumbled upon one of our men. Been caught in someone's crosshairs. Afterward the shooter must've come down from his perch...one of the soldier's hands was cut off and gone. We hid his body the best we could. The next day, another...his entrails cut out. It was going to turn ugly once our commanding officers found out what the guerrillas were doing. They would do something worse."

Mr. Sato took out his wallet and opened it. He handed Mr. Ono an old picture of a little girl of about four with large, shiny eyes, wisps of bangs blowing in a breeze, a flowery dress too big for her. "Looks like a little Filipina girl, doesn't she?"

"She's pretty."

"She's my daughter. But in that picture—only that picture—she's the spitting image of a little girl I knew during the War. Wondrous, isn't it?"

Then Mr. Sato told Mr. Ono about that little girl.

THE COMMANDING officers ordered the soldiers to slaughter villagers.

"Do it quick so they don't panic."

Hiroshi and his buddies lagged behind as the troops moved toward the first village. They fell back, took a path to the river, and found the children there. His buddies led them away, their only chance to escape.

He stayed with the smallest child, the one he often carried on his back. He was *her* horse. She wouldn't live long in the jungle, but he couldn't leave her. No telling what they would do to her. He pulled out his knife, knelt down, and believed she wasn't going to feel anything.

His hand on the nape of her neck...her soft hair...how warm she was. She looked at him with eyes as round and shiny as Bego's, his childhood companion.

He understood what he had to do.

No bayonet was going to tear through her...no bullets rip her body in half.

No knife!

He sheathed his, threw off his rucksack, pulled his flag from his waist. Moved like a madman.

He camouflaged his flag with mud...Folded it, scooped her up into it, tied her onto his back.

The child was going to cry or laugh and give away their position—he ran in the opposite direction of his buddies and the other children.

He could never go back. He was never going to get back home.

And what did that matter? If he killed her or left her there, how could he ever go home? How would he love his own children when they came into this world? He hadn't given his life to the Emperor to kill children. Other men had.

But he hadn't.

He would kill anyone who tried to hurt her.

There was no goddess in that jungle. There was nothing.

Only a matter of time and the jungle would take them. Until then, he was with her.

The little girl kept her head against his neck and held on tight. Her horse had never run so fast.

From some distance behind them came the rat-tat-tat of machine guns.

MR. ONO'S mouth had gone dry, his palms damp. He was a fool to think he could listen to what Mr. Sato had to say about the War...a little girl tied snug to a young soldier...to Mr. Sato.

Mr. Sato bent down, pressed his cigarette into some pebbles. Mr. Ono did the same.

"Strange to think of it now. Can you imagine a group of soldiers killing children? Children out here playing under these apple trees. They come marching and without a thought, kill the boys and girls. You are one of those soldiers. No one can imagine it. But I was there in that place. A hell of naked devils."

"Naked devils?" Mr. Ono had never heard the expression.

"Nothing to hide, nothing to fear. No pride, no shame, nothing to keep them as they are...devils. Even a devil has schemes. Even a devil wants to be more than what it is. But not a naked devil. A naked devil knows no bounds. There is nothing it won't do. There's nothing that will stop it."

Mr. Ono wished Mrs. Sato would call them in.

"At night, you could see bullets being fired. Like a river...of red-hot bullets. If they hadn't been deadly, I would've thought they were pretty."

Mr. Sato moistened his bottom lip.

"Drank from a small pool. 'Bout near killed me. Not like the forest springs I grew up with. Nothing tastes better...like it was from a fountain in heaven. But on that island, even the water was rotten. The day I left home, Grandfather gave me some dried gallbladder, thin as a few sheets of paper, from a bear. It stopped the runs. Hid it"—he smiled boyishly—"in the folds of my underwear."

Mr. Ono had heard stories from his father's friends. They had been able to keep only seals that were engraved with their family names—and their flags. Soldiers with photos of loved ones in war movies were romanticized fiction. The military had taken away everything.

"Fifteen months in an American POW camp. Good rations. We came back by way of the Inland Sea." Mr. Sato nodded toward his house. "Blue like her eyes. Docked in Hiroshima. Changed trains in your town."

Perhaps he wouldn't talk about the little girl anymore.

"Music was playing for us on the loud speakers. Real friendly of Osaka. Thought no one wanted us home. We hadn't won the War...hadn't died trying. Lots of us stood frozen on that platform, listening. I had stepped onto the train heading out when a couple of women put a small package into my hand and bowed. 'You've finished your work. Welcome home.' I stood with my mouth open wide, a certified country bumpkin, dumbfounded. Manjuu treats! Filled with azuki. I'd never tasted anything as good and sweet. Cried like a baby. I knew then everything would be all right for me. Those Osaka women were sure nice. Might've been your relatives."

"That would be something, wouldn't it?"

Mr. Sato turned away for a few long moments. Then he started.

"I was moving fast. Happy with my little bundle on my back. I didn't stop and look up into the trees...didn't stop to listen. The child patted my neck. Fun being up so high. Boys and girls like being up off the ground." He reached into the leaves and cupped his hand around a small, green apple.

"Her fist was about this size. Thought we'd be together a little longer. She tugged my ear...squealed...Someone in the trees heard. I lost my balance. And in that split second, her head was where mine should've been." He had wrapped her in his flag, laid her in the hollow of a tree, and prayed for her eternal peace after slitting the sniper's throat.

Mr. Sato looked at the picture again.

"Yamanokami brought her to me...The only way she could come back to me. Wondrous, don't you think?"

Mr. Ono murmured as quietly as the hum of the bees near the flowers.

"She saved your life."

Mr. Sato put his wallet back in his pocket.

"She let me—"

His sharp eyes met Mr. Ono's.

"Love my children."

Okinawa Song

MERYL wiped her eyes and looked up. Ayako was there.

Ayako opened the flag—one fold then another—stunned at how quickly she recognized the writing.

She let out a gasp and cried with the excitement of a child...the longing of a sister...the anguish of a woman.

Older Brother is home!

Her tears fell onto his flag. She kept unfolding. Larger and larger it became—would it cover the room?

She tried to stand but strength had drained from her.

Meryl was at her side.

Ayako leaned against her and tried to read what was on the flag. But she saw only the bloodstains. She didn't have his bones. She had his blood.

They held hands in front of the offerings, the flag on their laps, prayed and lit more incense. The fragrance calmed their spirits.

Ayako lifted her hand toward the offerings.

"Older Brother likes"—she picked up a cherry—"sa-ku-ra-m-bo." To the lilies she said, "Yu-ri." And then she touched the bunch of bananas. "Ba-na-na."

Meryl asked how to say banana in Japanese.

"Ba-na-na."

"A banana is a banana?...is a banana!"

Ayako squeezed Meryl's hand.

How Older Brother would laugh if he were alive.

They hung his flag on the rack in the alcove.

Meryl hugged Ayako and Ayako held Meryl's arms.

Then Ayako got her cassette player.

And in her hand was a note she had written. She pointed to each word and spoke slowly.

"*Favorite song. Okinawa song. Same as Older Brother's voice. Imagine sing for me. In song...someday we meet. In that place...are many, many flowers.*"

Tears were on Meryl's eyelashes. The voice on the tape. Same as Older Brother's.

Ayako took Meryl's hand. "I give you cassette. You have Older Brother's song. I have Older Brother's flag."

Notes plucked from the Okinawan jamisen filled the room and a voice that was also...

Meryl caught her breath.

Like Peter's.

Returns

Wet Feathers

THE PROFESSOR woke to the sound of pawing on the side of his mattress, let Freckles out into the early morning of his backyard, kept the patio door ajar, then went back to bed.

He was sure he was going to fall asleep again the instant his head hit the pillow. Instead his mind filled with Meryl.

Greg peered down the bed. His toes were sticking out from under the sheet as usual—but something stirred, pleasantly surprising him.

How long had it been since that happened?

A week ago—after he had first met Meryl.

He reached, imagined her in his arms, and his brow gleamed...as he picked up steam...for the I-think-I-can...when a character in his real-life story stole the climax.

Freckles jumped up on the bed, tail wagging, eyes laughing, floppy mouth shut, a wet feather sticking out of it.

"If you weren't a dog, I'd be a suspicious shade of red right now."

He pointed to the feather.

"Didn't get enough to eat last night?"

He put on his bathrobe and Freckles followed him outside.

Greg couldn't tell if she had swallowed the bird or not. She sat on the grass, lifted her paw. He stooped down and took it.

"Are you asking for congratulations on your hunting skills? More impressive than a tomcat's?"

Freckles pulled her paw out of his hand, placed her chin onto it...about to give him the prize!

Greg was ready for the worst—a half-mauled bird, warm guts, and a whiff of wet feathers.

Freckles opened her mouth and into his hand delivered a slobbery sparrow, flecks of uncertainty darted in its eyes. It ruffled its wet feathers...spread one wing, then the other. Freckles nudged it and off it flew.

Her soft mouth had been bred to retrieve fowl shot from the sky. Had evolution played tricks with her genes?

Greg hugged Freckles.

Catch and release. Something romantically philosophical was hidden in that idea...though the sparrow probably would've enjoyed the yard more without the front row seat to a set of doggy teeth.

The phone rang—Greg's first call from Meryl.

On his brow was a line of excitement, tempered with relief. He knew he was fooling himself about getting a phone call from her but wondered anyway. Would there be a few soft notes of I miss you in her voice?

She asked how he and Freckles were, told him that the flag had been returned, and said she had a favor to ask.

"I hope you don't mind."

Greg gently pulled at fluffs of feathery fur on Freckles' head.

"I'll do anything I can."

Starlight and dewdrops are waiting for thee.
—Stephen C. Foster
"Beautiful Dreamer Serenade"

A Rice Dumpling

THE DAY before Meryl's flight home, Jo and Fiona went with her to Nara Park again...to feed the deer. Afterward they stopped at a cafe and sat in a booth with seats made from tatami mats. Jo ordered each of them a bowl of green-tea ice cream topped with sweet azuki beans, whipped cream, and chewy mochi dumplings the size of large marbles.

Meryl wished a restaurant served desserts like that in Arizona.

"I suppose"—Fiona mashed her azuki beans—"you want the entire state of Arizona to become like Japan."

"Sure. The robatayaki, the hot springs, and the rice fields. Arizona should import them all."

"Hot springs and rice fields? Akita must have left quite an impression."

"At a lookout point there were so many mountains." Meryl told them about her husband. "I don't know how to explain it. But Peter was there. And in my mind I saw him riding his horse. Children were with him. Laughing and riding...on colts! They weren't in Vietnam."

She talked about the fireflies and the Satos, their apple orchard at the edge of a cedar forest, and about how she had lit incense for Mrs. Sato's brother.

"Mrs. Sato and I listened to a Japanese song, and she gave me the cassette tape. I wish I understood it. The singer's voice sounds like Peter's. It's...I suddenly knew...I know

Peter is with those children and...every living thing that his bombs...

"Mrs. Sato's brother is with them too. And my mother. I know I'll still cry for Peter, for those he...I'll still think about him, what his life would've been, how old he would've been on his birthday. I'm sorry I didn't stop him from going to war, from doing what he did. But for the first time, I believe Peter is where he should be, where he has to be. The only place he can be...where everyone will be." She thought of the flower field in Akita and what Mrs. Sato said about the song's lyrics. "Peter is with flowers, so many flowers. It doesn't make any sense, does it?"

"No, it doesn't." Fiona licked a dollop of whipped cream from her spoon. "But the everyday now barely makes sense. Nothing about the afterlife...if there even *is* an afterlife...can possibly make sense. It's the final frontier of unsolved mysteries. Our Creator is the worst storyteller. I hate it when a story doesn't have an ending. You waste time wondering what will happen next."

Jo asked Meryl to tell them more about Akita.

"The Satos live in a place called Ani. There's so much green there. Everything sparkles. I want to go back with my dog Freckles and live in that green for a summer, see the leaves change color in the fall, try to capture that on canvas. I think I'll ask the Professor to join us."

"The Professor?"—not quite in unison.

"Well, you see, there's a hunting culture—called Matagi. Scholars in Japan haven't studied it so I'm sure no one back home has. Byron's professor will be the first!"

"You mean the professor who explained the flag to you?" Fiona asked.

"Yes. He's taking care of Freckles."

Another Fiona question.

"A little over a week."

"I should say that's been a short time to know someone. You asked him to take care of your dog?"

"He said he would. And he took me to a travel agency. It was his idea to book the hotel near the language school."

"And what else"—Fiona counted three mochi dumplings in her dessert—"has the Professor done for you?"

Meryl told them he drove her to the airport and he was going to pick her up when she got back.

"What do you know about him?" Jo asked.

"Get to the point." A sticky, squidgy dumpling filled the pocket between Fiona's cheek and teeth. "Is he single, a great conversationalist, as swarthy as a pirate?"

Jo cooed, "A good kisser?"

"Yes to the first three. I don't know about the kissing. Probably never will. I shook hands with him. Twice."

Fiona pressed her lips together to keep the dumpling from becoming airborne. She swallowed, then bellowed, "Gaawd!" Every head in the cafe turned, but she didn't lower her voice.

"How did it feel?"

"What?"

"The handshake!" Jo cried.

"It was nice. Oh! He helped me when I was dizzy...put his arm around me."

Helped her! Fiona could see this was going nowhere fast. Meryl was as oblivious as a flea enjoying a bite on a dog.

That's it!

"What did he say about your dog?" Fiona was positive that even Meryl knew if a man loves a woman, he makes her dog a saint.

"He said she's a pretty baby and has manners. I imagine he praises every dog he meets."

"What did he say about your son?" Jo asked.

"Who cares about that?" Fiona sniffed.

"He said something about Byron being like a chivalrous knight and having immense kindness."

Fiona was about to quip, What do professors know?, but then...Bloody hell! Jo has hit the nail on the head. Men in love with women say the most absurd drivel about their dogs as well as their children!

But Meryl said, "He probably says things like that to all his students' parents."

Neither of the girls could wait any longer for Meryl to come to the obvious conclusion. They blurted out, "He's fallen in love with you!"

"He's a gentleman, that's all."

"You've probably already fallen in love with him, and you're too daft to know it."

"I do think of him, Fiona. That doesn't mean I'm in love, does it?"

"Do you remember Mr. Mazouzi? The French teacher from Algiers."

Meryl nodded and hoped she wasn't blushing.

"After your Mazouzi Dream—"

Jo kicked Fiona's shin.

"Ouch! She must have had the dream too. You said everyone does. Meryl, who did you think of after your dream?"

"Does everyone have...the Mazouzi Dream?"

"Yes. He's some kind of fertility god incarnate, but never mind. After the dream, who did you think of?"

"I'm not sure. But I remember seeing the Professor's face in my mind before I took a nap on a drive in Akita."

"He must be the one! What's his name?"

"Greg Gieschen."

Jo told her to hug him tight at the airport.

Meryl wasn't sure she could do that.

Fiona said, "You don't want to wake up one day in a cold sweat and realize that you hadn't seen the truth and the love right in front of you...that you were such a ninny...do you?

"Meryl"—Fiona was positive—"Greg is the answer to your Mazouzi Dream."

But Meryl steered the conversation in another direction.

"Mr. Ono is nice."

"Oh NO!" Fiona whined. "Changing topics to Mr. Ono?"

"Fiona, he's a safe driver and has wonderful friends and knows a lot." Meryl wondered if Fiona would listen. "He said your name more than once. I think he has fallen in love with you."

"Please, stop. Everyone says that." Fiona's emerald eyes dimmed to the color of her creamy green-tea dessert.

"Mr. Ono has a schoolboy crush. Has had it from the moment he set his woefully, retro-bespectacled eyes on me. Only an infatuation."

Meryl detected something in Fiona's voice that sounded like a clue.

Silvery spoons chimed in their empty dessert bowls. Jo paid the bill, then they headed to the train station.

Back in Namba near Midosuji, the boulevard lined with gingko trees buzzing with cicadas, they went to a clothes shop for sumo wrestlers and tall men.

Meryl wanted a cotton yukata for the Professor's thank-you present. She followed Fiona; Jo a few steps behind.

In Meryl's hotel room Jo handed Meryl a shopping bag.

"A souvenir from me and Fiona."

"It's not like," Fiona added, "one of Ms. Kawanishi's kimonos, but it will have to do."

Meryl blinked several times and pinched the tip of her nose. The good-bye to them was coming tomorrow. She opened the bag and pulled out a yukata. "Like the Professor's!" The floodgates burst.

"In case"—Fiona handed her some tissues—"you two become roommates in Akita. No squabbling over who wears the yukata."

MERYL spent that evening with the teachers at the robatayaki. And on the back street Elliot called the scenic route, she turned her head sideways searching for the cross-dressing prostitute in high heels, but she didn't see him under the neon signs.

She took pictures and couldn't wait to show them to the Professor—of the jolly Master and his sister, the mummified blowfish, the teachers drinking the elixir H_2Sho. One was of Elliot's sayonara under the red paper lanterns.

Then in Meryl's hotel room, the talk turned briefly to Byron's mystery woman and the endless number of Japanese lessons Meryl would languish through.

"At least a hundred," Fiona said, "to tell your daughter-in-law in her native tongue, 'Here's *my* potato salad.' "

Jo wrapped her arms around Meryl. "Byron's favorite!"

Darryl massaged their backs and rubbed their feet—even Fiona's—and had first dibs on sleeping next to Meryl.

When he was sure everyone had fallen asleep, he leaned over her—careful not to let his hair tumble onto her face. He wished she would fall in love again...simply because for Darryl, falling in love had always been great fun.

The H₂Sho clouding his mind led him to one idea that might work—be Meryl's Prince Charming. The evil spell that had kept her from falling in love would disappear with his kiss. At the moment his lips left hers, he was sure it had worked. But to be on the safe side, Meryl's prince kissed her again and once more, then fell asleep to the sound of her gentle breathing.

The next morning while Meryl took a shower, Darryl, Jo, and Fiona each called the school with excuses not to work that day.

Fiona sobbed like an Oscar-winning actress.

"My mother is dreadfully ill. I may have to fly back home."

Fiona didn't think it was much of a sin to say someone who was in heaven was dreadfully ill. Didn't thousands, if not tens of thousands of people around the world make up the same kind of excuse every day?

The secretary told her not to worry about work. "I'll cancel your lessons for next week."

The sobs stopped.

"Don't do that. I'm praying for my mother. God will answer my prayers." She faked a sniffle and fibbed again. "He always does."

The secretary agreed.

Then a few hours later, the door opened at Kanku International Airport and there was Mr. Ono waiting for them.

Middle Names

"A MYSTERY for your flight?" Fiona asked Meryl at the airport bookstore.

"No, I'm too excited. Too much to think about."

"Here." In Fiona's hand was the 100-yen Hello Kitty eye mask she had bought the day Meryl arrived. "Don't want you missing your beauty sleep."

They sat down next to Mr. Ono, Jo, and Darryl near the security checkpoint entrance.

Mr. Ono spotted Meryl's passport. He had never seen one from America.

She opened it and gave it to him.

"Why do you have three names?"

"Lots of people do. Jeanne is my middle name."

"MJQ," Jo said. "Modern Jazz Quartet. My favorite jazz."

Meryl winked at Jo. Hadn't Greg said the same?

Jo told Mr. Ono that her first name was really Geradine. Her middle name was Jo.

Darryl's was James.

Fiona stared at her watch. "I suppose you'll be wanting to know what my middle name is, won't you, Mr. Ono?" The minutes leading to their good-byes were filling with more emotion than she had imagined. "It's a simple name. Ann. My mum always called me Annie."

"Ani?" Mr. Ono said.

Next came silence, the kind that falls on a place when it's time to say good-bye.

They were in need of a joke, and so Meryl told them a favorite of Byron's...when he was eight.

"What's smaller than a teeny-weeny ant?"

"You've got to be kidding." Jo had heard it before.

"A teeny"—Meryl's voice jumped to the high pitch expected of those with antennae sticking out from their heads—"ant weenie."

Darryl put his hand on Mr. Ono's shoulder.

"Doesn't apply to me, my man."

The group stood up, and Meryl shocked the lonely feelings out of them with kisses on their lips and bear hugs.

Meryl waved good-bye through the windows separating the passengers from those staying behind. The four bowed deeply, as synchronized as department store employees welcoming shoppers at the start of the day. Their last glimpse of Meryl, on the down escalator to immigration, was her waving hand.

She settled into her seat on the plane and thought of how she had gotten there in the first place. Her cousin had sent the flag with a feeling that Meryl would fall in love—

Meryl brushed away a tear and put on her eye mask.

Well, she did.

Believe Anything

FRECKLES looked out the windshield, intent as an illusionist...Her gaze seemed to control the distance between Greg's car and the one ahead. Sunlight reflected off the hood. The late afternoon temperature hovered around 108 degrees. Greg had brought along a thermos and Freckles' water dish; after they picked up Meryl, they weren't going directly home.

"We've remembered everything, right Freckles?"—the favor Meryl had asked.

He parked near the terminal, kept the motor running, the air conditioner on, and crossed his fingers hoping a security guard wouldn't walk the short distance in the heat only to tell him that he was in a no-parking zone.

"Gate to baggage claim, five minutes. Maybe twenty if your mommy is the last off the plane."

He imagined Meryl in shorts bending over her suitcase and the glances her way...if only he could've seen her in the subway passages of Osaka, her blond hair sailing over the wave of jet-black heads. What an image! And what was the look on her face when she ate Japanese food? Did her eyes open wide at raw fish on a bed of daikon sliced so thin it looked like pieces of transparent string? Did she see women in kimonos? Did she have a chance to wrap a yukata around her body, the body he wanted to wrap his arms around?

He gently pulled Freckles' floppy ear.

"Your mommy will be here any minute."

Had she thought about him much? He hadn't been able to keep his mind focused on anything but her.

But Meryl had taken the flag to the soldier's family...had lit incense for him. And she had talked about her husband during their phone conversation. Was she still waiting for *him*?

Greg knew what it was like to believe with one's entire being...believe something impossible would happen.

The morning he woke and found that his wife had passed away in her sleep, he sent their children to school and told them their mother was getting up late. He sat by Janice...put his hand on hers. Wasn't she warmer than when he first touched her? He studied her face and swore her eyes moved under her lids...Was she dreaming? But Janice was dead. The bed was stained and it smelled. No, it reeked with a stench of something he didn't know. She was dead. Boyhood Bible stories came rushing back to him; Sunday school lessons flooded his heart. He hadn't believed in an afterlife or in God since he was a child, hadn't needed a moment of faith. But as he sat, clutching the bedcover near her face, he waited for her to rise from the dead. If Christ could do it, then by God, Janice could. She was going to beat death.

But he had been wrong.

And Meryl was wrong. Her husband wasn't coming back. If she had any love to give—

But was it even possible to win her love?

Greg's rival—the memory of her husband. Surely he was idealized in Meryl's mind...still as young as he had been when he'd kissed her and told her he'd be back before she knew it. Why shouldn't Meryl keep her heart locked? Greg had. The memory of his wife had kept him home.

What had changed?

Had he stopped loving his wife?

No.

Janice had loved him so naturally, so easily. He hadn't thought any more of her love than he had thought of the air he breathed. How had he lived without her?

Why had he fallen in love with Meryl? It was as natural as taking his next step.

He knew he could love her from a distance.

But he wanted more.

Wasn't Janice nodding her approval, giving him courage to act? If only Meryl's husband would do the same for her.

Freckles put her paw on his leg.

Greg asked himself if his brain had turned to putty from the glare of the sun.

"Love makes us believe anything, now doesn't it, good girl?"

She licked his arm as she would a wound.

"Miracle worker."

The history of humans and canines...how many souls comforted by these sweet beings? What outrageous fortunes conquered?

Greg turned his head toward the terminal.

"Stay here. I'm going to get Mommy."

A handshake for Greg. Kisses and hugs for Freckles. Bags in the trunk.

Then the three were on their way to the cemetery where Meryl's husband was buried.

"Flowers for Your Heart"
—Kina Shokichi

The River Flows

THE ONLY TREES at the cemetery were spiny-branched palo verde. Their tiny leaves had fallen months earlier. No shrubbery. No flowers. No lawn. The ground was as lifeless as those who had been laid under it.

Engraved steel plates, the size of a sheet of typing paper, spread over the land in rows like stepping stones. At first glance, overwhelming in number.

Rules had to be followed at that cemetery, for the sake of dignity. Nothing to distinguish one grave from another. Death was the great equalizer, and the cemetery where Meryl's husband was buried equalized the plots.

A reception area—two thick walls and a roof, a primitive shelter from the sun—vaguely looked like an incomplete, miniature Stonehenge. A map of the plots was there. But Byron had taught Freckles the way to Peter's grave. He had gone to the cemetery a few times every year, and Meryl's father still took Freckles whenever he went.

Freckles pranced ahead, then stopped.

Meryl saw her mother's name and at first, didn't know what it meant. Slowly realized. Yes, her mother was there too.

Meryl had thought it would be unbearable seeing her mother's grave...had imagined she would seep into the ground along with her tears.

Now, with Greg by her side...no, it was still unbearable. Her mother gone. Peter gone. But instead of falling to her knees and sobbing, she touched Greg's arm and talked to her mother as Mrs. Sato had talked to her brother when Meryl and Mr. Ono returned his flag.

She introduced Professor Greg Gieschen and told her mother she had just gotten back from Japan.

"Freckles is taking us to Peter."

Near Peter's grave, Greg set down an umbrella and two canvas bags. He took out a mat for Freckles and from the thermos, poured water into her dish.

"Thank you, Dr. Gieschen."

Meryl squatted down. Greg passed her the thermos and a small towel, and she began wiping her husband's marker.

The water pooled in the lettering.

Greg put a box of candles, a lighter, a small cup, and a garden trowel near her.

Under the shade of his umbrella, Meryl scratched out three small holes in the earth.

Could she remember what Mrs. Sato had done for her brother?

Meryl stood two candles in the holes, propped them up with small stones, and from her bag, took out incense sticks, propped them up between the candles, and lit them all.

Next, she poured water in the small cup and put it near her husband's name. She brought her hands together and closed her eyes.

But she didn't pray to God. She didn't ask for Peter's forgiveness because she hadn't kept him from going to war...didn't tell Peter that she forgave him for leaving her...for dropping bombs.

From the bottom of her heart, she thanked him for bringing her home.

She did what she had come to do...clean his grave marker, offer candles and incense, give him water. She wanted to believe she was too late...that he didn't need the water to quench his thirst, the fragrance of incense to lead him, the candles to light his way to paradise.

He was already there.

She opened her eyes to daisies, as beautiful as the ones Peter had sent on their wedding day. His note—*For your hair when you walk down the aisle.*

She blinked again and again. Were they really there?

"I didn't know what kind to get," Greg said. "These seemed to say, Take us!"

Meryl caught her breath. "Did the flowers talk to you?"

At the language school, hadn't darling Darryl told her that ikebana flowers talked to him? It was the evening Mr. Ono called...and she had met the man from Algiers, the one Fiona said was a fertility god—Mr. Mazouzi!

What images were conquering her mind? She was at her husband's grave...with another man...remembering other men! Was Peter playing a joke on her? Did he ask those daisies to catch Greg's attention? Could Peter see them? Was he pleasantly smirking because she was hot, sweaty, feeling somewhat uncomfortably confused and happy at the same time? She had dreamed of Mr. Mazouzi, slept in a futon next to Mr. Ono's, shared a bed with Darryl—kissed all three—and now, with Greg!

In his hands was his old cassette player.

Meryl fumbled with the tape that Mrs. Sato had given her. She wanted Peter to hear the song.

Or did she want Greg to?

She handed him the tape.

Notes soared into the desert sky, notes plucked from a stringed instrument.

Greg recognized the Okinawan jamisen.

Okinawa. His mind took him to its wartime past. How many soldiers had lost their lives on its beaches, in its jungles and fields of sugarcane? How many families massacred? The Japanese Imperial Army had forced the Okinawan boys and old men to the front lines, its sandbags, its barricade against the US troops. This Okinawan voice was one to be reckoned with...powerful, undefeated, and filled with love, peace, understanding, and hope. Had one of those boys survived the War, composed this song, and recorded it?

"Would you translate?" Meryl asked. "His voice sounds like Peter's, like he's singing to me."

Greg tried to keep his own voice from cracking. He felt as if he had been decked in the first minute of a prizefight. How could he win Meryl's love from a voice like that?

"The song tells of a distant river...of everyone traveling that river someday. Flowers bloom at the place they're going. So cry. So laugh."

Greg paused.

What was he doing?

The song may end by glorifying the fidelity of spirits in love and their blasted, blissful, eternal reunion! Meryl would never think of loving him if the voice of her husband said that.

He knew it was shameful, but he made up lyrics, which would work on her subconscious.

"Love the one you're with."

He cleared his throat. "English translations often sound trite." And wiped the sweat from his brow. "I'm not good when it comes to lyrics."

Meryl told him it was the most beautiful song she had ever heard.

"Flowers at the end of the river...Peter would like that."

She picked up one of the daisies. Peter had been in that flower shop and had whispered to the daisies and asked them to talk to Greg. Peter had sent her flowers.

And Greg had brought Peter's love to her. Yet...

Then Freckles licked Meryl's face. Greg stroked Freckles' back and said, "She's fond of the idea too."

He motioned to one of the canvas bags. "There are still more daisies. If you like, shall we give them to your mother?"

Meryl also lit candles and incense.

How her mother would have loved the scent of sandalwood.

"You'd Be So Nice to Come Home To"
—Cole Porter

Three Lifetimes

FRECKLES ran into the house first.

Greg took Meryl's hand in front of the romantic painting of Venice.

"Welcome home."

No one had ever said that to her in the house where she and Peter had planned to watch their family grow and grow up. Meryl had always been the one waiting.

Greg brought her hand up to his heart.

Meryl hadn't expected that either. What was next? Was it possible...Were Jo and Fiona right? Greg had helped make travel arrangements, driven her to and from the airport, spoken fondly of Byron, and taken care of Freckles because he had...fallen in love with her? Was he going to kiss her hand like a chivalrous knight?

But Greg didn't kiss Meryl's hand. Or even shake it. He brought it down and let go.

Or...was she right? Was he like this to everyone?

Greg's words came back to her from the first day they had met—see the beauty right in front of you.

Meryl felt like hollering, I see it!

His eyes—even dreamier than Darryl's. His hair—salt and pepper sensational. And his nose—like Mr. Mazouzi's!

What should she do?

The only thing that came to mind was eating green-tea ice cream with Jo and Fiona! Why? What had they talked about? Yes! Waking up from a dream...being able to see the truth.

But could *she* see the truth? Had her past tied a thick mask over her eyes, over her heart? Had false hope for her future kept it pulled tight? Was she unable to love?

She was no longer starry-eyed in love with a man who she had believed held her every wish, no longer a frantic mother striving to please the memory of her husband, no longer a daughter helplessly watching her mother's life slip away, wishing for a different future, regretting the past.

That moment, she was her own self—someone who wanted to know a lot more about a man she didn't know so much about. He hadn't gone to war. He wanted the best for her and had asked her to paint a picture for him and didn't mind that it was going to take her years to do. He liked her cooking. He went with her to her husband's grave, brought daisies. He loved her dog.

She didn't want Greg to go home.

But what if Jo and Fiona were wrong? He hadn't fallen in love with her.

What does a modern woman do at a time like this?

On cue Fiona's voice boomed in Meryl's mind.

"Blimey! Who cares if you're bloody right or wrong! Kiss him! Kiss him as if you've been in love with him for your past three bloomin' lifetimes! KISS HIM!"

Meryl held her breath. No, impossible.

Fiona's voice lowered. "It's not as if—"

If what?

"Does it matter?"

At the instant Meryl answered in her mind, she found that she didn't have to make a move.

To Meryl, his kiss felt as if he had been in love with her for his past three lifetimes and as if she was only...herself.

Finale

Kimono Time and Ms. Kawanishi

ABOUT A MONTH after Fiona said good-bye to Meryl and around the time Byron introduced his mystery woman to the teachers, Fiona got a call from London. Her father's health was failing.
    Sayonara, Osaka Camelot.
    She signed her resignation form, asked for lessons with Ms. Kawanishi and Mr. Baba—students Meryl had met—and told the secretaries not to tell any of the students that she was leaving.
    "They're so nice. Don't want them bothering with good-bye presents and sayonara parties."
    The secretaries did as they pleased.
    Ms. Kawanishi was sad at the news but had always thought that Fiona was destined for the London theater. She knew what kind of woman captivates an audience. In her youth, she had dreamed of a life playing the shamisen...after the War, had performed traditional Japanese dance.
    She easily decided on a good-bye present for Fiona, one of her kimonos—one she had never worn, but was saving for the right occasion. Her late husband had chosen it for her.
    Ms. Kawanishi had seen actresses in several Hollywood movies wear kimonos as dressing gowns and was sure Fiona would do the same someday—backstage, before a performance at a London theater.
    She took the kimono, which was kept in a paper cover, from the top tray of her kimono closet and tied a wrapping

cloth of textured silk around it, one dyed with a scene of the coming season. It reminded her of Fiona...golden luminous...shimmering like plume grass in the low autumn sunlight.

On the knot of the wrapping cloth, Ms. Kawanishi tied a piece of red cord, 'akaiito'; and in her English diary, she wrote its meaning.

The secretaries at the language school told her that her classroom, the one with the view, wasn't being used—she could wait there. Fiona was going to be her teacher that evening.

Ms. Kawanishi opened her English diary. But her mind soon wandered.

Would Fiona like the kimono?

Yes, Ms. Kawanishi thought so.

But Fiona would never cherish it as much as the women of her generation cherished their kimonos. They grew up in the days before the War when their mothers had said, "First your life, then your kimonos."

But times had changed. Ms. Kawanishi wore a kimono to only ikebana exhibitions or the Kabuki Theater.

Even Japanese women Fiona's age didn't feel the same about kimonos as she did or as her mother had. Her own daughters didn't. Kimonos were a "bother," "complicated to wear," and "too much to remember" with "too many parts."

What did modern women think was the most important thing they owned, next to their own lives? European fashion? Gucci, Dior, Givenchy, Chanel, Hermes? Her daughters casually volleyed designer names as if they were gossiping about cousins at a family gathering.

But for Ms. Fusako Kawanishi everything dulled compared to kimonos.

During her childhood, women had dressed in kimonos even when they went shopping. In those days, women's conversations often started with the topic of kimonos. She first noticed this on a mild autumn day...at a department store.

Fusako Morikawa didn't say a word as she held her mother's finger.

Osaka Men

"MRS. MORIKAWA! That *is* you!" Mrs. Toudou said—in a dark purple kimono.

She was one of the Morikawas' neighbors.

"You always look lovely." She patted Fusako's head. "Hello, little doll. Cozy and fluffy."

A shawl of white ostrich feathers was around Fusako's neck.

"Aren't you the happiest little girl, Ito-chan?"

Mrs. Toudou was from Semba, a district where refined families lived. The eldest daughters in Semba weren't called Ojoo-san—Missy—as they were throughout the country, but Ito-san or when the girls were small, Ito-chan. The kanji character for "ito," Fusako's mother had told her, means "string" or "thread."

"Ito-chan, show me your delightful kimono."

Wavy, pink and white camellias rippled in a field of mandarin orange as Fusako stuck her arms out to her sides and twirled around.

Mrs. Toudou oohed and aahed, patted Fusako's head again, and then...

"Mrs. Morikawa, is your kimono a tsumugi weave from Tooka City?"

Fusako's mother nodded yes.

"I knew it! Nothing fancy...thin stripes woven into the cloth. Rustic chic."

"My mother bought a bolt of it for when I got married—a reminder of the homespun kimonos women wear in our village."

"Once in a blue moon, kimono shops have it. Girls aren't weaving like their grandmothers used to. My brother went to Tooka City. Said the snow piles up to three meters high. What do women do in all that snow if they don't weave? I asked him to bring me back a bolt. And do you know what I got, Ito-chan?"

Fusako turned her head from side to side.

"Only talk of soba! He rambled on forever...Tooka City's full-flavored noodles and then something about how delicious they would be dipped in Kyoto's delicate dashi."

Mrs. Toudou glanced over Mrs. Morikawa's shoulder, "Mrs. Iijima!"

Another neighbor—kimono, light green.

Mrs. Iijima took Fusako's hand, spun her around, told her she was a princess, then took a good look at the haori half coat Fusako's mother was wearing.

"Such a nice feeling your haori gives."

Red camellias and dark and light green leaves circled round the light grey haori.

"It's dyed in the Kagayuuzen manner, isn't it? I'd love something in that color for my tsumugi kimono from Tooka City."

"You have one too?" Mrs. Toudou asked.

Mrs. Iijima nodded yes. "My husband sometimes goes to Kanazawa. I've asked him to bring back anything Kagayuuzen—would love an obi—but whenever he gets home, only talk of what he ate. He came back from Kanazawa last week stuffed. And with what, do you suppose?"

Three heads turned from side to side.

"Scallops, clams, oysters, and sea snails...in a bubbling hot pot. He said shellfish from the Japan Sea is so sweet."

"I've heard that too," Mrs. Toudou said, "and about the fish. The farther north you go, the better the seafood. Freezing cold, rough waves make everything delicious."

"Seaweed too!" Mrs. Iijima chirped.

And then the women decided on an afternoon treat, sweet azuki bean soup served with a side dish of savory kombu seaweed. Fusako squeezed her mother's little finger, and together they all went, the swish-swish of their kimonos and haoris joining their laughter.

IN her classroom, Ms. Kawanishi smiled at the memory and thought it was a shame Fiona hadn't modeled kimonos for her neighbors when she was a little girl.

And Fiona hadn't been taught that kimonos belonged to a complex, magical world Japanese women adored and were devoted to.

Nao's Haiku

IN that world the clock moved by kimono time.

Early spring 1940, the year Fusako turned seventeen, her mother announced, "It's time to start choosing kimonos!"— the ones Fusako was going to take with her when she became a bride and left home.

Nao knew that throughout a woman's life she may not always remember who she met or where or when, but she would always remember where and when she wore each of her kimonos.

Nao taught Fusako...

In nature, time passes as different flowers bloom. But for people, time passes as they dress in different kimonos. And because the hands of kimono time move a little faster than the earth spinning around the sun, the flowers blooming on a kimono come out sooner than those in the garden.

"Always wear kimono flowers before those same flowers start blooming outside."

Nao wrote haiku about kimono time.

One New Year:

towering pine stage
along with the dwarf bamboo
plum blossoms mingle

Everyone praised her handwriting.

Wisteria draped and irises unfurled in Nao's spring haiku. She dutifully attempted images of fireflies and hydrangea for the kimono rainy season, then skipped to summer with its sheer silk in rich colors and designs that stood out against a pale or white under-kimono.

Two lines went like this:

> *...scooping those nets to catch the*
> *shadows of lilies*

Autumn haiku—bellflowers, feathery plume grass, and falling leaves. Many kinds.

But during the kimono winter most kimonos were plain or had vertical stripes. And so, Nao put her writing brush away until the new year.

MS. KAWANISHI wondered if Fiona wanted a kimono like those in her mother's haiku.

Fiona's kimono had a sharkskin pattern, white pinpoints on a background the color of azuki beans. It was made of heavy silk and fully lined.

Wasn't it a good choice for London's damp climate?

What would her mother have chosen? She had fussed over plenty of kimonos...before the War.

Bolts of Silk, Undergarments, In-laws, and Obis

THE KIMONO shop owner and his assistant went to the Morikawa home several times. In a tatami room, they spread out bolts of silk and advised Nao on every detail she needed to know before making up her mind. She had an endless number of choices, each depended on which season and what occasion Fusako would wear the kimono...religious ceremonies, theater performances, tea ceremonies, art exhibitions, visits with relatives, acquaintances, and friends. Kimonos—formal and traditional or fashionable and fun.

Some silk was woven in fanciful patterns with dyed threads.

Some un-dyed silk had satiny patterns woven into it: cranes or flowers or drifting clouds, rows of stylized leaves, grasses and dewdrops. Some had a plain weave. For each of those bolts, Nao decided on its color(s) and on how it would be dyed...one flat color or a swirl of blended colors or a gradation...and on what pattern, if any, to be stenciled.

For a winter kimono or haori or a full-length coat, there was plush brocade velvet and also fluffy shibori silk, dotted throughout with tiny cloth bunches—thread twined around each bunch.

After the shibori silk was dyed and the thread cut from the tiny bunches, the silk had a puckered texture, looking like impressions of melting snowflakes.

Nao told Fusako, "The more puckers, the more expensive."

Fusako asked how long it took someone to twine the thread around all the tiny cloth bunches on a bolt of shibori silk that had the most puckers.

"About a year."

WHEN she was seventeen, about a year had felt like a long time. Ms. Kawanishi had known Fiona for...five years? She would check her old diaries that evening after she took a bath and washed her clothes and her lingerie.

Lingerie...not at all, thank goodness, like layers of kimono undergarments or a susoyoke underskirt.

Susoyoke was a rectangular piece of cloth she had wrapped and tied around her waist, going down to her knees.

Instead of panties—susoyoke.

How Ms. Kawanishi had begged her mother *not* to buy any for her new kimonos.

"MOTHER, I know susoyoke is tradition, but the wind races up between my legs. It gives goose bumps in the most secret places. Don't you think so too?"

Her mother told her that secrets should stay unspoken.

"Please, Mother! Buy me panties!"

Fusako's dramatics paid off. Her mother bought twice as many panties for her as she had bought kimonos—the nicest ones, going down to her knees.

IF Fiona saw a susoyoke or those long panties, what faces would she make?

Ms. Kawanishi covered her smile with her hand, though no one else was in the classroom.

Oh, those kimono undergarments!

Her mother had worried whether or not she had bought enough of them...had even wrung her hands over what a future mother-in-law would possibly *say* about them and about the rest of the kimono wardrobe.

WHILE Nao chose Fusako's kimonos, she imagined her daughter married into a fine family, without a care in the world. The colors and designs of the kimonos were going to mirror Fusako's joy.

But Nao wasn't completely living in the idealized world of kimonos. She had friends who were married to first sons and lived with their in-laws.

Because her husband was the eighth son, Nao never had to hold back tears while her husband's relatives whispered, "Lots of kimonos. All about the cost of one of mine" or "Like what Grandmother wore" or "Kimonos to disgrace the family."

Nao bought the best and most beautiful kimonos she and her husband could afford, in case Fusako married a first son.

ALL those kimonos her mother bought. All the obis!

Ms. Kawanishi wondered if Fiona wanted an obi.

They're difficult to tie if you haven't been taught and impossible to wear without obiage sashes and obijime belts. If she could only explain that in English to Fiona...and about obidome clasps too!

"IF the obi matches the colors of the kimono," Nao told her daughter, "it's a conservative look. If the obi is an unexpected color next to the kimono, then the outfit is for a fashionable affair. One obi can be worn with different kimonos. But remember, the obi is always more expensive than the kimono."

Whenever Nao chose an obi, she also chose obiage and obijime to go with it.

An obiage sash wrapped around the waist between the kimono and the obi and showed above the obi's top edge. Fastened or knotted at the front of the obi was a narrow obijime belt of thin woven cord or of heavy twisted cord.

Obidome, an ornamental clasp, accessorized the belt.

A jeweler brought a small chest filled with clasps to the house. Nao chose three for Fusako and added two of her own, each set in gold.

Emeralds for spring. Jade for summer. Red coral for fall, carved in the likeness of a suzumushi, the insect that sounds like a tiny bell ringing on the cool evenings of late summer.

The clasp for winter was a fragrant piece of carved sandalwood. Its shape, a single chrysanthemum blossom.

For any celebration throughout the year, one was of white pearls.

WOULDN'T Fiona look wonderful in pearls? Strings of pearls and coral beads and pendants of jade. Did she know that women didn't wear necklaces or earrings with kimonos?

There was no need to since kimonos were so eye-catching. But there were other things that went with kimonos.

Ms. Kawanishi's mother had bought all of them for her.

Finishing Touch

NAO picked out handbags, colorful shawls, embroidered and lace sun parasols, stylish umbrellas, and for very rainy days, a large umbrella made of bamboo and oilpaper.

There were stockings...

She ordered a few dozen tight-fitting, white tabi of different lengths, with varying numbers of fasteners that ran along the outside of the ankle—the more formal the occasion, the more fasteners.

Ozoori sandals...

So many. One pair was lacquered and inlaid with mother-of-pearl; another covered with a finely plaited panama; two had designs carved in stained wood; and one was trimmed in green lizard skin.

And there were suitcases...

Since Fusako would sometimes have to change into a kimono away from home—usually to attend a funeral—Nao ordered two kimono suitcases when she chose the silk for Fusako's kimonos for mourning.

She told Fusako to never wear those kimonos away from where the ceremony was held. "Everyone who sees you will be reminded of their lost loved ones."

BUT nowadays Ms. Kawanishi often saw people dressed in black at a department store on their way to or from a funeral.

Were there such customs in London? She hoped Fiona wouldn't have to think about those. No tears of grief for Fiona.

At times, Fusako Kawanishi felt that she had lived through enough sorrow for everyone.

THE WAR began and a year later, the kimono shop nailed its door shut.

Kimonos were no longer worn in public.

Fusako pouted. "Why be born Japanese if you can't wear kimonos? I might as well have been born in the Sahara. Why are we fighting this stupid war? Everyone should come back home."

Nao knew what Fusako found out much later. Anyone speaking against the War was dragged away and never heard from again.

She clutched her daughter's hands until Fusako felt as if her blood had stopped flowing.

"Never say anything like this to anyone. Never!"

Nao packed the new kimono wardrobe, along with bedding for the future newlyweds, in several trunks. Her family home in Nara Prefecture would be the safest place for them. Rumor had it that the Americans weren't going to bomb Nara because of its cultural heritage—as Fusako said of it, "Wherever you turn there's an old temple or shrine. Some on entire hillsides, even on mountaintops. Wasn't there anything else to build?"

At that time during the War, however, Nao's husband didn't want his in-laws to think he needed their help. Instead, he sent the trunks to his family home on the island of Shikoku.

The trunks were stacked to the rafters in a storage house near a terraced hill of apricot trees. In the summer of 1945, the storage house suffered a direct hit during an air raid.

Fusako wished she had seen the kimonos, even once. They were the keys to every dream her mother had dreamed for her.

Fusako would always remember what her mother said about those kimonos. One was sky blue with oak leaves fluttering across it...the leaves grew larger as they fell toward the hem. And there was a bingata kimono from Okinawa, in the vibrant colors of the tropics.

Decades after the War, Fusako saw a TV documentary about the military rule of Okinawa. Its citizens had been ordered to never surrender. And as the Americans invaded, women put on their treasured bingata kimonos that they had been saving for marriage. The dazzling procession climbed a path up a cliff above the ocean. One after another the women jumped. Kimonos caught the wind...moments later lapped against rocks and shattered bodies.

Fusako would always remember that too.

Nao mourned her daughter's kimonos for the rest of her life, spoke of them more often than of the people she knew who had been killed during the War. Each of those kimonos would have been the starting point for a light-hearted conversation...a mirror for the happiness in Fusako's marriage, an anchor for grand memories in her life. But most of all, they would have reminded Fusako of her mother.

MS. KAWANISHI was happy to give Fiona a kimono. Would the shimmering English woman cherish it?

Yes. Ms. Kawanishi felt certain—even if the kimono was only worn as her dressing gown.

Good-bye to Ms. Kawanishi

FIONA didn't want to tell Ms. Kawanishi that she was leaving. Even so, she was determined to teach her one last time. Their cultures, personalities, generations were each as different as any two extremes could be, but the women had grown fond of one another, at a private language school of all places, in a customer/employee, student/teacher relationship. The labels society had stuck on them had fallen off.

Fiona's plan—tell Ms. Kawanishi the news after the lesson, then slip out.

Ms. Kawanishi wasn't going to see her eyes fill with tears...or her face turn blotchy...or her nose swell.

Fiona stepped into the classroom.

Ms. Kawanishi was in a dark purple lace skirt, matching buttonless jacket, and a satin top trimmed with a narrow ruffle at her neck. Shiny white flowers showed in the lace where the satin was under it. Three interlocking, silver loops dangled from her ears. Her English diary, a pad of paper, a pencil, and a bundle wrapped in a golden yellow cloth were on the table.

Memories filled Fiona's heart.

Oh, how much fun she had in Japan! How much freedom! How much spending money! The bowing to her everywhere, the Master at the robatayaki telling her she was an exceptional beauty, her students bringing her sweets.

How clever she had been to leave London and come to the greatest country on the planet.

But the look on Ms. Kawanishi's face...hadn't Fiona's mother worn the same one after Fiona's first primary school stage performance—the sparkle of thrill in her eyes, the hesitant smile?

Something had ended. Something would start.

Fiona didn't come to Japan because she had made a clever choice. She fled London because her mother had died. She wasn't able to say good-bye or thank you or any polite nicety that even the most ungrateful daughters would've told their dying mothers if they had got a chance.

Ms. Kawanishi was tapping her finger at the edge of her lower lip.

"Yes, Ms. Kawanishi?"

"Nice...color."

Fiona's lipstick, the syrupy orange-raspberry color that seeps into summertime desserts, was a going-away present from Jo. "If you wear that on a date"—Jo had smacked her lips—"you might get *some*." Fiona promised herself to wear it only at work.

Fiona nodded toward Ms. Kawanishi's diary and asked her to read it.

Ms. Kawanishi waved her pencil over the pages but didn't say a word.

"Do you want me to read it?"

"No. Later. I read."

Ms. Kawanishi put a sheet of paper in front of her and started drawing.

There was a stone path, then a cherry tree...and then a pine. Cherry blossoms burst open at her pencil tip and pine needles shot out from it.

One of the cherry branches was touching a pine branch that was curving down to it.

"Every year grow. Closer."

"It's a true picture then?" Fiona asked. "These trees are somewhere?"

"A temple. This year after New Year." Ms. Kawanishi's pencil tip pointed to where the pine branch met the trunk. "I see—cut." She drew a line through the branch.

"But the cherry tree was touching it. Who would do that?"

"Perhaps, for New Year's flower arrangement. Not nice ikebana teacher."

"That's so..." Fiona wanted to say terribly tragic, but they were only trees after all. Even so, she felt an emptiness inside her.

"Will it grow back?"

"Cherry tree grows to matsu. Matsu waits. Do you know matsu?"

Fiona did. Darryl had taught her the noun matsu, "pine tree." Jo had taught her the verb matsu, "to wait."

Something Mr. Ono was always doing.

Whaaawt? Mr. Ono. Where in hell did he come from? Why think of *him* at a time like this?

"Yes, I know matsu. Both meanings."

Ms. Kawanishi cupped her hands around the part of the sketch where cherry blossoms bloomed along the pine branch.

"I hope you are always this. Always."

Fiona didn't know what to say.

Ms. Kawanishi put her hand on top of the bundle.

"This for you."

"But—"

"To remember Japan."

"But—"

"In London."

Tears welled up in Fiona's eyes and her nose filled. What she didn't want to happen was happening, but she wasn't angry with the secretaries for telling Ms. Kawanishi. In a way, she felt strangely at ease.

"Know you akaiito?" Ms. Kawanishi touched the red cord tied to the knot of the wrapping cloth, then read her diary.

"*Dear my teacher, Miss O'Shea. In Japan. Everywhere. Red strings tie all people we meet together. Some strings are weak. Some have tangles. Some strong. When you look at this red string, please know I am thankful for the one that ties together us.*"

She put the bundle in front of Fiona.

"Please, open."

Fiona untied the knot of the wrapping cloth and unfolded the bundle covered in paper.

"A kimono?"

"Please, again open."

"But Ms. Kawanishi...it's for me?"

Fiona opened the paper cover.

"Do like you?"

"Yes. YES! I've always wanted a kimono."

Fiona looked at the white pinpoints across it as though they held the secrets of her future.

Ms. Kawanishi lifted the front of the kimono enough to show the lining, a light shade of azuki, a warm pink, like the inside of a seashell.

Then Ms. Kawanishi took a handkerchief from her handbag.

"Thank you." Fiona dabbed her eyes and wiped her nose and wished with all her heart that when she was old, she would be as lovely as Ms. Kawanishi...but knew the chances of that happening were almost nil.

Ms. Kawanishi told her to wear the kimono in her dressing room at a London theater.

"Then I may never wear it. Can I wear it at home, please?"

"Now put on."

Fiona was too nervous to take it out and so Ms. Kawanishi did and helped Fiona put it on over her clothes. They looked out at the city in the soothing light of dusk, their reflection in the window.

Fiona gave Ms. Kawanishi a hug.

"Ms. Kawanishi, whenever I wear this kimono, I'll think of you."

Ms. Kawanishi patted Fiona's arm. "You and kimono. Now almost same color." Her hand covered her lips; she laughed softly and brushed away a tear.

"Sorry, my face turns red when I cry. Not good for an actress, is it?"

But Ms. Kawanishi loved Fiona's face. A face with a hundred masks, a face a stage actress should have. Abundant expressions, honest emotions. She hoped a man would see all of Fiona's masks someday.

Ms. Kawanishi turned her head, and the reflection of the kimono in the window moved her heart in a way she never would have guessed.

She wanted Fiona to see that man...not as an ideal or a disappointment...but for who he was...what she hadn't done with her shamisen teacher and her husband.

Jiro had looked like a jolly ogre made of apple jelly for sure. Her heart never fluttered near him. But the red string that tied him to her was the strongest one in her life. He had married her, fathered her children, given her kimonos to replace the ones lost in the War.

He had brought her peace.

Because for Ms. Kawanishi being able to wear kimonos meant a life of peace.

And peace was what she wanted for Fiona, for everyone, everywhere.

She took the kimono from Fiona's shoulders, put it on the table, and began folding it.

Fiona sat back down and wondered if she would ever know as much about life as Ms. Kawanishi did. What would it be like to live so long?

She breathed out a deep breath and asked Ms. Kawanishi what had been the happiest time in her life.

Ms. Kawanishi took Fiona's hand, thought for a moment, remembered years ago when she had asked the same question, then translated the words that had been spoken to her.

And the lesson was over.

Song of Tsukutsuku-boushi

DURING Fiona's last few days in Osaka, she also taught Mr. Baba.

The bell rang for their lesson to end. She told him she was going back to London. "I must. My father is getting old."

He didn't reply. But the wrinkles across his forehead deepened and his droopy eyes seemed even heavier.

Fiona worried that her feelings had garbled her words and was about to say them again when Mr. Baba stood up and bowed deeply.

She stood up almost as quickly and put out her hand. He held it while he spoke in Japanese. The emotion in his voice was unexpected.

He bowed deeply again.

"Mr. Baba, thank you. You're a marvelous student and taught me so much about Japan. Please keep studying English. And please do stay away from earthquakes and unattended bags. Good health to you and best wishes."

She pressed an envelope into his hand, wiped away her tears, and left the room.

THE SUNDAY after Fiona went back to London, Mr. Baba was at home.

For lunch, his wife made one of his favorites...a large bowl of udon noodles in a bonito dashi, topped with bite-size slabs of cod kamaboko, chopped green onions, and a thin piece of deep-fried tofu that she had flavored and stewed. His wife

served it with a bowl of white rice and homemade cucumber and eggplant pickles.
He had enjoyed her pickles for almost as long as they'd been married.

THE DAY after their wedding, his wife boiled salted water, cooled it in a covered bamboo bucket, then added rice bran—slightly browned—until it became mushy. Twice a day for a week she stirred it with her hand, pulling the mush on the bottom of the bucket up to the top, folding air into it.

Mr. Baba listened to the wet, sucking sounds of the mush. The same kind of sound had first been theirs, in the futon.

After the mush fermented, his wife pushed fresh vegetables into it, completely covering them.

A couple of days passed, then her pickles garnished their meals...from fall through winter, Chinese cabbage, turnips, daikon; from winter to spring, leafy mizuna and nanohana; and in summer, watermelon rinds, eggplants, and cucumbers.

She also added pickle food to the mush, dried peels to flavor it: apple and persimmon in fall; citrus in winter.

She plunged her hand into it once or twice a day, squeezing it through her fingers, turning it over, like a child playing with mud. Twice a week, she mixed in salt and rice bran.

Mr. Baba's wife had kept her bamboo bucket of fermenting pickles in the coolest part of their home during the first few years of their marriage. Later, the bucket became an enameled one in the refrigerator.

The Babas' grown children didn't touch the pickles. The sight of the bucket caused noses to crinkle, eyes to narrow, and "It stinks!"

They ate store-bought pickles—no matter how many times their father praised their mother's.

Nothing, the children stood their ground, could taste good if it had spent time fermenting in mud-colored mush *older* than they were.

AT lunchtime on that first Sunday after Fiona's good-bye, as Mr. Baba spooned grated ginger root onto his wife's pickles and wondered why his children had no sense of what was worthwhile in life, his wife said she had been at a temple the day before.

She had heard the song of the tsukutsuku-boushi.

At once, he thought of his lesson with Fiona in late August the year before.

"MR. BABA, what bird sings so beautifully this time of year? I heard it last week at Saidaiji Temple in Nara. A French cafe is nearby with cakes out of this world—one even had gold stars sprinkled on top...called Galaxy or some such silly name. Anyway, at the temple I heard an amazing bird."

"Can you mimic the sound?"

"Impossible. It was making two sounds at once. Each had a different beat. The softer sound was going clack, clack, clack and at the same time a louder tweeeep, tweeeep, a crescendo of that, then a long tweeeeee-ap, tweeeeee-ap. And then it stopped. A minute or two later it started over again."

Mr. Baba leaned back in his chair. "A tsukutsuku-boushi."

"What does it look like? Must be exquisite with that voice. How big is it? Does it have a long beak? What color are its feathers?"

"It has no feathers."

"A bald bird? Wouldn't it be cold in winter?"

"Pardon me. I don't know the English name." He thumbed through his pocket dictionary. "Here. A ci-ca-da."

"Are you sure?"

"Yes...but it's different from the noisy ones. It sings goodbye to summer."

"That magical sound came from a bug?"

MR. BABA finished his pickles and took a bite of rice and a slurp of noodles. After lunch he reread Fiona's letter.

Dear Mr. Baba,
Enclosed is a picture of me before I came to Japan.

She was standing in Trafalgar Square. His daughter had been to London, and he had a photo of her in about the same spot.

If you are ever in London, please look me up.

London?

When Mr. Baba retired, he and his wife planned to travel to the northern island of Hokkaido...see the horizon, sunrise, sunset, the stars in the Milky Way—things they couldn't see because of the buildings and smog in Osaka.

He put away Fiona's picture.

If he and his wife went to England instead, what stars would they see there?

fruit before flower
sprout before seed
spring following summer
how out of sync life will be...If you leave
—Kotaro Takamura, "To the Woman N"

Vanquished

FIONA expected to say a brief farewell to Mr. Ono at the language school, hoped he wouldn't ask her out for coffee. Why he might shake her hand or pat her on the shoulder. Or—God forbid—hug her close and kiss her like Meryl did at the airport.

But Mr. Ono was out of town covering stories and had cancelled his lessons. He had no idea she was leaving.

When the secretaries told Fiona that Mr. Ono wasn't around, she nearly blurted out, It's probably for the best.

She didn't want to see him. She kept telling herself that he was going to be a memory and perhaps someday, an amusing one. Her lips curled up at the thought.

She packed—a sumo hand towel and bento lunchbox, a Hanshin Tigers baseball cap, ticket stubs from a number of concerts. Mr. Ono had told her how to get all those tickets, had even given her some.

Because of everything he had done for her, Fiona wondered for a split second if Mr. Ono was as annoying as she thought.

"He most certainly is. I've been thinking about him since I opened my suitcase. And I've got to concentrate on the future. But Mr. Ono is always lurking about in whatever murky nooks there are in my mind. How can anyone be more annoying than that?"

She refused to be bothered by thoughts of him any longer.

"The wannabe mystery writer may figure out a way to get to London. Until then, memories of Mr. Ono are vanquished. He's finished. Banished from my mind. The End. It's over. The curtain drawn."

THE WEEK after Fiona left, Darryl told Mr. Ono that she was in London taking care of her father. "She said to tell you good-bye and thank you."

"When is she coming back?"

Darryl had never looked so melancholic, so crestfallen. "She's not."

Mr. Ono's mind went blank.

Her glowing hair, her fiery emerald eyes. Nothing. Her voice, her British accent.

Gone.

During the days that followed, Mr. Ono felt worse than any of his fictional characters ever had. He was in anguish.

Mr. Ono stopped writing his novels.

He drank mixed juice at the coffee shop decorated with teddy bears and union jacks.

And when his telephone rang, he begged the phone lines to make the call be from Fiona.

It didn't, however, occur to Mr. Ono to follow Fiona to London. And why would it? He had never in his life imagined being away from the best country in the world.

Well...his country was only perfect if he ignored everything that wasn't perfect about it...cult terrorists, nuclear power plants, ineffective politicians, not to mention the typhoons pounding into them each summer. And how about what's under the ocean? Unpredictable plates that forever move and every so often, belch up earthquakes and tsunamis.

Mr. Ono believed Fiona would come back.

The strings that had kept her in Osaka would absolutely pull her back—her friends and students, her high salary and easy work schedule, 100-yen shops, trains on time, cheap cigarettes. Only in Japan, he was sure, could she defiantly twist noodles around a fork instead of using chopsticks and no one would make fun of her.

Mr. Ono told himself she was coming back. She didn't.

He went to Akita and stayed at his friends' ryokan, but Okamisan's welcoming smile couldn't cheer him and soaking in his favorite hot spring brought tears of loneliness. He drove to Hachimantai Plateau and stared at the wind-whipped firs, gnarled branches twisting out from one side of their rugged trunks. Those contorted trees summed up what he was without Fiona.

Half a man.

He drove to Ani, his adopted country home, the place he and Meryl had taken the flag.

Ann, Fiona's middle name...she had told him at the airport. Her mother had called her Annie.

Ani and Annie...the same most beautiful sound. Fiona. His life now. His home.

From the roadside, he stared at the Satos' apple orchard. The branches had become heavy with what any poetic observer would imagine as merry ornaments dangling from the edge of a cedar forest. But Mr. Ono didn't. Mr. Ono thought about what Hiroshi Sato had told him...the bay that had turned as red as red can be...the little girl bundled on his back who his daughter looked like in the old picture he kept in his wallet.

Mr. Ono imagined what he would do if he had to march off to war. He would be on the next flight to London. He would tell Fiona...But he wasn't marching off to war. He was going back to his office, to his apartment, to Osaka. His country was at peace, would always be at peace. Somehow, he didn't know what to do in the middle of his staid life.

He bowed toward the Satos' orchard, then drove to the airport.

AT work the next day, colleagues were poking fun at their English conversation skills. "They won't send us. What a relief. Who wants to leave the best city in the world?"

Mr. Ono was puzzled by the outburst of hometown devotion until he spotted a memo from personnel...for a position at the newspaper's foreign bureau...in London.

Japanese Lessons

DURING August, Byron left Japan. In transit, he phoned his mother. He and his bride would take a taxi home from the airport.

"What? Whose idea is that?"

Byron said it was his wife's.

"That's OK with you?"

"Yeah."

"You don't want your mother meeting you at the airport?"

"No."

Meryl sat next to Greg in the living room, waiting for the two to arrive. She didn't want to sound like a mother-in-law, but...

"They're not even here yet and she's making all the decisions."

Greg didn't point out that it had been only one.

"Byron's friends don't know who she is so that means she wasn't a student at the language school. Do you think I'll have to study Japanese to tell her to please consult her husband's mother on everything?"

Greg put his arm around her, whispered a few words in Japanese, then said he was more than happy to give her all the private lessons she needed.

Innuendo wasn't Meryl's forte.

"Thank you, but you'll be busy with your own classes soon."

She started again on her daughter-in-law.

"Fiona called her *Byron's mystery woman.* I love mysteries, but not when I'm in the middle of one. Why didn't he introduce her to Darryl and Jo and Fiona? If only I knew what they thought of her." Meryl sighed. "If only he had married one of them."

"Maybe he did."

Meryl told Greg that Darryl was too busy with ikebana to be interested in marriage and Jo thought the only reason to marry someone was for the uninhibited pleasure of sex with one trusting partner.

"I have artistic and modern friends."

"You talked about sex?"

"I listened. I don't think my son is enough of a sexual animal for Jo."

Greg didn't tell Meryl that mothers don't always know everything about their sons.

"How about Fiona?"

"She's fond of Mr. Ono." Meryl put her head on Greg's shoulder. "My daughter-in-law probably can't speak a word of English."

Meryl muttered some Briticisms.

"Poppycock? I thought that word only survived in musty British flicks."

"Noooo. I'm almost positive Fiona said it."

"Bully for her!"

Then the taxi honked. Meryl rushed to the window, Freckles and Greg right behind.

It was as she had imagined her husband coming home. But Peter didn't get out of the taxi. Byron did, like a magician in a disappearing act reappearing in a different costume. Meryl's dream of Peter vanished.

Their son had come home.

She blinked her eyes. Byron wasn't the same as he'd been when they said good-bye years earlier. He wore an attractive confidence that was nurtured by someone he loved. His wife must be wonderful. Meryl expected a petite woman as pretty as a Japanese doll to appear from the taxi. Instead a pair of dewy, bare legs in high heels swung out.

"Jo!"

She was wearing a low-cut, slinky dress, and her exuberance glowed from every visible pore.

Meryl grabbed Greg's arm. "Jo came along! Maybe Darryl and Fiona came too—for the fun of it. And Mr. Ono! Do you think another taxi is on the way?"

She ran out of the house, threw her arms around Jo, and had all but forgotten her son's bride. "Jo! You're here! I have so much to tell you." She took Jo's hands and whispered, "You and Fiona were right. Greg loves me!" and in a loud voice, "I hope you're staying a long time."

Byron was at Meryl's side and kissed her. "I was thinking the same."

She looked past him.

The taxi drove away. There wasn't a pretty doll with jet-black hair in sight. No one was speaking Japanese.

That could mean only one thing.

"Jo! You're the mystery woman! I don't have to take Japanese lessons! All that worry for nothing. Why didn't you say something?"

Jo told her that she didn't know Byron was thinking of marriage until Meryl had talked about his fiancée at the Nara Hotel. Byron was positive she would say yes when he had written the letter asking about married student housing—the letter Greg had told Meryl about. Byron proposed after he got back to Japan from his trip to Vietnam.

Meryl hugged Jo again and gave her a couple of kisses. Thank goodness Jo was her daughter-in-law. They wouldn't have to spend any uncomfortable time getting to know each other. After all, they had slept together, in the same room, twice...the first time, in the same bed!

But even unspeakable joy didn't keep Meryl from wishing for more...like a child after opening her last Christmas present.

She wanted Fiona to also be her daughter-in-law. Darryl, her son-in-law. Oh, and Mr. Ono!

She bear hugged Byron and thought—Blimey, if only you had been quadruplets.

My Love, one more lifetime with you.
—Hajime Kitamura and B. Jeanne
"Another Beginning"

So Yummy

ONE MORNING when the sun was still thinking about what colors to dress the sky, Meryl dreamed.

She was near a brook in a forest. In the rippling water, fish caught the sunshine like silver trinkets. And from the shadows...

Kyorororoo.

A leaf flitted down toward her, then turned into a whimsical ruddy kingfisher, rusty brown and marked with a splash of sky blue.

Its long beak sliced through the water. In an instant, back out it flew, landing on a shiny, black stone—beak empty.

During the brief struggle, bird and fish had set off a swarm of glittering, swirling bubbles...thousands flowed...over rocks, under vines and ferns beaded in dewdrops, around mossy bends...traveling on into a river, toward an endless ocean.

Meryl saw the bubbles from beneath the water...she had become the water.

Some bubbles floated, reflecting the world in their half-spheres. Some clustered like grapes. One burst into another. The two became one.

And in her dream, Meryl had a peaceful understanding about loss.

A bubble disappears. Suddenly it is the water, still flowing, still in the same direction, still together.

Thoughts tumbled around in her sleepy head.

Then the tip of Meryl's nose twitched.

But it wasn't the smell of musty earth or damp leaves or forest flowers in the air.

It was coffee.

WHILE his bride lingered under the covers, Greg was in the kitchen, draped in the yukata from her.

He poured coffee into his cup, the one his first love had used.

And raised it—

She had shown him love in the simplest things.

He said thank you, then took a sip.

And marveled.

It had been only a few months since Meryl brought him the flag.

Greg raised his cup again.

And now, every morning he made her coffee.

He adored the luster in her eyes when she spoke the melodious Osaka dialect she had remembered from her trip. "Oh-key-knee. Oh-e-she nah—!" "Thanks. Soooo yummy!"

From the kitchen window, he saw that it was going to be another fine day, then went to wake her.

B. Jeanne Shibahara lives in Nara City, an ancient capital of Japan.

Printed in Poland
by Amazon Fulfillment
Poland Sp. z o.o., Wrocław